T5-CCL-771

"Call Me 'Matt.' I Would Prefer That."

"Why?" she asked. He was looking at her in a way that made her feel breathless, even though the width of the room separated them. "Does everyone call you by your first name?"

"No, but I want you to. May I call you 'Becca'?"

"My name is Rebecca." Her heart was beating so fast she was certain he must hear it.

"I know. But I want to call you something no one ever has before. We are going to be very important to each other and I want you to know that from the start."

"I don't know you," she protested in a whisper. "And you don't know me."

"We know each other," he told her softly. "We knew all we needed to know from the very beginning. All that's left are the little bits and pieces that have to do with memories and dreams."

Dear Reader,

We, the editors of Tapestry Romances, are committed to bringing you two outstanding original romantic historical novels each and every month.

From Kentucky in the 1850s to the court of Louis XIII, from the deck of a pirate ship within sight of Gibraltar to a mining camp high in the Sierra Nevadas, our heroines experience life and love, romance and adventure.

Our aim is to give you the kind of historical romances that you want to read. We would enjoy hearing your thoughts about this book and all future Tapestry Romances. Please write to us at the address below.

The Editors
Tapestry Romances
POCKET BOOKS
1230 Avenue of the Americas
Box TAP
New York, N.Y. 10020

Most Tapestry Books are available at special quantity discounts for bulk purchases for sales promotions, premiums or fund raising. Special books or book excerpts can also be created to fit specific needs.

For details write the office of the Vice President of Special Markets, Pocket Books, 1230 Avenue of the Americas, New York, New York 10020.

Willow Wind

Lynda Trent

A TAPESTRY BOOK
PUBLISHED BY POCKET BOOKS NEW YORK

Books by Lynda Trent

Embrace the Storm
Embrace the Wind
Willow Wind

Published by TAPESTRY BOOKS

This novel is a work of historical fiction. Names, characters, places and incidents relating to non-historical figures are either the product of the author's imagination or are used fictitiously. Any resemblance of such non-historical incidents, places or figures to actual events or locales or persons, living or dead, is entirely coincidental.

An *Original* publication of TAPESTRY BOOKS

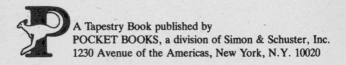

A Tapestry Book published by
POCKET BOOKS, a division of Simon & Schuster, Inc.
1230 Avenue of the Americas, New York, N.Y. 10020

Copyright © 1983 by Dan Trent and Lynda Trent

All rights reserved, including the right to reproduce this book or portions thereof in any form whatsoever. For information address Tapestry Books, 1230 Avenue of the Americas, New York, N.Y. 10020

ISBN: 0-671-47574-6

First Tapestry Books printing November, 1983

10 9 8 7 6 5 4 3 2 1

POCKET and colophon are registered trademarks of Simon & Schuster, Inc.

TAPESTRY is a trademark of Simon & Schuster, Inc.

Printed in the U.S.A.

In loving memory of Oletha Petty,
who brought happiness into the lives
she touched for 101 years

Willow
Wind

Chapter One

"I SEE YOU, JIMMY LITTLE!" REBECCA SIMP-son exclaimed. "Drop that candy!"

The boy thrust the rock candy into his coat pocket and bolted for the door. Rebecca threw down the bedspread she was folding and ran through the store in hot pursuit. She dodged the new clothes dummy she had just set up, skirted the counter that held the spring cali-coes, and ran past the row of vanity mirrors in which she had seen the reflection of the cul-prit.

Jimmy slammed out the front door on a dead run, but since the silver bell had not stopped jangling before Rebecca reached it, she thought she just might catch him red-handed this time.

Intent on the youthful thief, she ran headlong into the man about to enter the store, and both landed in a heap in the doorway.

"Pardon me, ma'am, I seem to have gotten in your way," the stranger observed wryly. He sat up and dusted the sleeves of his coat before resting his forearms on his knees to gaze at her.

Rebecca ached all over from her fall, and instead of speaking, found herself staring at the man. He had blond hair, the color of raw honey, and his eyes were the illusive green of a forest in late summer. When he smiled, as he did now, his features transformed from rugged into handsome and his teeth were white against his tanned skin. She suddenly became aware that she was sitting in full view of the street with her skirt hiked up almost to her knees. With a blush, she scrambled to her feet and smoothed her gray skirt, dusting the black piping and straightening her white pleated blouse. The man also got to his feet and brushed the street dust from his trousers.

"I'm so sorry," Rebecca stammered as she fought to control her blush. "I didn't see you and I thought sure I could catch Jimmy this time." She was rambling in her embarrassment and she closed her mouth abruptly.

"This time? You mean you do this often?" he asked in mock horror.

"You aren't hurt are you?" she asked belatedly, but before he could answer, she glared across the street where the boy had disappeared down the alley beside the feed store. "He comes in several times a week and grabs a handful of candy. He always gets out before I can catch him. This time I nearly had him."

"Maybe he's hungry?" the man suggested as he studied her angry face.

"He's not hungry, he's the sheriff's son, and the sheriff's son can do no wrong in this town." She looked up at him. "Are you hurt?"

Their eyes met and Jimmy Little evaporated from her mind. Time seemed to hang suspended as they gazed at one another.

"No," he answered after a pause, breaking the silence. "I'm not hurt. Are you? You took quite a fall."

"I'm all right." She still ached from head to toe but continued to ignore it. Realizing she was staring again, she pushed open the door behind her. "Please come in. My name is Rebecca Simpson."

"Matt Prescott." He surprised her by presenting his hand for her handshake. She took it and felt his fingers encompass her own as an odd tingle ran up her arm.

He wasn't unusually tall, not even six feet by her reckoning, but he had an impressive physique. His shoulders were broad and his chest deep, so that his white shirt was stretched taut across his muscles, and she was certain his coat was tailored to fit him. In contrast, his waist was lean and his hips narrow, but his legs looked hard beneath his well-cut trousers.

"Is something wrong?" he asked.

"No. No, of course not!" she replied with a blush. "I was only wondering . . . that is, I have never seen you before."

"That's quite probable. I've been in town"—he hesitated as he checked the gold pocket watch he carried in his coat pocket—"only about an hour now." In the guise of looking around the store, he studied her. She was a small woman, probably in her mid-twenties, but there was no wedding band on her hand. This was surprising in view of her beauty. She wore her dark hair in a heavy bun on the nape of her neck, and her chocolate brown eyes were the sort to mirror even her most fleeting thoughts. Her skin was the color of rich cream, and he guessed she had to be very careful lest it tan. Although her clothing was somber, and more suitable for an older woman, her figure was slender and graceful.

He smiled. "This is a nice store. Do you and your husband work here?"

"I'm not married," she said before she thought. Then, to soften her seeming abruptness, she added, "The Emporium is an old store, but then so is Mellville."

"That's one of the things I like about this town. It feels settled, secure." His hazel eyes swept over her face in a way that made her feel shy and almost beautiful.

"I apologize for running into you like that," she said to cover her lack of composure. "It

4

was so foolish of me. You're certain you aren't hurt?" For some reason her pulse was racing and she felt unaccountably breathless.

"I'm quite all right, and I suspect there is nothing foolish about you." He couldn't take his eyes from her face. She seemed hypnotizing to him and it took a moment for him to realize he had probably spoken far too intimately to this stranger. "What I mean to say is that I'm here in regard to the sign saying you have a room for rent."

Rebecca looked at him blankly, then smiled, and a dimple appeared in her cheek. "You want to rent a room?"

"I'd like to see it first, but yes, I need a place to stay until I can buy a house and get settled in."

"You're moving to Mellville? Whatever for?" Again she shut her mouth quickly, but a bit too late. Always she had been inclined to say exactly what she thought. She had been on the verge of also telling him she had all but forgotten about the For Rent sign in her parlor window. "I didn't mean to say that. Outspokenness has always been a failing with me."

"That's quite all right. I wouldn't expect you to share your home with a stranger and not know why he's there. I came through here a while back and I liked the town, so I decided to build here."

"In Mellville?" She looked at him in astonishment. "It's just an ordinary town."

"You mean you haven't heard about the railroad? I should think everyone in town would be talking about it."

She shrugged. "I've heard talk, of course, but I doubt anything will ever come of it."

"The way I heard it, it's a sure thing. The rail will connect Dallas and Shreveport with points east, making big cities of them both. Since Mellville is on a line between them, I'm sure it'll come through here as well."

"Perhaps. Just a moment and I'll take you over to see the room." She left him examining the counter display and hurried to the back. "Nell? There you are. I need to be away for a few minutes, so will you watch the front while I'm gone? Someone wants to look at the room I have for rent."

"Why?" Nell stared at her as if the idea of a renter were bizarre.

"He's a stranger in town." Rebecca plopped her wide-brimmed straw hat on her head and secured it with a hatpin. "I won't be long."

"He?" Nell asked. "It's a man?"

"Good-bye, Nell," Rebecca said firmly.

Matt Prescott was waiting patiently and smiled appreciatively as she came down the aisle of bolt goods. "If this isn't a convenient time, I can come back later," he said.

"This is fine. My assistant said she would look after the store until I get back."

He reached past her and opened the door to let her precede him. His eyes followed her as if

6

she were a desirable woman rather than the town's spinster.

Spinster was a word she had unfortunately become accustomed to hearing in reference to herself. Certainly it was preferable to old maid, but she deplored it anyway. During those years when her friends were being courted, Rebecca's stern father had kept her at home with one excuse after another. By the time all the girls in town were becoming brides, her father was an invalid and there was no one to look after him and the family business except for her. There had been no time to see to her own interests, and now that her father was gone, there were no suitors left to call upon her. The few bachelors around were more interested in younger women, and the older widowers sought the companionship of those of similar age. Thus, Rebecca, at twenty-five, had been placed on the shelf.

Matt walked her to a buggy drawn by a sleek gray gelding, and helped her onto the seat with as much gallantry as if she were the belle of the county. Rebecca glanced at him from under the brim of her hat. Why was he treating her like this? Should she trust him?

"I saw your sign as I rode into town," he said as he reined the gray down the street. "Could you give me some idea how much the room rents for?"

"I'm asking thirty dollars a month, no meals included."

"No meals?"

"I don't like to cook."

"I've never talked to a woman who admitted she couldn't cook," he commented with interest.

"Not *can't* cook. I said I don't like to cook. My mother died when I was barely in my teens and I've spent all the years since in the kitchen. Several years ago my father had a crippling stroke and I had to go to work in the store *and* cook."

He looked at her profile. The sun filtered through her straw hat brim and made a golden pattern on her face. Her lips were naturally pink, and health bloomed in her soft cheeks. To his surprise, he longed to reach out and touch her, to see if she were as soft and warm as she looked. "Do you make a practice of telling strangers you live alone?"

"No, but I rarely see a stranger. Everyone in town already knows I live by myself. It's hardly a secret."

He frowned. "That doesn't seem very safe. Besides, won't people talk if a single woman rents a room to a bachelor?"

So he wasn't married! She had been wondering. "No," she said reluctantly. "Five years ago, I would have created a scandal by renting to you. Even two years ago there would have been raised brows. Now, however, your reputation is safe."

"Mine? I was referring to yours." He turned

to look at her as the horse trotted briskly down the brick street.

A wry smile tilted her sensitive lips. "Perhaps you're not accustomed to the ways of a small town. All too often we are bracketed into slots and given a title. The Widow Johnson over there has remarried, but she still retains her title of Widow. That house on the right was the home of Nate, a man with the mind of a child. The whole family moved away two years ago, but that is still Nate's house. For the same reason, if you eat at Cooper's Boarding House, you are really eating at Branson's. Mrs. Cooper died, but the Bransons weren't able to convince anyone of the change in names, so they put Cooper's sign back up. You might say that this town is kind of old-fashioned."

"I see," he said as he turned down a tree-lined street. "And your title?"

"Rebecca Simpson, Spinster."

Matt looked at her searchingly. "How on earth did a mistake like that come about?"

"I'm not too sure of that myself. First I was too strictly guarded; then I was too busy. Suddenly here I was, the town's paragon of virtue. Unfortunately, it wasn't my intention to remain single." Suddenly she realized her mouth was again running away with her, and she stopped talking.

Matt looked down the road, then back at her. "Why do you do that?"

"Do what?"

"Stop talking practically in the middle of a word. It's rather disconcerting."

"Not as disconcerting as it would be if I kept talking," Rebecca said with resignation. "I know this for a fact. I've even sent some ladies fumbling for their smelling salts after a brief conversation." She nodded toward a white picket fence. "Pull in here."

Like her neighbors', Rebecca's house sat back from the street and on an ample lawn. Oak trees lined the gravel drive, and azaleas made a dense hedge. The lawn was lush green, and several dogwood trees bloomed in drifts beneath the taller magnolias. The house was white and gleamed with fresh paint. All the windows were flanked with blue shutters, and the eaves and peaks were embellished with gingerbread trim. A wide porch started at the bay window on the left and skirted the two-story house in a gallery of welcoming shade. A porch swing hung on the front section, and a big yellow cat was sunning lazily on the front steps. The Room for Rent sign he had seen earlier was displayed in the bay window.

Matt drew his horse to a stop by the hitching post and went around to help Rebecca down. "I can see why you set people on their heels if you always say what you mean."

"I'm sorry," she said automatically. "I'm far too outspoken."

"Not for me, you aren't. I like it." Although she had safely reached the ground, he continued to hold both her hands. "I tend to say just what I think, too," he said quietly.

Rebecca pulled away, her heart pounding. Nothing in her entire experience had ever prepared her for someone like Matt Prescott. Even though the day was cool, she felt unusually warm, and her normally precise mind was fluttering like a captured bird. To hide her confusion over the gentle note in his deep voice, she hurried toward the house. "The room is on the second floor," she babbled, "and gives you a lovely view of the front street. It's a northern exposure, so the sun is no problem in the summer. It's well ventilated and stays quite comfortable, even in August."

"That's nice. What does your room overlook?" he asked conversationally.

"The orchard. In back of the house." She looked at him, and the amusement in his eyes made her hurry up the steps as she searched her reticule for her keys. The cat blinked up at her and deigned to move his tail a fraction of an inch.

"Your cat, I presume?" Matt observed as he stepped over the inert animal.

"Yes, that's Samson. He let's me pretend to own him, but it's really the other way around." The shady porch enveloped them and she bent to fit the key in the lock beside the etched glass door panel.

"No Delilah?" Matt teased. "That's a real pity."

"Every cat in the neighborhood looks like Delilah to him," she laughed, then closed her lips firmly. She had to learn not to rattle on like that!

"There!" he accused. "You did it again!"

Rebecca didn't reply as she opened the door wide. She was beginning to wonder if she was making a mistake by renting the room to Matt. For some reason she felt too relaxed with him and ended up saying far more than she should, so she reminded herself to be cautious as she removed her hat and placed it on a peg of the hall tree. Yet it was as if she had known him before, he was so familiar. "The parlor is in here. You're welcome to use it whenever you please. That room beyond is the library and you may use it as well."

The parlor was sunny and cheerful, with the usual number of chairs and a settee upholstered in shades of blue cut velvet. A hooked rug softened the oak floor, and even Matt's inexperienced eyes told him someone had spent countless hours in its creation. Two marble-topped end tables flanked the couch and supported lamps with matching stained-glass shades in a floral design of red, blue, and cream. A side table between two of the chairs sported a bowl of silk flowers of pleasing, but improbable, design. The room was pretty, but not welcoming.

Matt went to the library and looked in.

Immediately he felt drawn into the room. The walls were lined with oak paneling that made the room seem alive. Vibrant blue and red and gold splashed from the upper panes of the fan-shaped window and lay in pools of color on the soft leather chairs. A large rolltop desk presided in one corner and two walls were filled with leather-bound books. Slowly he walked in.

"This is my favorite room," Rebecca said as she followed him. "After my father's stroke, I began sitting here every night. First to wade through the muddled records for my father; later to read."

He looked at her in surprise. "I thought the parlor would be more appealing to a woman. It's so . . . feminine," he finished lamely.

"It's fussy. I only keep it because I must. My mother decorated it the year she died and it's been kept more or less the same ever since. I only go in long enough to clean it, or to sit when the Women's Guild calls on me."

"The Women's Guild?"

"It's a sort of social and garden group, really. I talk to them in there because the chairs are quite uncomfortable and they don't stay long." Again she heard inappropriate words falling from her mouth and she sighed.

Matt grinned. "I like the way you say exactly what you mean. No shilly-shallying around with vague innuendos."

"I could stand a bit more vagueness, Mr. Prescott."

"Call me Matt. I would prefer that."

"Why?" she said. He was looking at her in a way that made her feel breathless, even though the width of the room separated them. "Does everyone call you by your first name?"

"No, but I want you to. May I call you Becca?"

"My name is Rebecca." Her heart was beating so fast she was certain he must hear it. The gold of the window fell on his hair and gave him the look of a medieval knight.

"I know. But I want to call you Becca because it suits you. Also because I want to call you something no one ever has before."

"Why?" she said softly.

"Because we are going to be very important to each other, and I want you to know that from the start."

Neither moved, and the silence between them was charged with expectancy. At last she said, "I'm not a woman to take lightly, Mr. Prescott. While I may not like my title of Spinster, I prefer it to that of Harlot."

"I don't like either label. And I'm not proposing that you resign one by acquiring the other. I know a lady when I see one, Becca, and you have nothing to fear from me."

"I don't know you," she protested in a whisper. "And you don't know me."

"We know each other," he told her softly.

14

"We knew what we needed to know right from the start. All that's left are the little bits and pieces that have to do with memories and dreams."

Still the room separated them, but Becca felt his embrace as surely as if he held her in his arms. What he said was true. From the moment their eyes had met, she had known something special was to come. After a pause she said, "I guess I had better show you to your room." She turned to go and his voice made her hesitate.

"My name is Matt."

"Matt," she repeated. With a small smile she preceded him out of the room.

They again crossed the formal parlor and returned to the entry. She led the way up the steps and hoped he wouldn't notice the worn threads of the stair runner. The banister was walnut and felt satiny smooth beneath her hand. The wainscoting was painted white, and above that was a pale yellow wallpaper with garlands of spring flowers. Would it seem too fussy and feminine to him? He was so ruggedly handsome the house appeared frilly in his presence.

At the head of the stairs she turned left and opened the dark, varnished door to the larger bedroom. It had been her parents' room and seemed to be the most logical to rent. She went in and stepped aside for him to enter.

His shoulders seemed to fill the doorway as he came into the room, and again she was aware of the magnetism he held for her. He looked around approvingly.

The wallpaper was ivory with chocolate and burgundy stripes, and the wainscoting was stained walnut. Several small rugs in rich tones warmed the well-polished floors, and the windows were draped in burgundy fabric. Becca pulled open the curtains and raised the window to allow the spring air into the room. The four-poster bed was a tall, old-fashioned one made of oak. The counterpane was spotlessly white and billowed over the feather mattress beneath. The tall wardrobe, dresser, and rocker were also oak and looked as if no dust had ever settled upon their surfaces.

Matt turned to her with a smile. "It's even better than I had hoped. I'll take it." She still stood by the window, with the sunlight turning her skin to glowing transparency. Ruddy highlights appeared in her hair, and in her eyes as well. Matt felt a stirring deep within him. Were all the men in this town blind, to let such a woman remain single? He had been half surprised at his own outspoken words in the library—though he wasn't known as reticent under any circumstances—but now he wondered only that he had not said more. For he suddenly knew beyond a shadow of a doubt that this was the woman for whom he had searched all his life.

"The price is fair? I've never rented a room before, but it's less than Mrs. Branson charges at the boarding house. Of course there are no meals here." He was looking at her as no man ever had and she grew nervous. Who was he, anyway? Was she foolish to allow a perfect stranger to move into her house, and her with no male protector? Yet she had no fear of him, only this odd, hurrying sensation as if unspoken decisions were being made. "Will you be moving in right away?"

"Yes, if that's all right with you. As you may have noticed, I have my trunks in the buggy."

"Of course. That will be fine." She hadn't paid attention to anything but him, and they could have ridden to the house in a dog cart for all she had noticed. "I'll leave you then to get settled in. I work until five o'clock and I'll be home then." She crossed to the dresser and opened a small drawer beneath the candle stand. "Here is a key to the front door and another to the back. The barn is behind the house and you may use any of the stalls for your horse."

"I'll drive you back to the store."

"I couldn't put you to such a bother. I always walk back and forth. It's really not that far."

"I would consider it a pleasure." He inclined his head slightly in a courtly gesture but never took his eyes from her face.

Once more Becca felt the stirring sensation and cautioned herself to be prudent. She had no illusions about her station in life and she wasn't eager to be made a fool. There was a confidence and polish about Matt Prescott that told her he could have his pick of women, even without his handsome face and well-turned body. Why would he be interested in her? All her life she had heard her parents describe her as an ugly duckling in comparison to several of her cousins. Matt's attitude confused her.

She gave him a cursory tour of the kitchen and dining room and he opened the door for her as she replaced her sun hat. The gray horse pricked his ears as Matt spoke to him, and Becca noticed that both the horse and buggy looked expensive. The buggy was shiny black patent leather with discreet touches of cherry red over the mud skirts and was topped with a black leather sunshade. It looked quite new.

"I never asked where you're from," Becca said as he took his seat beside her.

"Memphis, Tennessee. I was in business there these last ten years. However, my partner had several grown sons and he wanted to make it a family business, so I let him buy me out. By the way, I was noticing that building that used to be a feed store across the street from the Emporium. Could you tell me who owns it and if it's for sale?"

So he was in the feed and grain business. She wouldn't have guessed that to look at him. "It's owned by Harvey Willis, and, yes, it's been on the market for several months. You can usually find Mr. Willis over in the little park across from Cooper's Boarding

18

House. He's retired now and he and his old friends like to sit there on the benches and tell how they could have won the war sooner if they had just had a say."

Matt glanced at her. "I notice you're wearing mourning. Is that for your father?"

"Yes. He died last year of a stroke. We thought we'd lost him right at the end of the war when he turned up missing, but later we heard he was in a hospital, and it was nearly a year before he finally got back home. He never really recovered, though. He never talked about the war, either."

"I tried to get involved in that mess, but I was just a boy and the army didn't want me in the way. My oldest brother found me and hauled me back home and made me promise him I'd stay there. When he didn't come back from Shiloh I wanted to go avenge his death, but the promise I'd made him kept me away. And it's probably a good thing, too, as I was only ten years old at the time." Matt again noticed the darkness of Becca's clothing, and continued, "You said your father died last year. Will you be in mourning much longer?"

Becca looked at him from under her hat brim. That was a rather impertinent question. "He has been dead not quite a full year now. After that I'll put aside my mourning."

"Good. I want to see you in bright colors."

The words were on the tip of her tongue to put him firmly in his place, but she couldn't, in all honesty, voice them. She disliked the drab colors and wished to be rid of them, too, although it would be more proper for her to continue wearing the subdued shades in view of her single status. Her thoughts turned longingly to her favorite blue dress, folded away in tissue paper with lavender, and carefully stored in her cedar chest. Perhaps she would air it out and wear it as soon as her year was up. Well-drilled guilt made her bite her lower lip. As if he had followed her thoughts, Matt smiled and urged the horse to a smooth trot.

He reined the animal to a stop at the Emporium's front door and held up his finger to halt her automatic exit from the buggy. Once again he handed her safely down to the street. As if this were the most ordinary thing in the world, he smiled at her.

Becca was well aware of three women who were clustered in front of the bakery shop, and knew they were all speculating on the stranger. With a sudden burst of savoir faire, she smiled up at him and tilted her head coquettishly. He wouldn't know she was filling a need long denied her in spurring the town gossips; for once she wouldn't be dismissed as merely Rebecca Simpson.

He looked over her head at the abandoned feed store. It was in an excellent location, being a stone's throw from the town's central crossroads and with ample room to park buggies and horses. Already he was full of plans for his new enterprise.

Because the gossips were nonchalantly edging closer, Becca said in a clear voice, "I know you must be tired from your journey, Matt, so I won't keep you."

"It has indeed been a tiring day. But I don't ever recall a more interesting one." He smiled down at her. Even though he wasn't particularly tall, he still towered over her small body.

On inspiration, Becca said, "I'm serving supper at eight. Will you eat with me?"

Amusement glinted in his eyes and he said softly for her ears only, "I thought you didn't cook."

"Sometimes I do," she said in a low tone. Had she gone too far in her endeavor to set the gossips on their ears?

"I would be delighted," Matt responded in a rich timbre that was keyed to reach the group of women. Before Becca knew what he was about to do, he took her hand and kissed it.

Becca drew in her breath as his lips caressed her hand. Not only did the gesture feel far more intimate than it looked, she knew he had seen through her little game.

"Let them stew over that," he whispered as he released her fingers. Louder he said, "Eight o'clock then. I will be looking forward to it." His mellow Southern accent gave the words a lilting quality and his eyes made them intimate.

Becca blushed and hurried toward her shop. She hoped the triumph was worth the embarrassment.

Chapter Two

BECCA STRAIGHTENED THE YELLOW LINEN TA-
blecloth and strategically placed her plate to
hide the mended spot. She had refrained from
using the ivory china and instead had set the
two places with the damask rose dishes she
used every day. The deep pink border and
primroses looked cheerful against the table-
cloth, but not contrived. Becca was determined not to appear grasping or starved for
affection.

She paused and frowned. Did that descrip-
tion fit her? Perhaps she had become as needy
as Miss Peabody, the church organist! Becca
picked up a plate and, after a surreptitious
glance at the hall door, looked at her wavery
reflection. In the plate's distortion, her eyes
looked huge and dark, her face as pallid as a
ghost. The sound of approaching footsteps

startled her and she dropped the plate onto the table with a clatter and hurried back to the kitchen.

Thankfully, nothing was burning. She poked experimentally at the batter-encrusted steaks and stirred the green beans. Should she have cooked something more exotic than this? She chided herself for being silly. After all, she was only cooking supper for her boarder.

"Can I help?"

Matt's deep voice made her jump and she nearly tipped the beans off the stove. She turned to stare at him. Never in all her life could she recall seeing a man in the kitchen. "Help?" she asked uncertainly.

He rummaged through the cabinet until he found the black iron oven-door handle and then, with obvious familiarity, latched it onto the door and pulled it open. "I think the cornbread is done."

Becca groaned. She had completely forgotten about the bread. Before she could grab the hot pad, Matt had doubled the cup towel and brought the pan up to the cabinet. Whistling a tune, he turned the yellow disk onto a plate and began to slice several golden wedges. Becca was so surprised, she almost burned the meat.

Hastily she forked the steaks onto a platter and poured the beans into a bowl. The sweet potatoes were baking on the oven shelf and were already soft inside their crisp skins.

"Where do you keep the serving spoons?" Matt asked.

She mutely pointed to a drawer. Even with the cool spring night, the kitchen was uncomfortably warm. Becca patted the moisture from her brow with the corner of her apron. Her apron! Quickly she whisked it off and tossed it to the straight chair by the door as if speed would make him unaware she had ever worn it. She smoothed her skirt as he fumbled for spoons in the drawer. "I didn't expect you to come in here," she said in explanation as he turned and looked from her dress to the apron.

"Why are you acting so nervous?" He reached around her to put a spoon in the beans.

"I never saw a man help put a meal on the table, at least not one who knew what he was doing. It's rather startling."

His laughter filled the room. "A man doesn't live thirty years and not know how to cook unless he's an imbecile. A bachelor learns these things pretty fast. And besides, I rather enjoy cooking."

"You've never been married then?"

"No, I never found the right woman." He gazed at her thoughtfully. "Are we ready to eat?"

She nodded and picked up the bowl of beans and the one of potatoes. A man cooking had never occurred to her. She had just assumed he would have hired someone.

They went into the cooler dining room and sat down. Again Becca was assailed by doubts. Her father had always prayed loud and long before every meal. Should she be the one to do it, or should she skip it altogether? To her immense relief, Matt bowed his head and said a short grace as comfortably as if he were the host.

"What kind of meat is this?" he asked as he tasted the crisply battered morsel. "This is really good."

"You've never had chicken fried steak? You must not have been in Texas very long."

"Only a few days." He helped himself to a sweet potato, split it open, and put a wedge of butter to melt on the orange surface. "I spent some time in Jefferson, but it's already an established town. I want one I can grow with —like Mellville."

"Then you think the railroad really will make a stop here?"

"They're bound to, as near as I can tell. If the tracks miss Jefferson, they have to pass through here to get to Dallas. Public opinion in Jefferson is against the railroad, so they will probably vote to keep it out and stick to having just the river port. Mellville is the only other logical route."

"I'll believe it when I see it. More beans?"

"You're a good cook, for someone who doesn't like it. Next time I'll cook for you."

Becca's fork paused halfway to her mouth. Could he be serious?

"Don't get me wrong now. I know board isn't included in my rent. I just meant we should do this again. All right?"

"Yes. I'd like that. You know, maybe I was a little hasty in not including meals. Not that I mean for a moment that I'd expect you or any man to cook for me, but . . ."

"Why not?"

"Why not what?" she asked in confusion.

"I'm a good cook. You have already told me you don't care for it. Why don't we share the food expense and the work?"

"I couldn't possibly do that! What would people think?"

"It's proper for a single woman to rent to a bachelor, but not proper for him to cook her a few meals? Come now."

His hazel eyes sparkled as if he were enjoying himself. "Why don't you just say what you feel?"

After a lifetime of being told to do exactly the opposite, Becca looked at him in puzzlement. Then she tossed tradition to the winds and said, "It sounds like a good idea to me."

"Fine. That's settled. Incidentally, I found Harvey Willis this afternoon. He was on a bench in the park, right where you said he would be. We had to do some horse trading, but I now own the old feed store. Tomorrow I'll start hiring carpenters to do the work."

"So soon? You certainly don't waste any time, do you!"

"Not when I see something I want." The

words sounded intimate and she looked up from her plate to find him watching her. Abruptly he said, "Would you like to work for me?"

"Me?" Visions of working in a feed store caused her to blink. Most of the sacks of grain weighed as much as she did. "No, thank you."

"You're sure? I'll pay good wages."

"I'm as busy as I can possibly be where I am," she said tactfully. She could scarcely believe he was serious.

"All right. If you change your mind, let me know."

"Apple cobbler?" she asked, as she rose from the table.

"Sure. I'll never turn that down."

Becca took their plates into the kitchen and scooped the dessert into bowls. When she turned, she nearly ran into Matt, who was bringing in the remains of supper. "Now what are you doing?"

"Clearing the table," he said, gesturing with a bowl. "What does it look like? That cobbler sure smells good."

"It's only made from dried apples. When the fruit ripens on my trees out back we'll have fresh ones." She watched him over her shoulder as he efficiently scraped the leftovers into a pan. A new idea suddenly dawned on her. Maybe he had been a chef in Memphis. That would explain everything. But why would a chef want to sell cow feed?

After supper, they went to the back porch.

He had insisted on drying the dishes while she washed, and Becca was positive she was dreaming. The night air was almost uncomfortably cool, but each breeze brought perfume from the flowering orchard just beyond the yard. In the center of the fence was an immense willow tree whose weeping boughs swept the new grass.

Becca sat on the rail and leaned her head back against the porch support. A nearly full moon glided from behind pewter clouds and silvered the willow. The orchard's blossoms seemed to float like an army of wraiths. "It's a beautiful night," she said contentedly. "I can smell spring everywhere."

Matt leaned on the rail behind her. "This place is unusual. The first time I saw it, I knew I was home."

Assuming he meant the town and not her backyard, Becca smiled. "I've always liked Mellville. Some day I want to travel and see all the places I've read about. Mountains, oceans, castles. But I want to come back here when it's all over. This is home."

"You grew up in this house?"

"Yes. I was born here. My special place was under that willow tree. When it's fully leafed out, it makes a sort of room in the center with leaves for the walls and roof. I used to pretend it was magic. I decided that if I whispered a wish when the wind was blowing, the wish would come true."

"Did they?"

"Sometimes. Often enough that I kept believing it for a long time."

"I'll bet you were a lovely child."

"Probably not. My cousin Hetty is prettier. My cousin Lilly May is smarter. My cousin Beatrice got the blue eyes. All of them are taller."

"I think you're just about perfect," Matt said quietly.

For a while Becca was silent. Then she said, "Don't tease me, Matt. I want us to be friends, but I don't need or want idle flattery."

He came to stand beside her and turned her face around to meet his. "Becca, if there's one thing you need to know about me from the start it's that I don't say anything unless I mean it. You're a beautiful woman. You're also intelligent and straightforward. Do you believe me?"

"Only the last two. And modesty would have me deny them."

"You're also hardheaded and sometimes wrong."

When she opened her mouth to object, he kissed her, gently silencing her with his caressing lips. Once when Becca was twelve, she had been kissed by a schoolboy. This was nothing like that. Matt's palm cupped her chin and his knowing lips sent rivers of fire through her veins. Sensuously, he stroked her cheek with his thumb and made her world reel drunkenly.

At last he lifted his head and gazed deeply

into her eyes. His were dark and stormy with an emotion that had never touched her until this night. A muscle flexed in his jaw and he seemed to be holding himself in check, but only with great difficulty.

"What's happening to us?" she whispered, as if her voice might shatter the emotion that engulfed them.

"I don't know, Becca," he murmured. "I never believed it could happen like this. I've heard of it, but I never thought it was really possible."

The air around them seemed to crackle with tension. "I don't understand. I don't want to know yet. But I'm happy and fearful, all at the same time." He still held her face tenderly in his palm and his thumb continued to send shivers through her.

"Which are you mostly, happy or fearful?" he asked with gentleness.

"Happy. I think."

He smiled tremulously. "I'm more fearful. You'd better go in now, Becca." He bent and kissed her lightly, and his mouth lingered on hers for a moment. "Go while you still can."

Hesitantly, Becca slid off the railing. At the door she stopped and looked back at Matt. He was silhouetted in silver against the dusky bulk of the willow. "How long have we known each other?"

He grinned at her but he still looked perplexed. "Not nearly long enough to feel like this, love."

The endearment hung between them. At last she said, "Good night, Matt."

He didn't trust himself to answer until she was well into the house. "Good night, Becca. Sleep well."

The crickets made an answer to the wind as Matt sat on the rail Becca had just left. He was busily readjusting his opinion of love at first sight.

Chapter Three

BECCA STRETCHED LIKE A CAT IN THE DOWNY billows of her feather bed. It was Sunday morning and she could hear a rooster crowing somewhere down the street. Pale sunshine drifted through her open window and a breeze wafted the snowy curtains. She snuggled deeper beneath the mound of silk patchwork comforter and smiled. She had dreamed about Matt Prescott all night. The details were shadowy, but she still felt comforted and happy.

The spring air beckoned her to the window and she got up and padded barefoot across the highly polished floor. Beneath her and beyond the backyard spread her small orchard, the limbs puffy with fragrant blossoms of pink and white. The rail fence was covered with blackberry brambles. Beside it was her vege-

table garden where glossy turnip greens com-
peted with poles of beans and cucumbers.
Although she didn't like to cook, she did enjoy
gardening, and hers was one of the finest in
town.

On the side road beyond the orchard she
saw the milk wagon. It was pulled by an
indolent dappled horse that wore a straw hat
closely resembling the milkman's. The wagon
was painted white with red letters that were
faded with age. Both the wagon and the horse
were relics of her childhood and were as
much a part of the early morning scene as the
mockingbird that sang in the large willow
beside the back porch.

Becca shivered in the cool air and wrapped
her arms around herself. Although her nightgown was long sleeved and primly high
against her throat, it did little to warm her.
Quickly she crossed the room and slipped the
gown over her head. Her long, thick hair
swept her rounded buttocks as she pulled a
dark brown merino dress from her wardrobe.
Becca stepped into her lace-trimmed bloomers and tied the ribbon snugly about her
slender waist. Then she pulled on her lacy
chemise. She put on her cotton petticoat and
tied it in place, then slipped the dress over her
head. It was warm against her cool skin, and
she deftly fastened the row of tiny jet buttons
up the front. The neck closely encircled her
throat and she embellished it with a jet
mourning broach, such as had become stylish

with the death of Prince Albert several years earlier. She could admit to herself that she was looking forward to putting away the broach containing her father's hair, and the dreary clothing.

As she sat at her dresser and brushed her long, dark hair, she thought of Matt. Had he meant all the words he had said to her yesterday? It was hard to believe that it could be true. The mirror reflected her image no differently than it had on any other morning, yet inside, for the first time in her life, Becca felt beautiful.

Her chocolate eyes softened as she drew the brush through her hair. It lay in silken strands over her breast as she daydreamed. With a sigh, she started to gather it together behind her head. From long practice, she braided her hair, then wound it in a thick bun at the back of her head. She secured it with a few long pins and looked back at the mirror. Without a doubt she looked better with a less severe style, but it would be scandalous for a woman of her age to leave her hair unbound. The brown merino did nothing for her either.

Becca lifted the somber skirt between her thumb and forefinger. It was trimmed with black cording and was as dark as her hair. There was only a month left in her mourning period. Thirty days.

From the open window she heard a melodious whistle in the strain of "Greensleeves."

Becca lifted her chin defiantly and began stripping off the dull dress.

She opened her cedar chest and pulled out her favorite blue gown. It was as light as thistledown and sprigged with tiny green leaves. Delicate lace edged the Eton collar, sleeves, and tucked bodice. Becca pulled it over her head and fastened the minute pearl buttons. Already she felt less burdened. She slipped on stockings and her calfskin shoes and deftly worked the fastenings with her buttonhook.

Would Matt think she had gone out of mourning only for him? That she was so lonely she would jump through a hoop for a few compliments? Becca looked back at the dour merino. If he did, then he did. Resolutely she hung away the dark dress. In moments she made up her bed and left her room.

Across the landing from her door was Matt's room. The door was closed as it had been for a year, but what a different emotion it now stirred in her! Instead of an overbearing invalid who had nothing but complaints for her, it now enclosed a man who made her heart race. Again Becca wondered if she were being foolish. After all, she knew nothing at all about Matt Prescott.

Keeping her steps to a sensible gait, she went downstairs and began frying a chicken for a picnic dinner as she made her breakfast. Out the window she could see Matt in the orchard.

He wandered among the fruit trees and listened to the hum of the bees that swung from flower to flower. The scent was almost cloying in the midst of the trees and promised an abundant harvest in a few months. He noticed some vegetables in an adjoining patch but couldn't have told their names. Gardening had never been a pastime for him. Not when markets sold all he needed for food.

A blue jay flew in the tree beside him as if he were inspecting the future crop for plunder. When Matt moved, the bird fluttered away, sending a few petals floating to the ground.

Matt strolled back through the low gate and over the lush grass. It was already taller than it should be and he decided to cut it for her later that day. He wondered if she would see that as an invasion of her privacy, or as the thoughtful gesture he intended it to be.

Three wooden lawn chairs, with their paint peeling, sat in the shade of the willow, and he tried to imagine which one had last offered her a place to rest. He grinned. Two days ago the name Rebecca Simpson had meant nothing to him. Now it embodied all he found desirable in a woman.

He stood beneath the willow and looked up. The rough gray trunk soared up and branched into graceful arms. The leaves were only beginning to open, but already he could see the suggestion of an emerald dome. When it was in full leaf, the tree would be magnificent. Best of all it had sheltered the child Becca, and given her a gift of magic.

"I've been told willow trees are unlucky," she said just behind him. "I never believed it, however."

When he saw her, he caught his breath. She was even more lovely than he had allowed himself to believe. A pale rose colored her cheeks and the sunlight brought deep fire to her hair. "You've left off your mourning," he observed.

"Yes." She touched a feathery tendril of leaves. "My year is almost finished and the day is so lovely."

"I'd like to think you left it off because of me."

Becca's slender fingers hesitated in her caress of the leaves. Then she said, "Would you like to go on a picnic today? We could drive down by the river after church." She looked up at him. "Do you go to church?"

"Yes," said Matt, who hadn't been to church in months. "I just started."

Mellville had two churches, one Baptist, the other Methodist. One had a larger building, the other a taller spire. They were separated by a hard-packed dirt road. Becca attended the Methodist Church.

Matt tied his horse with the others at the long rail and helped Becca down from the buggy. Behind him he could hear the murmur of the other churchgoers and was reminded of a hive of bees. Becca smiled up at him from beneath the floppy brim of her Sunday hat. The brim's shade made her look as fresh as a misty morning, yet mystery lurked in her almond-shaped eyes. Her smile created the elusive dimple in her cheek, and Matt looked away quickly. He wanted to put her back in the buggy, whisk her away to the riverbank, and love her until the smile was permanent on her face. Instead, he tucked her hand in the crook of his arm and led her up the wooden steps. The crowd parted before them.

All through the sermon, Becca was aware of the attention she had generated. Long accustomed to fading into the background, she shifted uncomfortably. Perhaps, she thought, she had misjudged the town's opinion of her in regard to her taking in a boarder. But what boarder looked at his landlady with that unsettling glint in his eyes? None she had ever heard of in Mellville.

During the hymn her hand brushed his and she nearly dropped the book. During the benediction his arm radiated its heat against hers and she missed every word the preacher was saying.

As they filed out, the preacher, flanked by his wife, examined Matt through his spectacles and drew his mouth into a firm line. Then he looked pointedly at Becca's blue dress and his lips narrowed even further.

"I hadn't realized your dear papa had been gone an entire year," he said testily.

Becca's chin raised and her hand tightened on Matt's arm. "He hasn't been, Reverend Dobson. Not for another month yet. I'd like to introduce you to my new boarder, Mr. Matt Prescott." She decided she might as well take the bull by the horns.

"Your boarder, you say? Is there a Mrs. Prescott?"

"Not yet," Matt said with strained patience.

"I see."

Becca summoned a disarming smile and nodded good-bye to the preacher and his wife. Matt led her back to the buggy as the crowd again drew back to let them pass. His identity was already spreading through the crowd and the whispers were clearly audible. A blush stung Becca's cheeks as she realized she wasn't quite as far above scandal as she had assumed. A muscle tightened in Matt's jaw, but he handed her into the buggy and smiled encouragingly at her.

Anger was beginning to replace embarrassment as her friends' and neighbors' speculations reached her ears. When Matt climbed to the seat beside her, she surprised him by again taking his arm and giving him a dazzling smile. He called to his horse and sent them trotting down the road as the small congregation looked on.

When they were out of sight, Becca released

his arm and assumed a more decorous position.

"I liked it better when you were sitting closer," Matt observed.

"I don't know what made me do that."

"No? I do."

She glanced at him and saw anger in his face. "They don't mean to be like that. It's just that we see so few strangers in Mellville."

"If you ask me, it has less to do with my being a stranger than it does with the fact I'm living under your roof."

"But it is, however, my roof. Mellville will simply have to accept it."

Matt looked at her. Although her voice was calm, her face was pale and her eyes glinted with battle. "I could go elsewhere."

"No, you couldn't. That would feed the gossips even more after only one night."

"You're probably right. I guess I'll start looking for a house tomorrow."

Becca was silent for a moment, then said, "As you wish. Turn here and follow the road by the river."

Soon the pasture and scrub oaks were replaced by taller pines and then a glade of large oak trees, sweet gum, and sycamore. He stopped the buggy in a grassy meadow. Leaves laced like stained glass over their heads and turned the sunlight to pale emerald as Matt helped Becca to the ground. The grass was long and silky in its wild abandon, and several lemony butterflies skipped over pink buttercups and purple violets. A broad stream gurgled and splashed over shallow rapids to deepen into a peaceful current only a few feet further downstream.

Matt lifted the basket of fried chicken, deviled eggs, and potato salad out of the buggy. Becca spread the quilt over the billowy grass and laid out the dinner as Matt unhitched the horse and led him to the water. Once the animal was tethered in the deep grass, Matt joined Becca on the quilt.

She had removed her hat in the cool shade and was pouring iced tea from a large fruit jar into two glasses. Her full skirts mounded like the petals of a flower and made her graceful waist seem even smaller by comparison.

"Do you have any idea how beautiful you are?"

She looked up at him with a startled expression. "I'm not beautiful. Why do you say that I am?"

"You really mean that, don't you. Who convinced you of such a thing?"

She looked at him for a minute, then said, "When I was a child, my mother often told me of a little girl who had freckles and straight hair the color of thick molasses. This little girl was a very plain child and she learned to be a dutiful daughter who was very sweet and giving to her parents. After a while I figured out the story was about me."

"That couldn't be true."

"But it was. My hair is exactly the color of blackstrap molasses and is Indian straight. My freckles faded, thank goodness, but if I go in the sun without a hat, they come back to haunt me."

He looked at her steadily. "I think that's one of the worst things I ever heard."

Becca smiled at him wryly. "Then I must assume you've led a very sheltered life." She offered him the plate of chicken.

"Let me tell you another story. This one is about a little girl whose hair is as dark as polished walnut and who has angel kisses across the bridge of her nose. She once lived in a cave with ogres, who were jealous of the little girl's beauty, so they told her she was plain and selfish and almost convinced her. Then one day a prince came riding up in a buggy drawn by a gray horse—make that a silver steed—and whisked away the girl, who was really a beautiful princess. What do you think of my story?" He continued to gaze at the water as he ate, but Becca knew he was aware of her every movement.

"I prefer your version. Did the prince and princess live happily ever after?"

"Yes." He looked at her and his hazel eyes asked questions she was afraid to hear.

"Have another deviled egg." She lowered her eyes and pretended to be interested in the quilt's familiar pattern.

Matt looked back at the lazily drifting

water. "I'll bet there are fish in there. Do you like to fish?"

"I don't know. I've never tried."

"Never?" he asked in a shocked voice.

"I have no brothers or uncles who would have taken me. Besides, there were always music lessons or sewing lessons or art lessons. All the things parents consider indispensable in bringing up a daughter."

"Well, now that you're brought up, you should learn to fish. I'll teach you."

Becca smiled. "I'd like that."

"Then it's settled. As soon as the weather gets warmer, I'll show you all there is to know about creek fishing." He helped himself to another piece of chicken.

When they had finished, Matt helped Becca put the remains of the picnic into the basket. He returned it to the buggy as she shook the crumbs from the quilt and spread it again on the grass. He lay back and closed his eyes and let the music of the water lull him. Becca watched him from the corners of her eyes. He looked so confident, so at ease. It was hard to believe she had known him scarcely one day. She had never met anyone who could settle down so comfortably in such a short time. He fascinated her. Cautiously, she risked a more straightforward look and found his eyes upon her.

"Will there be trouble for you after today?" he asked. "We stirred up quite a commotion at church."

"That will do Mellville good. We haven't had a to-do since Ollie Hanheimer eloped with Rosie Johnson."

"But will it cause a problem for you?"

"Probably not. After all, I'm the Spinster. Remember?"

"That's not the impression I got in church." He wondered if the owner of the Emporium would chastise her for her untoward behavior. Would it cost Becca her job if he continued to rent from her? He wondered if there was a way to ask that tactfully.

"What about you? Mellville seems to be casting you in the role of Rake. Are you worried about what this will do to your reputation with the ladies?"

"Do you think I'm a rake?"

"No, of course not."

"Then I'm not worried."

Becca glanced back at him. "You really ought to be serious about this. Once people make up their minds around here, they stay made up."

Matt sat up and rested his forearms on his knees and looked at her. "I don't care what anyone thinks about me. All I want is assurance that I haven't compromised you."

"Nothing has happened between us," she said uncertainly. Except for that one kiss that had set her soul winging. And the way he had of looking at her and sending her pulses hammering. Other than that, nothing at all.

"People may not believe that. Then what?"

He leaned toward her and pulled her chin around so that she looked at him. "Have I hurt you, my Becca?"

"No," she whispered. "You wouldn't hurt me."

"You believe that?" His eyes were upon her lips and there was a tenseness about him.

"I don't know why, but yes, I believe that. There's no hurt in you." He raised his eyes and she saw the gold flecks in their moss green depths. Her heart beat so hard she was certain he must hear it. "Yet somehow, you frighten me. I don't think I'll ever be the same again." She realized she was admitting far more than she should and she closed her mouth abruptly.

He chuckled and stroked her velvety cheek. "You did it again. Closed your mouth as if you're afraid too many words will fall out."

She blushed. "I talk too freely."

"No, you don't. I want you to be able to tell me anything." A breeze caressed them and he felt himself drawn toward her as if the cool air made them one. She didn't pull away, and he gently lowered his mouth to hers. Soft lips parted naturally beneath his and her breath was hot against his cheek.

As he kissed her, Becca's world seemed to spin. All the dire warnings she'd ever heard, about being too approachable to men, and especially strangers, fled from her mind. She knew only that his lips sent shivers over her and that it seemed so right. She tilted her head as he gathered her to him and her arms instinctively encircled his shoulders and waist.

Gently he laid her on the quilt, his lips still rendering her powerless. She heard a low moan escape him as she returned his kiss with her own untried ardor. She felt no shyness, no fear, only a growing need to give herself even more freely to him.

Matt drew back to look at her and gently brushed her cheek with the back of his hand. Then he again claimed her willing lips. As her eagerness increased, he took her lower lip gently in his teeth. Then he kissed her upper one. Experimentally, he ran the tip of his tongue along the incredible softness and tasted her sweetness. Becca moaned and met his tongue with her own.

"Becca," he murmured as he left a trail of kisses along her jaw and nuzzled her shell-like ear. "Have you ever . . . That is . . ." For once words failed him.

"No," she said, understanding. "I haven't. Not ever."

He drew back and read the honesty in her eyes. "In that case, lady, you have a rare talent." He grinned and lowered his head to taste her lips once more.

But his words made Becca recall herself and she forced herself to turn her head. "Matt, please. I don't know what has come over me. Until last night, I'd never even kissed a man. Now . . . I can't do this."

Using tremendous willpower, Matt rolled away and pulled her to a sitting position. "I don't want you to think I'm only after a tumble in the grass," he said firmly. "It's not like that at all."

Flushed from the emotions he had awakened in her, Becca ran her hands over her skirts in a self-conscious gesture. "Then what is it?"

"I've fallen in love with you." He said the words as simply as if they were a statement of the most obvious fact.

"Love? With me?"

"Of course with you."

"How can that be?" Her voice sounded weak as she struggled to believe what she wanted so desperately to know.

"I don't know. All I'm sure of is that I do love you. I knew from the very beginning. Don't you feel it, too?" His eyes probed into hers and she saw his worry that his love might not be returned.

"Yes. I feel it—something. But love? How can we call it love so soon?" Her eyes pleaded with him to give her proof. Some logic she could cling to.

"All I know is what I feel," he said quietly. "I was awake most of the night, trying to make some sense of it. Finally I told myself that I had imagined it, that when I saw you in the morning I could put it off as a flight of fancy, or even pure animal lust. But when I did see you, it was impossible for me to deny

47

it. I love you, Becca. I've known lust before, and I can tell the difference."

"You certainly don't mince words, do you!" She was too shocked to blush.

"No, I don't. Before you get the wrong impression, let me hasten to assure you that I want you as much as I love you." He was smiling now and laugh lines fanned at the corners of his eyes. "I want to love you in all the ways a man can love a woman. To make you feel desired and cherished every waking hour. But I know you have to have time. You take whatever time you need, Becca, but when you're ready, come to me."

She stared at him, her lips slightly parted. "You are serious, aren't you?"

He nodded. "I am. Whatever has happened to us is too big for either of us to overlook or ignore. If you feel what I do, then there's no denying it."

"And if I don't?"

"Then I'll go away and not bother you again."

Becca gazed at him as even more of her social training crumbled to dust. "Don't go," she said.

"And what about your friends and neighbors? I saw them whispering about us this morning. You may think you've been relegated to the role of ancient Spinster, but I think you're wrong. They were all willing to believe the worst of you."

"I don't understand it. Everyone has always been so good to me. How could they think I'm any different just because I took in a boarder? Of course," she said with a smile, "you don't look like a typical boarder. You look more like a hero from one of Jane Austen's novels."

He reached out and took her delicate hand. It lay trustingly in his and he stroked her tapering fingers and traced the faint blue veins along its back. "Maybe it's best if I move to Cooper's Boarding House. It's not far and yet it will lend respectability to our courtship. For I do plan to court you, Becca," he said when she looked at him. "I intend to win you over and teach you to love me."

"Do you imagine that will be too difficult?" she asked in a low voice.

"I think you already love me in your heart, but not in your mind. It's all happened too soon for you. Am I right?"

She nodded. "I can't say the words you want just yet. But when I do say them, it will be for the first time and I will mean them forever. I'm not one to use words such as those lightly."

"Then you agree that I should move to Cooper's?"

"If my reputation of twenty-five years can be destroyed by lodging a boarder, even a devilishly handsome one, for only one night, then it isn't worth having. Let Mellville say what it will. I don't want you to go. Besides," she finished lamely, "Cooper's charges much more than I do and the food is rumored to be bland."

He grinned. "You find me devilishly handsome? You never mentioned that before."

Becca blushed and looked away. "My tongue needs a brake. Yes, I find you quite handsome."

"If anything, I wish you spoke more freely, not less. I want you to be able to say anything at all to me."

"No one has ever said that to me in my entire life," she marveled. "Are you certain you're real?"

"I'm as much flesh and blood as you are, my Becca. And to me, it's you who are too good to be true."

Their eyes met and held in an eternity of a moment. The stream murmured in approval and a breeze stroked Matt's dark gold hair. Yet they were aware only of each other and the dawning love in the other's eyes.

"We must go," he said softly as he raised his hand to touch her face.

Wordlessly, she nodded. As he harnessed the horse, she stood and folded the quilt. His moves were graceful with lithe strength, and the horse stepped trustingly into the traces. Becca watched him and tried to make sense of the turn her life had taken.

Most of all, she was afraid he was leading her on, not telling her the truth. She had long become accustomed to hearing she was the most unlovable of children. So why would a man like Matt Prescott fall in love with her at first sight? It made no sense at all. Not if he was telling her the truth.

So what did he have to gain by courting her? She forced herself to admit that she was rather well-off financially, in that she owned the only dry goods store in town. The Emporium would never make her wealthy, though she was comfortable. But did she appear affluent enough that a man might want to marry her for her money? It seemed unlikely.

"You look worried," Matt said as he came to her. "What's wrong?"

"Nothing, really. I was only thinking. Tell me about yourself. Why do you want to settle in Mellville?"

"Originally, as I've already told you, because Mellville is sure to become a railroad stop. Now it's because of you."

"Suppose the rails don't come through here and the stop is in Jefferson instead?"

"I don't think it will be. And there's still you. Even if Mellville is missed entirely, I don't want to leave now. But it won't be."

"I don't see how a depot will make much difference. This is still a small town."

"It is now, but when it can be reached by rail, businesses will be built here. The land is cheaper here than in Dallas and people will want to buy here. Once goods can be shipped from here by rail, Mellville will start to grow. You'll see."

"And if it doesn't, then what?"

"Then we'll have to decide whether we want to stay here or move to wherever else the rails do go. But we will decide together."

Becca looked at him long and carefully. "It's all happening too fast. I'm afraid."

"Of me?"

"A little. You aren't like anyone I've ever met before. You seem so confident. So . . . strong. I feel things with you that I've never felt before. It's overwhelming and rather frightening."

"I never want to frighten you."

He was standing close to her and she felt her body sway toward him as if he were a magnet. The sun gilded his thick hair into a cap of gold and lay on his burnished eyelashes. His eyes were the topaz green of fall leaves. "I need . . . time. Time to think," she protested weakly.

"Take all the time you need. I want you to be sure."

"I can't think at all when you look at me like that." Becca drew a long steadying breath. "Maybe it would be best if you move to Cooper's for a while. I don't want to make a mistake. Not about something as important as this."

"All right. I'll move there tomorrow. There's no time today before sunset."

She looked at the sky and saw that the sun was indeed low and that long shadows were stretching across the silky grass. "Tomorrow then," she agreed. At the words, her heart felt heavy. She didn't want to think clearly if it meant his absence. The realization stunned her. What she was feeling wasn't logical or even reasonable. But she couldn't back down now. "Tomorrow," she repeated for her own benefit.

As he helped her into the buggy, she felt saddened. Perhaps he would take this to mean she didn't care for him at all. Could she bear to be without him now that she was falling in love with him? She had not admitted this before, even to herself, and her mind turned away from it quickly. She would see him again. He had said he would come to court her; besides, Mellville wasn't so large that she wouldn't see him often. But would it be the same after he left? New love seemed so fragile, as if it were no more substantial than a soap bubble. Could it continue to grow? All the way back to town, Becca was silent.

Chapter Four

BECCA UNDRESSED SLOWLY. FROM BEYOND the thin wall she could hear Matt doing the same. She slipped off her dress and hung it in the wardrobe. Because she didn't feel in the least sleepy, she decided to rearrange her wardrobe. She took her lighter-colored garments from the cedar chest, shook them out the window to remove the dried lavender, and hung them in place of the drab mourning clothes. As she folded away the last black dress and firmly closed the lid of the chest, she heard Matt close a drawer in the adjoining room.

A small frown puckered Becca's brow, and she sat on the chest to remove her shoes. Was he packing even now? The thought brought her pain.

I've got to get hold of myself, she thought

firmly. This must be faced reasonably and with propriety. At the same time a rebellious part of her mind demanded to know why.

She removed her garters and rolled her stockings down. Barefooted, she sat on the chest and made no effort to sit erect or to keep her knees together. There were far more important things on her mind than etiquette.

Once years ago she had known a boy named Charley Barnett. He had been boyishly handsome with a shock of red hair and a quick sense of humor. She and Charley had secretly "walked out" a few times, and he had even held her hand in the dark stretch between the church and her house. But her father had heard of the budding romance and had told Charley in no uncertain terms that his advances were not welcome. Because he had chosen to do this on Main Street at noon, word spread quickly. Rebecca Simpson was to be avoided by all young men lest similar embarrassment occur. Becca had been too mortified to leave the house for days. When she finally did, Charley's ardor had cooled appreciably, and he never walked her home again.

She hadn't thought of Charley Barnett in years. He had moved away and married a girl in Jefferson. Although Becca had been only eighteen at the time, her spinsterhood had begun on that day. Long-buried anger at her domineering father surfaced. If only he had allowed her to have a normal childhood, so much of her unhappiness would never have happened. She would probably be married to Charley and raising redheaded babies by now.

But she wasn't married to Charley and no longer wished she had been. Matt's footsteps sounded on the wooden floor and she looked toward the wall. Her father would approve even less of Matt, with his virility and easy confidence. Matt wasn't a man to bow to anyone. Becca suspected that if her father had upbraided Matt on Main Street rather than Charley, the outcome would have been far different. She smiled as she pulled the pins from her hair.

The umber masses cascaded down her back and she ran her fingers through it. She much preferred her hair loose and flowing, yet even as a child she had had to wear it braided in pigtails. Someday, she decided, she would leave it loose. As long as she didn't leave the house, who would know?

She stood and finished undressing. The room was cool with the late evening so she hurried into her gown. It was one of her favorites, with mock pearl buttons up the front and delicate embroidery on the bodice. The gown was more suitable for a trousseau than a lonely room, but since she had seemed unlikely to have the former, she had made it anyway. Like her hair, which she wore unbraided at night, no one would ever know.

She lay down and pulled the covers over her before she blew out the small lamp. At once darkness washed over the room and was gradually dispelled by moonlight. A fat moon hung outside her window and set silvery blue light over her bed. Becca crossed her arms behind her head and watched it slowly rise.

Sleep eluded her. She could no longer hear Matt moving about, so she assumed he too must be in bed. The thought sent her mind in most unmaidenly imaginings.

Becca rolled to her side and closed her eyes, but they opened again. Tomorrow he would move to Cooper's Boarding House and she would again be alone. The problem was, she didn't want him to go.

She turned to her other side and stared at the wallpaper by her bed. She knew each posy, each leaf, each minute rose. They marched across her walls in unerring rows of permanent springtime. For years those same roses had made unfading garlands and would continue to do so. Unchangingly.

With a sigh, Becca flung herself onto her back, her arms outspread. In this position, both her hands fell off the narrow bed. Above her, on the ceiling, were cousins of the same roses, only in small clumps.

Seven years ago she had lain exactly like this and stared at those same roses, then bright with newness, and wondered if she could die of embarrassment. She had hoped she might expire of a broken heart over Charley, but she hadn't. Either love had been too weak or her spirit too strong, but she had survived. Seven years. She hadn't realized it had been that long ago. Since then, her life had settled into a dull predictability. She had gone to work at her father's Emporium; he had had a stroke and she had become its ruler; he had died, and now it was hers. But Becca wanted more from life than yard goods and notions and predictability. She wanted love.

Was he asleep by now? She had heard no sounds for a long time. She wondered if he slept in a nightshirt as her father had. Somehow she couldn't imagine him in one, but what else was there?

She recalled the golden depths of his hazel eyes and how green they looked in the sunlight. How his hair gilded and ruffled softly in the breeze. Unlike most men, he had used no pomade to keep it in place, and it looked as soft as her own. Mentally she traced every facet of Matt's face, from his broad brow, to his chiseled lips, to the strong column of his throat. The memory of his kisses rose to haunt her and she closed her eyes.

Charley Barnett had never been adventurous enough to kiss her, but she knew instinctively that it would have been nothing like the magic of Matt's kisses. Even now, hours later, she felt weak just thinking about them.

Was this love, she wondered? Could it be anything else? She had never experienced what Matt had termed "animal lust," but she had often heard about it in church. Unless she was very mistaken, this wasn't it. True, she ached for him and his embrace, and even his gaze made her long for more. But it didn't stop there. She wanted to talk to Matt. To tell him all her dreams that she had never confided to anyone else, to entrust him with her secrets. Not only that, she wanted to hear his innermost hopes. To help him accomplish them. Although his strength was obvious, Becca felt oddly protective toward him, and yet she didn't mind the thought of being protected by him. Since she had been reared to be a bulwark to her parents, this was unusual indeed. Becca had been carefully trained to be the family support, and while she might regret the load, she was taught never to relinquish it. Until she met Matt Prescott, she had never considered that she might. The sensation of being cherished and nurtured was new to her, and she found that she liked it.

Becca sat up and looked around the room. She had slept within these walls every night of her life except for rare visits to her Aunt Agatha in Jefferson. Beside the door stood her dresser; by the window, her wardrobe loomed in the dusk, and beside it but invisible in the shadows was the cedar chest. Last was her narrow bed. Nothing else. The room was hers and hers alone. Forever.

Without hesitation, Becca threw back the covers and got out of bed. The room seemed to be pressing in on her and she felt confined. Thinking a glass of milk might lull her to sleep, she padded barefoot across the floor and opened her door.

At the same time, Matt opened his and they stood face-to-face across the landing.

Matt's lamp sent a rectangle of gold across the oak floors and made a black well of the staircase. He wore his pants and a shirt unbuttoned to his waist. Becca could see his deeply tanned chest, which contrasted sharply with the white shirt. His hair was tousled as if he had run his fingers through it, and his eyes looked dark and haunted.

"Don't leave me," Becca heard herself whisper. "Don't ever leave me."

"Becca," he murmured.

"I love you," she said simply.

Matt caught his breath as if her words had had a physical impact.

"Do you know what you're saying?" he asked hoarsely.

"I don't care anymore. What you said was true. This is more than we can turn our backs on. A love like this happens very rarely and the only sin would lie in disregarding it.

"If what we have lasts only a month or even a day, it must be the way it is. I don't see how so strong a love could continue for a lifetime, but even half of this is more than I thought I could feel." She smiled tremulously. "It could diminish greatly and still be more than I ever expected."

"Then you want me?" he asked incredulously.

"I want you."

He held out his hand to her and met her

halfway across the landing. "You can still turn around and go back, my Becca," he said as he gazed hungrily down at her. "I'll think no less of you."

"If I intended to go back, I would never have said what I just did. Will you let me come to you?"

Matt touched her face as if she were made of the finest porcelain. Emotions thundered through him at the sight of her looking up at him so trustingly. Her dark eyes were soft with love and her hair made a silken cape behind her. He knew he should try to reason with her and send her back to her room, but to do so would take superhuman strength. He bent and lifted her in his arms. She was light and warm, and her body seemed designed to fit in his embrace. She lay her head on his shoulder and her slender arms encircled his neck. A wave of love rushed over Matt and made him tremble at its impact. Tenderly he carried her into his room.

He lay her on his bed and turned the lamp down low. Her glorious hair fanned out on the white pillow and framed her heart-shaped face. When he touched her cheek his hand was unsteady and he smiled wryly. He couldn't recall ever having been shy with a woman, but then, he had never before been in love.

"You're so beautiful," he said gently. "Your eyes are like dark jewels and your skin glows in the lamplight. When you smile like this, you have one dimple, and it never shows at any other time. How could anyone so perfect ever fall in love with me?"

"Because you're Matt Prescott," she whispered. "If you were anyone else, it would never have happened. I'm only perfect for you, as you are for me," she answered with the wisdom of love.

"Then you truly love me?"

"With all my heart. And you love me?"

"From the first moment I saw you."

She laughed softly as her hand stroked his cheek. "The first time you saw me, we were sitting on the sidewalk."

"You were beautiful then, too. Battle fire was in your eyes and you were going on about a young thief."

"Jimmy Little finally did me a good turn." She was silent as she studied the way his eyelashes fringed his eyes and how the hazel depths were dark now in the dim light. She wanted to remember every single detail about him. Then, if this incredible love didn't last forever, she would have him printed indelibly in her heart.

"You look as if you're memorizing me," he said with a smile as he lifted a long strand of her flowing hair.

"I am. You have the same look."

"If you ever tire of me, I want to be able to remember you just like this," he replied.

Hearing him repeat her thoughts so exactly

made Becca melt inside. "Will this last, Matt?"

"Yes. It's too strong not to." Slowly he lowered his head and tasted her lips. "After seeing heaven, to lose it would be too cruel." He studied her face to see if she were less certain than he had admitted to being, then again claimed her mouth.

At the touch of his warm lips, Becca felt her last reservations flee forever. Warmth spread through her and seemed to brand her for his own. She met his kiss with growing abandon and put her arms around him to hold him close. His arms encircled her and he lifted her to him. When their lips parted, he embraced her so strongly she seemed about to merge with him, and she hugged him close as she buried her face in his shoulder.

Matt's fingers plundered the night of her hair and he nuzzled his face in its fragrant depths. "Becca," he murmured hoarsely. "My Becca, I love you so."

Again his lips found hers as love pounded through his veins. She was so small in his arms that he feared he would hurt her in his passion. Yet she matched his excitement and held nothing back. Matt ran his hand down her back as he supported her against him. She was gracefully slender, but as his hand caressed her ribs, he felt the swell of her full breasts. He had learned long ago that a shapely dress didn't always cover a well-endowed bosom, but her breast was firm and soft beneath his hand and her nipple grew taut as he cupped the supple mound.

She murmured with pleasure at the caress, and Matt began to gently knead her soft flesh. Untried she might be, but she knew instinctively how to love him. She arched her back to give him better access and entwined her fingers in his hair as she kissed him.

Slowly Matt released the buttons that held her gown primly shut. One by one they opened for him. He laid her back on the pillow and kissed each inch of skin as he discovered it. Her hands stroked his back and made no move to stop him as he revealed her untouched flesh.

With ragged breath he paused and gazed deeply into her eyes. "You're sure, Becca? You want this too?"

"Love me," she whispered. "I want you as badly as you want me."

He opened the last button and ran his fingertips over her creamy skin. Almost reverently he pushed the fabric aside for his first view of her. The dusky pink bud of her nipple crowned her rounded breast in a glory of femininity. Gently he ran his fingers over the incredibly smooth skin and saw her nipple harden even tighter. Slowly he lowered his head and took the bud into his mouth. His eager tongue loved the hardness and the satin skin surrounding it and he heard her moan with pleasure.

Not lifting his head from her, Matt pulled

the gown from her shoulder and she slipped her bare arm around his neck. He ran his hand over the supple skin of her arm and shoulder and let his tongue flick over her nipple with maddening slowness. Only when she arched against him and pressed her body to his did he pull her gown from her other shoulder and do the same honor to her untouched breast.

Becca felt fires of molten desire kindle in her as he nuzzled at her in ways she had never imagined, and she wondered briefly at the wanton ecstasy she discovered. Then his hot tongue again found her aching nipple and she forgot about everything but Matt and the passion he was so knowingly building.

His shirt was a barrier, so she pulled it out of his pants. Eagerly she pushed it from his shoulders and tasted the faintly salty essence of his skin. His muscles were hard beneath her lips, but his skin had the texture of fine satin. Hungry to know more, she ran her hands over him and marveled at the power she felt beneath her palms. Heavy muscles rippled over his broad back and dipped into the shallow trough of his spine.

Matt paused in his loving to ease her nightgown past her hips and to gaze down at her. His expression of awe told her she pleased him as he finished removing his shirt. His chest was broad and looked bronze in the mellow light. Lean muscles ridged his belly and his breath was coming quickly, as if he had been running.

"I never knew anyone could be so perfect," he said at last. "Your clothes don't do you justice."

Standing, he unbuttoned his pants and removed them, his eyes alert to any sign of trepidation on her face. There was none. Becca boldly surveyed his erect manhood, his lean hips and well-muscled thighs, then returned to the font of his desire. "You're beautiful, too. And much more than I had expected."

Matt laughed softly. "Your body was made to be loved by my body. I'll not hurt you."

She looked up at him in surprise. "I was told it always hurts."

"And you wanted me anyway?"

"I love you. A little pain is nothing compared to the need I have to be one with you."

He lay beside her and smoothed the hair back from her face. "It need not hurt at all, love. The first moments may be a little uncomfortable, but after that, you'll feel only pleasure. But that," he said as he nibbled her ear, "comes later."

"How much later?"

"When you're far more ready than you are now."

Becca couldn't see how she would ever want him more than at that moment, but his hand had begun making slow circles about her breast and his lips were tracing fire along her neck, so she didn't ask questions. His fingers seemed to know better than she did what would give her pleasure, and his lips and tongue kindled desires in her that she had never known. She heard a moan of passion and realized it had come from her own lips. Still he urged her to greater joy.

His lips centered on her nipple, drawing it into his mouth, releasing it, only to draw it in again. Becca arched against him and her hips moved in an instinctive rhythm of love. Slowly his hand moved lower, massaging her flat stomach and encircling her navel, then lower still. When he nudged her legs apart, Becca opened to him eagerly. But he only stroked the sensitive skin of her inner thighs.

Passion shook her when he finally touched the seat of her arousal, and he chuckled softly at her willingness. "There's never been a woman more made for love, my Becca. You're all I ever dreamed of and more." His fingers sent flames through her and she felt a tightness and trembling deep within.

"I love you," he professed. "God, I love you."

He knelt between her thighs and gently guided himself to meet her passion. She felt a slight resistance and steeled herself for the pain, but it never came. Instead she was aware of a completeness she had never known before, and he moaned as their union became complete. After a moment's pause to let her become accustomed to the new sensation, he began to move within her.

As the newness fell away, Becca's passion increased until she seemed to soar in Matt's arms. Higher and higher they flew on a wave of molten love. Suddenly, incredibly, the wave crested and Becca felt as if the universe had exploded within her. She cried out in ecstasy and heard Matt call her name. Wave after wave of satisfaction thundered through her, leaving her weak and shaken, but smiling broadly.

Matt looked down at her and after catching his own breath said, "You look happy. Like a woman in love."

"I am happy," she sighed as the delicious warmth flowed through her. "And I'm very much in love."

"No regrets?" he asked as he kissed her cheek and then her ear.

"None at all." She stroked his shoulder and ran her hand over the expanse of his chest. "You won't leave me, will you?"

"I'll never leave you." He pulled her head over to lie comfortably on his shoulder.

"Not even to go to Cooper's Boarding House tomorrow?"

"No, we're going somewhere else tomorrow."

"Where?" she asked sleepily.

"To church to get married."

Her head shot up. "Married?"

"I believe that's the usual procedure when two people are in love. Don't you want to marry me?"

"Of course. But I didn't think it would be so soon. Are you serious?"

"No man in his right mind talks marriage unless he is. Especially at a time like this." He looked up at her with love shining in his eyes. "Miss Simpson, will you do me the honor of becoming my wife?"

"I'd be delighted, Mr. Prescott. And I won't even make you ask me the usual three times before I say yes."

"Nothing will come between us now, love. Not ever. By this time tomorrow you will be Becca Prescott, Beloved Wife."

"I'm looking forward to the demise of Rebecca Simpson, Spinster," she laughed contentedly as she snuggled down by his side. "I love you so much." She slept cradled in the security of Matt's strong arms.

Chapter Five

MATT PRESCOTT DREW HIS HORSE TO A HALT IN front of the wood frame parsonage. A glance at his gold pocket watch told him it was ten o'clock. By now Becca would be arranging to take the rest of the day off. He smiled as he recalled their hours of loving. She was a rare one, his Becca, and he could still hardly believe she was his.

He tied the gray horse, and as he went up on the porch he patted at his pocket to check that the tiny gold ring he had just bought was still safely tucked away. Getting the preacher to marry them that afternoon couldn't take too long. That would give him ample time to pick Becca up at the Emporium, take her to dinner at Cooper's, then return to the church for the private ceremony. With a smile of confidence,

Matt rapped on the door. At his second knock an imposing woman with steel gray hair and an ample bosom opened the door and greeted him coolly.

"Morning, ma'am. I'm Matt Prescott and I've come to see Reverend Dobson."

"The reverend is busy. I'm Mrs. Dobson. Is he expecting you?" She kept the screen door firmly closed.

"No, ma'am, not exactly, but I want him to perform a wedding for Miss Rebecca Simpson and me."

Mrs. Dobson's double chin dropped. "Rebecca Simpson is getting married? Since when?"

"What's going on, Margaret?" a voice called from inside the house. "Is someone at the door?"

"Did you know Rebecca Simpson is getting married?" his wife tossed over her shoulder. To Matt she said crossly, "Might as well come in. The reverend is already interrupted."

"Thank you," Matt said with forced politeness. Hat in hand, he followed the broad woman down the short hallway.

"What's that about somebody getting married?" the preacher was saying. "Ezra Simpson's daughter?" He looked up from his papers and stared for a minute at Matt, then slowly rose. "So it's you. Mr. Prescott, I believe?"

"That's right." Matt's eyes flicked over his

unexpected adversary. "Miss Simpson and I plan to get married and we would like you to perform the ceremony."

"When?"

"Today." Matt was fast losing his patience.

"Today! That's impossible! What's the rush?" Dobson's eyes narrowed suspiciously.

"There is no 'rush,'" Matt said coolly. "We are in love and see no reason to waste time."

Mrs. Dobson snorted as she stood with her arms folded over her chest. "How long has she known you, young man?"

"Not very long, but long enough to know." When she snorted again, Matt scowled.

"You have to see our side of it," Dobson said. "We've known Rebecca all her life and her parents before her. Now here she is all alone in life and she's vulnerable. By all rights she should still be in mourning for her father, not planning a whirlwind marriage."

"Are you refusing to marry us?" Matt asked incredulously.

"It's just that we don't know who you are," Mrs. Dobson put in. "A woman alone has to be careful. Where did you meet her?"

"I rent a room from her. What difference does it make? I'm Matt Prescott from Memphis, Tennessee. Becca Simpson loves me and I love her. We are both consenting adults and I can't believe I'm standing here trying to justify marrying her!" Matt's voice had raised steadily and his eyes flashed with anger.

"There's no need to lose your temper, young man," Dobson said with maddening slowness.

"Obviously there is one reason to advise against such a union," his wife intoned as she drew herself up. "Rebecca Simpson never had a public outburst of anger!"

"If you won't marry us, we'll go to your competition across the street!"

Dobson leaned forward and looked at Matt disapprovingly. "Here in Mellville we don't refer to our brothers in the faith as competition. Where did you say you're from?"

Matt leaned his palms on the desk and met the preacher's glare. "Memphis! And you?"

Mrs. Dobson whipped a handkerchief from her sleeve and waved it under her own nose as if she felt faint.

"Perhaps you'd better leave, dear," Dobson said as he slowly stood. "I want to talk to him man to man." As soon as the woman bustled out and the door closed behind her, Dobson said, "Rebecca will never countenance being married in any church but this. Your threats fall on deaf ears." He drew himself up and struck a pose worthy of the pulpit.

"Then what do you propose that we do?" Matt asked in a menacing voice. "You have two people in love and wanting to do the right thing. They live alone, unchaperoned, in the same house. Already there's vicious gossip starting to circulate. What do you suggest?" His voice was scarcely louder than a whisper, but its impact was greater than a shout.

Dobson exhaled and slowly sat back down. "You could find another room. Perhaps at Cooper's?"

"No. Try again."

"She could have a relative move in with her as well?"

"There is no one, as you well know," Matt gambled. "And if there was, it would take weeks to find a suitable cousin or aunt and move her in—if the cousin or aunt was even willing. Any more suggestions?"

"You refuse to move out?"

"I do."

"What about her good name? You seem determined to smear it with mud!"

"Not me! I want to marry her. What will people say when they hear you refused to marry us and left us no choice but to live in sin?"

"Live in sin! I never suggested you were actually . . . Now see here. That's black-mail!"

"That's right."

Dobson sputtered with outrage and rubbed his spectacles vigorously with his handker-chief. "Blackmail! You want to get married today, you say? What's the all-fired hurry."

"Because there's going to be a night tonight, and another tomorrow. Unlike you, I really *am* thinking of her reputation."

"All right! Come by today at three. I'll meet you at the church and I'll have the papers with me. Now get out of here!"

Matt grinned and straightened up. "Thank you, Reverend Dobson. I appreciate it." He turned and left promptly before the preacher could have second thoughts. As he passed Mrs. Dobson, industriously dusting the hall tree by the study door, he said cheerfully, "Congratulate me, Mrs. Dobson. I'm to be married today at three o'clock."

As he left the parsonage he was whistling.

"I can still hardly believe it!" Becca exclaimed as she gazed up at him. "It's my wedding day! Are you certain Reverend Dobson didn't object to such a remarkably short courtship?"

"If he had objected, would we be on our way to the church?" Matt asked evasively as he opened the front door for his bride-to-be.

"I simply can't believe it!" Becca looked back at the familiar parlor. "The next time I come in this door, I'll be Rebecca Prescott." She tilted her head up to his and said, "Do you mind that there will be no friends or relatives?"

"I prefer it this way." He tenderly cupped her small chin in his hand. "What about you? Will you regret not having all the bustle and scurrying around and being the center of attention?"

"No," she laughed. "I don't regret it. Years ago it would have been what I wanted, but now I only want to be your wife."

"Twenty-five is hardly ancient, Becca."

"It is in Mellville." She tiptoed to kiss him briefly. "I don't even have a trousseau."

"You won't need one if I have a say in it." He grinned suggestively.

Although she blushed, Becca nodded. "You'll have your say."

"Let's go."

Becca pulled on her white kid gloves and adjusted her wide-brimmed straw hat. She wore an apple green dress of watered silk with deep ruffles of ecru lace at the cuffs and rounded neckline. The lace cascaded down the bodice to form flounces like a frothy waterfall on the visible underskirt. Her hat was trimmed with a broad silk ribbon of the same shade of green. Her hair and eyes seemed velvety dark by comparison, and her translucent skin glowed healthily.

When she was seated in the buggy and Matt whistled to the horse, she looked longingly in the direction of town. The road to the church was in the opposite direction. Sensing her need, Matt grinned and reined the horse toward Main Street first.

Although Becca greeted her friends with a casual smile and a nod of her head, she felt delight course through her. Many frankly turned and stared at her in her best dress, riding beside the handsome stranger who had set the town agog. Even the gray was a beauty with its proudly bowed neck that required no check rein, and it had a spanking gait. Becca knew the town would be speculating before they were out of sight. Becca, who had always prided herself on never being a target for gossip, smiled.

"You have a broad streak of the theatrical in you, Miss Simpson," Matt observed.

"So do you, Mr. Prescott. I never asked you to drive through the middle of town."

"No? I could turn off on this side street," he offered.

"Once around the park, please," she said regally.

The spring air was warm on her cheeks, and only a few cotton-ball clouds floated in the azure sky. Wild flowers vied with luxuriant grass on the town's park lawn and scarlet geraniums bloomed along the walk. Never had Becca seen a more perfect day for a wedding. She glanced over at Matt and felt her heart swell with love. She would make him a good wife, she vowed to herself. She would never let a cross word to him pass her lips.

At the edge of town they circled back through the fields to the church. Soon they saw the white spire and simple frame building across from the newer and larger one of red brick. Becca tightened her grip on Matt's arm.

"You're not having second thoughts, are you?" he asked anxiously.

"No, I was afraid you might be. I've heard men detest weddings, even their own."

"Not me. I'd fight for the chance to marry

you." He glanced at the parsonage behind the church and hoped Dobson would show up.

Becca smiled contentedly in the knowledge Matt would never be put to the test. Who would ever dispute his claim to marry her? Still, it was nice to hear him say so.

They tied the horse at the front rail and, arm in arm, entered the church. Reverend Dobson was distributing hymnals in the racks in the empty pews and he looked up at their entrance. He eyed Matt distastefully, then gave an exaggerated sigh. As if this were a signal, his portly wife appeared through the side door. With her was her friend, Mabel Henshaw.

"You need witnesses," Dobson commented. "Come down to the rail, please."

With a smile up at Matt, Becca started down the aisle. Suddenly he stopped. "Wait here," he said.

Becca watched him dash out and heard the outraged murmurs behind her. In no time he was back, a bouquet of wild bluebonnets in his hand. As shyly as a young boy, he presented them to Becca.

Tears of happiness blurred her vision as she took them from him. "Thank you, Matt."

"I wish they were orchids," he told her softly. "Someday they will be."

Her eyes shining, she answered him truthfully. "I prefer these."

He offered her his arm, and together they walked down the aisle. Reverend Dobson met them at the prayer rail and began the familiar ceremony. Becca glanced sideways at her groom. The wind had ruffled his hair across his high forehead in a way that was less than stylish but utterly appealing. His nose was straight and narrow, giving him the aspect of a Greek god. Even though he wasn't smiling, his finely sculpted lips tilted slightly at the corner. His jaw was deep and hinted at more than a strain of German blood, and his neck was solid and rounded with muscle. Becca's eyes moved to his deep chest, and memories of the night before made her jerk her gaze away. Distracted, she tried to catch up with Reverend Dobson's dry monotone.

She, Rebecca, promised to take him, Matt, forever and ever. The vows were exchanged and Dobson firmly closed his black Bible. They were now husband and wife. Becca lifted her radiant face for Matt's kiss and she noticed his hand trembled on her chin. Their eyes met and held, then closed as their lips came together in a salute that was rather too long for the Reverend Dobson's patience.

Without taking his eyes from his bride's face, Matt handed the preacher two dollars. Hand in hand, he and Becca left the church.

"I forgot to thank Mrs. Dobson and Mrs. Henshaw for being our witnesses," Becca exclaimed as they drove away.

"A bride is allowed to be forgetful on her wedding day . . . Mrs. Prescott."

Becca laughed with sheer joy and laid her

head on his shoulder. Matt peered happily around the brim of her hat and wondered if all grooms were so well pleased with their lot in life.

"Let's go for a ride in the country," he suggested. "Here we are married and we've never done that."

"I'd love to. You pick the road so it's an adventure for us both."

Within the hour they halted in a field covered with clover and wild flowers. Becca laid her bluebonnet bouquet on the seat and let Matt put his hands on her waist and spin her to the ground.

All around them, the field rolled on in gentle undulations. A forest of tall oaks and gum trees partially encircled the huge meadow. A short distance away was a tumbledown cabin —the only sign that anyone had ever passed this way before.

They strolled to the cabin and Becca knelt to smell the profusion of small pink roses, now reverted back to wild brambles. A few pale iris waved like crepe paper in the breeze, and a chinaberry sapling had taken root just inside the doorway.

"Who do you suppose lived here?" Becca said dreamily as she leaned back on Matt.

He removed her hat and slipped his arms around her before he said, "Someone who was very happy."

"How do you know?"

He nibbled her ear and said, "He brought

her roses. As old as this cabin seems to be, they must have had a long journey. I'll bet whenever these roses bloomed she thought of him."

Becca looked up at him. "Matt Prescott, you have the soul of a poet."

"Love does that to people." His hands crept higher to cup beneath her breasts.

"You shouldn't do that! What if someone should see us?"

When he quit laughing, he made a sweeping gesture with his arm. "Who can see us, love? There's not another soul within miles." He deftly brushed the froth of lace aside and began to release the buttons of her bodice.

"What are you doing?"

"Guess."

"Out here? In the open?"

"If anyone comes by we will see them long before they can see us."

"There's a flaw in your reasoning," she told him, "but I don't care."

Her gown dropped to the ground, and her petticoats, shoes, and stockings followed as Matt removed his coat, shirt, and shoes. As the wind caressed her nearly bare skin, Becca paused and looked up at him. "I love you," she said softly. "I love you with all my heart."

Matt kissed her gently and pulled her to him in a rapturous embrace that nearly took her breath away. His skin was warm and firm beneath her palms and she clung to him as if she would never let him go.

Matt released her at last and slowly pulled her chemise over her head. Her skin was pale ivory in the bright sunlight and her taut nipples were darker than the roses behind them. Matt loosened the ribbon that held her bloomers and they joined the petticoats. Carefully he removed the pins from her hair and let it fall free like the mane of a pagan goddess.

With unschooled fingers, Becca unbuttoned his trousers and eased them down. "You don't wear anything beneath?" she asked in surprise. She had done enough washing to know her father had worn long johns the year around.

"Only in the winter. Do you ever use corsets and lacings?"

"No. I'm already too thin."

"No, you're perfect."

They stood in the cool air, as unencumbered as two people could be. Then Matt took Becca in his arms. For long moments he merely held her. Then his passion overtook his awe and he kissed her with growing urgency as his fingers set fires in her sensitive breasts.

Becca moaned and moved her hips seductively against his hard manhood. Her knees were weak and she trembled at his tender onslaught. Sensing he was awaiting her signal, she knelt on her petticoats and pulled him down beside her. They gazed long at each other, loving with their fingertips and soft words until neither could bear it any longer.

They became one beneath the brilliantly

blue sky, with a field of fragrant flowers for their bed. Their union was all the sweeter for her newly acquired experience and richer for the band of gold that encircled the third finger of her left hand.

Afterward, they dressed slowly, bedecking each other with clover and buttercups as if they were children. Becca wove a garland of Indian paintbrushes and white clover for his hair and adorned her own hat with wild roses and violets. Attired once more in the semblance of civilization, they wandered back to the buggy.

"Someday let's buy this land," Matt suggested, "and build us a house right there on that hill."

"All right, we will," she said playfully. "And I'll have an orchard of fruit trees there and one of pecan trees over there."

"So close to the barn?" he protested. "The horses will eat the crop."

"Then we'll plant the pecans down the drive in a double row."

"We're going to have a wonderful life together," he prophesied. "Why don't we start it by going on a honeymoon?"

"I can't leave town," she said in surprise. "I have to work."

"Won't your employer give you some time off? It's not every day a woman gets married. Who is he? I'd like to talk to him."

"I'm him. That is, I own the Emporium."

"You do?"

"Of course. I thought you knew that!"

"No, you never mentioned it."

Then he hadn't married her for her property. The thought had crossed her mind. "Perhaps Nell could open and close up for me tomorrow, but I really can't be gone longer than that. The bills are due out this week and it's time to place my next order for merchandise."

"I understand. After all, I'm in business myself. If you want a store to keep you, you have to keep it. By the way, I need to start tearing down the old feed store I bought. Since we can't leave town, I guess I'll get the workmen on it tomorrow."

"Tear it down? Whatever for?"

"It won't do for my business. The floorboards are warped from storing heavy grain and the whole place smells like a barn."

This seemed to be a strange complaint from a man in the feed business, but she smiled and laid her head on his shoulder. "Then you'll only replace the flooring and inside walls?"

"Oh, no, it will have to be taken down to the ground," he said as he glanced at her curiously. "I'm building a fine new building. One that will attract customers from miles around."

As he would have the only feed store within ten miles, Becca had no doubt that he was right. She secretly wondered if farmers cared one way or another about a fancy front for such a commodity, but she was too much in love to argue.

"I think my freckles are back," she observed as she wrinkled her sunburned nose.

"They are, and they're beautiful. Let's see if you can say the same about my broiled back." Matt grinned at her and kissed her forehead. "It was worth it."

As they neared town, they passed another couple out for an evening drive. Becca smiled and nodded a greeting but the other couple only stared.

"Why do you suppose they were looking at us like that?" she said as she examined her dress for any loose buttons.

Matt's grin broadened as he caught sight of her wild-flower-bedecked hat. "Search me," he replied.

Chapter Six

THE NEXT FEW WEEKS PASSED IN A HAZE OF happiness. Becca became accustomed to Matt dropping in the store for a quick kiss or a hasty conversation. Many of the topics could easily have waited until they were at home, but it pleased her that he found excuses to see her so often. And with him overseeing the new building every day, he didn't have far to walk.

The old feed store had been leveled to the ground and the new one was being erected in its place. Instead of the cheaper lumber, Matt was building with red brick from the nearby quarry. Becca had to smile when she looked at it, for it would easily be the most prestigious building in town, and much more elaborate than any feed store had a right to be.

She knew very little about building and she

usually contented herself with watching the progress from the Emporium's small paned windows. Carpenters and bricklayers swarmed over the construction, and within weeks a white lintel was added over the front door and also over the gaping holes where the windows would stand. When painters were added to the work force, Becca could only shake her head in wonder. At this rate, farmers would be too intimidated to buy there. She considered telling Matt as much, but decided against it. After all, she thought, he knew the feed business from past experience and she was only familiar with dry goods.

Business had been good that day. Becca had had a sale on ginghams and every woman in town had flocked to the store. During the dinnertime lull, she rolled the uncut fabric straight on the heavy bolts and stacked them on end upon the bolt goods counter. She was struggling with a roll of cotton ticking when Matt came striding down the aisle.

He lifted the large bolt, found a space, and deposited it for her. "Come look at my windows," he said with excitement. "They just arrived from Dallas."

Becca was tired and she saw nothing remarkable about windows, but his excitement was contagious and she smiled. "I guess I can spare a few minutes. Let me tell Nell I'm leaving."

Matt's hand felt warm on the small of her back as he escorted her across the brick street. As they reached the sidewalk, the workmen were lifting in the first window. It was a sheet of plate glass.

Becca stopped and stared. "What kind of windows are you putting in?"

"Plate glass. It's so much nicer for a showroom window. How do you like it?"

"A showroom?" she laughed incredulously. "In a feed store?"

"What feed store?" Matt asked in confusion. "I tore the feed store down."

Becca looked from Matt to the huge expanse of glass, and back to Matt. *"This* feed store, of course."

"I'm not building a feed store. Where did you get that idea?" He grinned down at her as if she were teasing him.

"Then what are you building?"

"A dry goods store, of course."

Becca's mouth dropped open. "A what! Why are you doing that?"

"To sell my merchandise. Honey, you must have known I'm in the dry goods business."

"You never told me that!"

He stared at her, then looked at his store as if to reassure himself that he was right, and looked back at her. "Becca, I'm in the dry goods business."

"You can't be serious! There isn't enough business in Mellville to support two stores."

"There will be when the railroad comes through." He watched the window being secured; then the workmen lifted the other one into place.

"Matt, the tracks may not even come through here, and if they do, they may not stop!"

"I don't think there's much chance of that happening, but if they don't we will still be all right. We'll just move your merchandise into the new building and keep on as before."

"What! We will do no such thing!" Becca gasped. Several passers-by turned to look in her direction. In a lower voice, she said, "The Emporium has been in business here for thirty years. I'm not going to move it."

Matt looked down at her with interest. "Are you angry, Becca? I've never seen you lose your temper before."

"No!" she said through clenched teeth. "I'm not angry. But you're crazy if you think for one minute I'm going to let my own husband set up in competition with me!"

"You are angry. I can tell." He reached out and touched her cheek. "There will be enough business for us both."

Becca slapped his hand away and glared at him. "So you're going to do it anyway? I won't stand for it." A group of curious onlookers was gathering.

The small muscle tightened in Matt's jaw. "I don't need your permission, Becca."

She became aware of the attention they were getting and jerked her head up. "We will discuss this at home, Matt!"

"There is no discussion," he said firmly. "But I will see you later."

His dismissal made her anger flare even higher, but she clamped her lips shut. With a toss of her head, she strode through the growing crowd. Humiliation fanned her temper. Tonight the Prescotts' public argument would be the subject of many supper conversations.

She stormed back into the Emporium and began straightening the bolts with a vengeance. Nell wisely retired to the storeroom.

As news of the disagreement spread, more customers arrived at the store. Becca spent more time evading curious questions than she did in cutting cloth. It seemed many a matron wished to repeat the old adage: Marry in haste, repent in leisure. Becca managed to keep from retorting, but by the end of the day, she was exhausted.

"Is it true?" Nell asked as they were pulling down the shades for the night. "Is Mr. Prescott opening a dry goods store?"

Becca frowned at her, then at the new building across the street. "Not if I have anything to do with it, he isn't."

Nell clucked and shook her head dismally. "It sure will be bad for business if he does." She was a thin woman with lank hair and a long face, and even her stance implied probable defeat.

"Then I'll just have to see that he doesn't," Becca snapped. She rubbed her forehead tiredly. Never had she talked short to an

employee. "I'm sorry, Nell," she said con-
tritely.

"That's all right. You've got a load on your
mind." Nell continued to stare at the red brick
building and clucked again.

Supper that night was nearly silent. Becca
spoke only when asked a direct question and
made no effort at small talk. Matt was almost
as quiet as she was. Afterward, they sat in the
library as was their custom and Becca went
over the receipts from the Emporium and
made out the bills to her customers on accounts. At least she tried. But all the time she
was aching inside from the estrangement she
felt between Matt and herself.

At last she threw down her pencil and said,
"I can't stand this anymore. Are you going to
talk to me or not?"

"If you want to," he said warily.

It was a beginning. Becca's eyes narrowed
speculatively and she smiled. "Let's go upstairs."

Matt laid down the book he had been pre-
tending to read and said, "I was hoping you
would say that."

Becca's mind was on battle strategies as
she preceded him up the stairs. All her life she
had heard one woman or another tell how she
got her way with a balky husband. All she had
to do was refuse him until he gave in. Becca
smiled broadly.

Once in their bedroom, she had Matt help

her unbutton her dress down the back. Then she took her time about undressing, and released her hair from its bun before she slipped on her prettiest nightgown, a soft lawn one that flowed seductively against her body. From the corners of her eyes, she saw Matt had missed none of her performance. Before fastening the neck, she bent to spread back the covers, allowing him a glimpse of her breasts. Then, as if unaware she had done so, she primly buttoned the front.

Her hair made a frame for her face on the pillow, and the feather mattress billowed around her like a cloud. When Matt lay beside her and propped up on one elbow to look down at her, she smiled. It would have been easier to ignore her attraction to him if he slept in a nightshirt, she realized, but he never slept in anything at all.

"You forgot to turn your lamp out," he observed.

"I know. I thought perhaps we could talk for a while."

"All right," he agreed as his fingers stroked her hair. "You start."

"I apologize for the way I spoke to you today. It was wrong of me." His fingers were caressing her cheek now and she found it difficult to remain detached.

"I accept your apology. If I didn't tell you I was opening a dry goods store, I'm sorry." He nuzzled her ear where he knew she was most susceptible. "I thought I had."

Becca decided to change her strategy. Perhaps denying him wouldn't be as effective as seducing him. Already he was sending shivers up her spine and her body was quickening toward him. "It was my own fault for not understanding."

Matt looked at her, then continued in his progress down her neck.

"But, darling, you have to admit Mellville isn't large enough—as it stands—to support two dry goods stores. Don't you agree?"

"Yes, I do."

"However, I've been thinking. A café would be perfect here."

He raised his head and regarded her thoughtfully. "You're right. Cooper's is the only place to eat out and the food tastes like cardboard."

Becca smiled and allowed the dimple to appear in her cheek. "Then you think a café would be better?"

"Yes, as a matter of fact, I do. Then when the railroad comes through, we can go back to two dry goods stores."

"I completely agree." Becca sighed happily. Getting her own way had been even easier than she had expected. The new plate glass windows would be perfect to show the satisfied diners at their meals.

Matt smiled as she put her arms around him. He had always suspected she wasn't cut out for the dry goods business, and a café would be the perfect solution. He could see the old Emporium now, with gingham curtains at the windows and happy customers eating one of Becca's lemon pies. He couldn't have come up with a better idea himself.

Becca decided she liked fishing. The wide branch of the Little Cypress meandered beneath her feet and coiled back on itself like a huge serpent. The towering trees made a cathedral hush over the glade and it was easy to believe no other eyes had ever seen this place except Matt's and her own. A shiny black bug made a vee of ripples across the glossy water, and a few yellow leaves floated on its surface. Becca leaned contentedly against the trunk of a mossy oak and watched Matt.

He sat on the grass a few feet away and was baiting his hook. "Do you feel a bite yet?"

"Not yet, Matt."

"Keep your eye on the cork, and when it goes under, pull back."

Obediently Becca watched the round brown cork that drifted on the water. She had not been so relaxed in months. Maybe years. Matt's cork settled to the water a few feet from hers and he leaned forward to watch it, his forearms resting on his knees. He had removed his coat and hung it over one of the oak's limbs and his sleeves were rolled to his elbow. Becca saw the strength in his exposed arms and hands and she smiled.

"The cork is over there," he reminded her.

"I know." The only part of fishing Becca didn't like was baiting the hook. Matt had done it for her the first time and had talked her through it the next. Becca had quickly figured out she could enjoy all the pleasures of fishing without the baiting by simply fishing with a bare hook. So for nearly half an hour she had lazed by the river and watched Matt string one worm after another on his hook.

"I can't understand why you aren't getting any bites," he said, as his cork quivered from the unseen activity. "Maybe the worm is gone."

"It's fine, Matt. I checked a few minutes ago," she answered promptly. "I'll just be patient."

Matt's cork disappeared in the amber water and he pulled in a perch almost as long as his hand was wide.

"Seems a little small," Becca observed.

He took the fish from the hook and tossed it back in the water. The fish vanished with a flick of its tail. "There's a big one in here. I can feel him." Matt tossed his hook out and caught the fish's twin.

"We can have the leftover roast for supper," Becca consoled him.

"I've got my mouth set for fresh fish." He looked over his shoulder at her cork. "Are you sure you still have bait?"

"Everything's fine over here." She looked up at the canopy of green leaves. The sun spangled in brilliant sparks but scarcely penetrated the dome. The banks had a warm, earthy smell of dirt that knows little sunlight but a lot of moisture. The steep slopes of the bank were lacy with ferns and emerald mosses. "How deep is it here?"

"About waist deep, maybe more. It's a good hole for catfish. Maybe we aren't fishing deep enough." He hauled in his line and raised his cork.

"Don't laugh, but do you know what I have always wanted to do?" Becca said dreamily. "I want to learn to swim. Not out where anyone could see me, of course, but just to learn how."

Matt looked over at her and grinned. "I could teach you. I've been swimming since I was a boy."

"But where could I learn?"

He thought for a while. "We saw a cow pond out north of town, remember? It wasn't near a house. Maybe we could go there about sundown."

Becca thoughtfully regarded her motionless cork. "Do you think it's private enough? I would have to strip down to my undergarments."

"We can ride out and see. Of course, it would be best if you weren't wearing anything at all."

"Then I would never get as far as the water," she laughed. "I know you better than that, Matt Prescott."

From the woods came the sound of a mockingbird, trilling his complicated song in blissful abandon. "Do you still like your horse?" Matt asked when the last notes died away.

"She's wonderful." Shortly after their wedding, he had bought them each a saddle horse. This gave her more freedom than the bulky buggy. Her horse was a palomino mare with a lively disposition; Matt's was a bay, a color considered more suitable for a man. They still owned the gray, but no one would ever dream of saddling their buggy horse.

"Maybe we should breed her this fall," Matt said thoughtfully. "Even though the war missed this section, there is still a shortage of horses. A good colt could bring in some extra money. Especially if it has a smooth enough gait for a saddle horse. Harvey Willis has a fine animal. If you want to do it, I'll talk to him."

"I think it's a good idea," Becca replied with a smile. If her father had mentioned the subject of breeding to her mother, she would have needed her smelling salts. Becca liked the way Matt talked to her as an equal. The concept was daringly innovative and she knew she could never discuss it with any of her friends.

A lone dirtdobber flew down to the damp bank and began gathering a minute load of mud to build his house. His glossy black wings hummed over his deep red body and he flew away without a glance at the two humans who shared the stream with him.

"You haven't had so much as a nibble in an hour," Matt said suddenly. "Let me see your hook."

Becca pulled on the cane pole, but the line seemed to be stuck in the water. She frowned and leaned back harder. "Matt! Matt, I've got a fish!" she cried out.

"Pull back! It must be a big one!"

She did as he said, and the pole made an arch in the air. Still the taut line refused to budge. "It must be huge!" she exclaimed.

Matt tilted his head to one side. "There's nothing in this whole stream that is all that big." He came to her and put his hand on the line. "It feels like a stump to me."

"Are you sure? I felt something move," Becca said excitedly.

Moving nearer the bank, Matt wrapped the line around his hand and pulled as he leaned forward. The end of a submerged branch, slimy with mosses and rotted leaves, surfaced and slid back into the water. He turned to grin at her, and as he did, the damp bank crumbled beneath him. With a yell, Matt tumbled backward into the stream.

Becca blinked as the water splashed up at her, and she leaned forward. "Are you all right?" she asked anxiously as he surfaced.

Matt got his feet beneath him and stood up. From the top of his head on down he was dripping wet. "I'm just fine," he growled. "Just great."

Seeing he wasn't injured, Becca felt a giggle start to build in her. She tried to disguise it as a cough, but laughter welled up. Tears of mirth filled her eyes and ran down her cheeks as she looked down at Matt.

"It's not all that funny," he commented.

"It is from up here," she assured him. "Here, let me help you out."

She tried to give him her hand, but he was several inches below her. With inspiration, she took her lace-edged handkerchief from her pocket and waved the far corner to him.

Matt held the bit of cotton between his thumb and forefinger and said, "Do you plan to pull me out with this? I'll wade downstream and climb out where the bank is lower."

"There's no need to do that. I can get you out right here." Becca stuffed her handkerchief in her pocket and looked around. "If I can find a limb, I can pull you up with that." No broken branches were on the ground, but her hand encountered a muscadine grapevine. It was an old one that climbed far up into the tree, with heavy loops and broad leaves. She grasped the scaly section that was nearly as large around as her wrist, and reached for Matt with her free hand.

"Be careful!" he cautioned as he saw her intent.

As is the nature with muscadine vines, the lower end wasn't anchored to the tree nearly as tightly as was the top end. It swung outward in an erratic curve, reached its limit, and dumped Becca into the creek. Matt gallantly tried to break her fall, and both went under the muddy water.

Becca came up sputtering, and the first thing she heard was Matt's laughter. Rivulets of water streamed from her hair and hung on her eyelashes. Her wet dress weighed an extra ten pounds with all the mud and water, and her feet were sinking in the oozy river bottom.

She did the first thing that came to mind and pushed Matt backward. His laughter turned to bubbles as he sank. She looked up at the grassy bank and was contemplating her escape when his hands fastened around her ankles. With a shriek, she went under and saw ocher bubbles rise past her.

Matt stood up and hauled her to her feet. "Want to learn to swim now?" he suggested. "We're in the right place for it."

She caught her breath and tried to glare at him, but the ridiculousness of the situation got the best of her. She looked wryly from Matt to the bank, and said, "How are we going to get out of here?"

"I could push you from behind," Matt suggested. "This time use the fishing pole to pull me out."

She put her foot on his cupped hands and tried to get a grasp on the bank, but the mud was as slippery as the inside of a rain barrel and she fell back onto Matt.

"Now what?" she said when she came up and got her feet planted in the muddy bottom.

A crackling in the underbrush signaled an arrival, and Becca swung around to see Cyrus Johnson standing on the bank. All her life Cyrus and his wife, Birdie, had prophesied she would come to no good end. Becca dug her elbow into Matt's back to let him know they had company. "Good afternoon, Mr. Johnson," she said cordially. "How are you today?"

Cyrus spit a stream of brown tobacco juice discreetly into the bushes and stared at the wet couple. Then he looked around as if he wasn't sure his eyes weren't playing tricks on him.

"Afternoon, Mr. Johnson," Matt repeated after Becca. "Nice day."

"What in the hell are you folks doing in the creek?" the older man finally asked as he scratched his head. "Begging your pardon, ma'am."

"We're fishing," Matt said nonchalantly.

Cyrus squatted down and looked from them to the two poles and the can of worms. "Catching much?"

"No, sir, not too much. I had a few perch, but they were too small to keep."

Becca was struggling to keep down her laughter.

"Want me to help you out?" Cyrus offered, extending his hand. Beneath his feet a few clots of mud peppered into the water.

"No, no," Becca exclaimed. "We're just fine."

"Yep, we're fine," Matt echoed.

Cyrus stood and cocked his head. After a bit he said, "Well, I guess I'll be on my way then. You're sure I can't help you any?"

"Thank you anyway." Matt turned downstream and offered his arm to Becca as if they were strolling down Main Street.

"Give my regards to Mrs. Johnson," Becca called gaily over her shoulder.

"Yes, ma'am. I'll do that." Cyrus watched in amazement as the Prescotts waded downstream.

"I suppose this will spread all over town," Becca muttered under her breath.

"I can't think of any reason why it should," Matt reassured her. "What could be less remarkable than a married couple out for an afternoon's stroll?"

Becca leaned forward to dislodge her sodden skirt from a submerged root. "You're probably right. Is my hair straight?"

"Not a strand out of place," he assured her. "I doubt Mr. Johnson noticed anything unusual at all. Besides, it would have been much worse if he had come upon us in the meadow by that old cabin."

Becca groaned. "Just keep walking, Matt. I think I see a low bank ahead." She was beginning to wonder if marriage was quite as respectable as she had always assumed.

Chapter Seven

"MATT, I'VE BEEN THINKING," BECCA CALLED out as she scattered feed to her greedy chickens. He looked up from the loose board he was nailing to the barn. "We should be making plans about the new café. Neither of us wants to run it, am I right?"

"I know I don't. I don't know the first thing about it." He put a nail to the board and drove it home in two strokes.

"Neither do I. Mrs. Henshaw—you remember, she was one of our witnesses?" Matt nodded as he reached for another nail. Becca continued, "She is one of the best cooks in town. I wonder if she would be interested in managing the café."

"Maybe. We could ask her and see."

Becca broadcast the grain and watched the plump white and Dominique hens scramble for the food. The rooster, a rust red with tail feathers the green-black shade of a beetle and a comb as fiery as blood, pecked at the corn. He had a vile temper and sharp spurs, and Becca always kept an eye on him. "We could make it look so nice. I can just imagine it with potted-plants in the windows and starched curtains to match the tablecloths."

"Plants? In a café?"

"Why not? I think it would look pretty and give it a homey atmosphere."

"I never saw plants in a café."

Becca, who had only seen one café in her entire life, said, "I'm certain it'll look nice. I was thinking of Boston fern."

"Will it get enough light?" He tried to remember how much sunlight filtered through the Emporium's small panes.

"Of course it will." She recalled his huge glass windows and suppressed a smile. Matt must not know much about plants. While the chickens pecked and clucked contentedly, Becca wiped the grain dust from her hand and went from nest to nest gathering eggs and putting them in the syrup bucket that had held the feed. She avoided the nest in the nail keg where her best brooding hen watched her with a baleful eye. To keep the other nests active, she had put a milky china doorknob in the straw. The hens, not being the most clever of creatures, continued to deposit eggs beside the "nest egg."

"We also need to employ a cook and some

waitresses," she continued as she placed the warm eggs carefully in the bucket. "Mrs. Henshaw may agree to manage it, but she will never hire on as cook. Granted, she's very good in the kitchen, but I don't know if she'd be willing to cook all day long. Maybe we can get some farmer's wife for that, or a widow." She put the bucket on the shelf beside the row of nests and opened the wooden gate. "There are several teenage girls here in town. Maybe they would agree to work as wait-resses."

"We can ask around and see," he agreed as he tested the next board. "I've noticed Wally Henshaw is a pretty fair carpenter. I think he could build the tables. The chairs are more difficult, but I could send to Jefferson for them."

Becca took a larger, empty bucket and looped the bail over the spout of the large water pump beside the barn. She worked the handle and water splashed into the bucket. "Wally will be glad for the work, I imagine. I've heard a rumor he wants to get married before long." She unhooked the bucket and, holding out her other arm to balance the weight, carried it back to the chicken yard.

"I could get the sign painted," Matt suggested as he sat down to run a whetstone over his hatchet. "That way, it's all ready whenever we can open." He picked up a cedar log that had once been a fence post and began slivering it into kindling.

"That's a good idea." Becca lifted the lid from the chicken's water dispenser and poured the bucketful into the thick cylinder. Water flowed into the tray it sat in until the air holes in the tank were covered. The watering contraption was too heavy to be turned over by the chickens, and the tray too narrow for them to wade in it. As they drank, the tray would be automatically refilled by the reservoir. Becca replaced the lid and shook the remaining water out of the bucket.

"You know," she said as she returned the bucket to the shelf, "you certainly are being nice about this café business."

Matt looked up at her and smiled. "You're the one who is being understanding," he told her fondly.

She carefully took the eggs from the feed bucket and put them in the fold of her apron. "We have a good marriage," she said with contentment. "How would you like some egg custard for supper?"

"That sounds good. Maybe some red beans and cornbread?"

"I'll put the beans on and make the custard if you'll do the bread," she bargained.

"It's a deal. I'm nearly through here."

Becca crossed the yard and looked back to see Matt still cutting kindling. Her heart warmed at the sight. Already she found it hard to remember she had ever lived without him. Surely, she thought, he was the very best of husbands. She was positive most men would still be arguing about keeping the store for dry goods, rather than bowing to logic. Matt looked up and she waved to him.

He returned the wave and tossed the handfuls of kindling into the wooden crate used for that purpose. She was a good woman, his Becca. Many women might have been in an uproar over having to change an old family store into a café, though that made the most sense. But not Becca. She was as even tempered as a pearly dawn. Matt put away the hatchet and easily lifted the box of kindling to take it to the house. While the beans cooked, he planned to carry her off to their bedroom. The thought brought a happy whistle to his lips and he lengthened his stride.

Becca watched the progress of the building across the street. It gave her a great deal of pleasure to see the gleaming picture windows. Once Matt installed the kitchen equipment, they could eat dinner there instead of walking the few blocks to the house or eating a snack in the back storeroom.

Nell joined her and said, "It looks like the café is progressing nicely. Who has Mr. Prescott hired to manage it?"

"I think he'll ask Mrs. Henshaw," Becca replied. "I put back a bolt of that new white eyelet for curtains. That will look so fresh and clean, don't you think?" She saw workmen carry a large sign, with its back toward her, across the flat roof. "Look, his sign must be finished."

As they watched, the men reversed the sign and lowered it into place. The delayed sound of their hammers, a bare second after each impact, sounded across the street.

Nell's breath was drawn in sharply and Becca felt the blood leave her face as she read, "Prescott's Dry Goods."

"Dry Goods!" Nell exclaimed. "I thought it was to be a café!"

"I'll be back," Becca said firmly. She jerked open her door and marched across the street. At the sidewalk she called up to the workmen, "Don't nail up that sign. There's some mistake."

The men looked down at her, at each other, then shrugged. The hammering dwindled away.

Becca hurried through the new ornate wood doors with the oval glass inset. At once the smell of new paint tickled her nose and mixed with the fragrance of sawdust. Matt was in the back supervising the construction of long counters. Becca paused and doubt began to creep upon her. "Matt? May I talk to you?"

He looked up and smiled at her. Pride of ownership was in every move as he skirted the sawhorses and lumber and came to her.

She led him outside and pointed up at the sign. "Look what it says. The painter made a mistake."

He read the words carefully and shook his head. "What do you mean? It's all spelled right."

After a second's hesitation, Becca laughed. "I don't mean it's misspelled. It should read 'café,' not 'dry goods.'"

Now Matt paused and looked curiously at her. "I'm not opening the café—you are."

"Me! I own the Emporium!"

"Honey, don't you remember how we discussed this? You suggested we open a café."

"Not in the Emporium. Here!"

Matt looked up at the idle workmen and called out, "Keep nailing up there."

"Don't you do it!" Becca countermanded.

The men hammered a couple of blows and were quiet again.

"Becca, you know we discussed this. Harvey Willis has almost finished your new café sign."

"You ordered me a new sign? Without consulting me?" She stared at him aghast.

"Of course. We talked about signs just the other day. Besides, you can't keep the old one, or people will continue to think it's an emporium."

"And they will be right! The café goes in here!" She stabbed her finger toward the new building.

"No, it doesn't." He glared up at the men on the roof. "Get to work!"

"Don't you dare hit one more nail, Wally Henshaw, or I'll tell your mother!"

The young carpenter grinned broadly at his fellow workers, who laughed.

"Leave my carpenters alone!" Matt demanded. "They're working by the hour."

"We need to discuss this, Matt!" she suggested between clenched teeth.

"The only thing I'm going to discuss is how many tables to put in the Emporium!"

"Not one single table goes through my door, Matt Prescott. I have an established business. I'm not about to give it up and put in a café." She frowned at the three ladies who had paused on the sidewalk within earshot.

"Neither am I. Prescott is a name well known for dry goods in Memphis. I have experience! I built up my business from the beginning; I didn't inherit it!"

"You're not in Memphis, Matt! This is Mellville, Texas, and here *my* name is well known. The Emporium is an established landmark!"

"It's old and outdated."

Becca's jaw dropped at his blasphemy. "Outdated! I carry only the most current goods! My patterns are the latest fashions. Nell creates hats especially for my customers. Do you plan to make ladies' hats, Matt?" This last jab she threw in as free advertising for her latest innovation, as once more a crowd was gathering to observe the Prescotts' eccentric behavior.

"I plan to hire a milliner," he defended his store.

"Nell is the only one in town," Becca retorted haughtily. "And *I* have her!"

"I took out an ad in the Jefferson paper." This wasn't strictly true, but he planned to arrange for one before the day was finished. "And," he added for the crowd's benefit, "I'm hiring a dress designer and seamstress."

"You wouldn't dare!" Becca gasped. "They'll cost you a fortune.".

"No, they won't, and the specialized service will bring me more customers. Instead of ready-made clothes from a rack, my ladies will be able to have an original—and not have to sew it themselves." He nodded decisively and waited for her next gambit. He had always thought clearly under fire, and thanks to Becca, his plans, which before had been only vague ideas, were now taking firm shape.

Becca opened her mouth to retort and shut it abruptly. Some things were best said at home. Besides, the crowd was growing. Lifting her head, she said, "We will see about this, Matt. My customers are loyal!" With a twitch of her skirts, Becca retreated to her store. She thought she heard someone applauding, but the sound was drowned out by the banging of hammers.

Nell met her at the door. "What did he say? It looks like the sign is going up."

Becca marched to the storeroom and grabbed the bolt of eyelet material. "It is. I'm adding this to our stock."

"Then Mr. Prescott is opening another dry

goods?" Nell gasped. "Right across the street?"

"He seems to think he is." Becca glared at the blue-and-white sign. "He doesn't yet realize that we are well known and trusted throughout the county. Who would want to buy clothes in the old feed store when they can come to the Emporium?"

"He tore the feed store down," Nell said doubtfully. "The new one looks nothing like it."

"That place has always been associated with feed and grain. Memories are long in Mellville," Becca snapped. But she had to admit the store looked good, even if the unostentatious sign didn't compare to the Emporium's red-and-gold one. "By the way, Nell, can you sew?"

"I do fairly well," Nell admitted doubtfully. "Mostly I do handwork."

"I think I'll put my sewing machine in the back room by the millinery goods. Some handmade dresses might go over well. Especially if we put smocking and embroidery on them."

"I never heard anybody ask for homemade dresses," Nell replied.

"That's *hand*made," Becca corrected, "and we may be about to see a demand for it. Also, I think I'll embroider some pillowcases and hand towels for the gift counter."

"Sounds like you expect Mr. Prescott to be some competition," Nell observed.

"Probably not, but why rest on our laurels?" Becca wished she felt as confident as she sounded.

Dusk settled softly about the tall, white house. The promise of rain had the trees whispering among themselves, and the breeze brought the scent of roses to Becca. She sat on the long porch swing and tried to reconcile her thoughts and her feelings.

When he had walked in the front door after work, Matt had been cheerful and as loving as a new wife could want. There were no visible effects of their public argument a few hours before. Not only had he helped her cook supper, but he'd whistled as he did so. Her own demeanor had been coolly reserved lest he think she took his traitorship lightly. She still rankled at the idea of her husband opening a competing business.

The blue-gray sky brightened briefly with a distant storm, but no sound reached her ears. Lamps were being lit along the street, making circles of gold on the grass and street beneath, yet the light barely penetrated her shady lawn. Her roses were in full bloom and the various colors bobbed like giant butterflies in the gloaming. The cooler night air made them seem even more fragrant. Huge four-o'clock bushes of the deepest pink edged the porch, and the night-blooming flowers gave off a scent as heady as the more highly regarded roses.

The tranquil scene was relaxing Becca as it always had. She felt the day's strain fade as minute lightning bugs skipped across her yard, appearing, then vanishing, only to show up several feet away. Again the sky paled momentarily to show towering castles of leaden clouds.

"Mind if I join you?" Matt asked as he came out onto the porch.

"Of course not." Becca felt herself tense and she regarded him with caution. Was he about to resume their argument? She pushed the floor with her foot and started swinging as Matt sat in the porch chair.

He inhaled deeply and let his breath out on a contented sigh. "It's a beautiful night."

"It's going to rain," Becca contradicted.

"You're still mad at me?" Matt questioned as if he were surprised that she might be.

"Now that you mention it, yes, I am. I think it was pretty underhanded of you to do what you've done."

"Becca, opening a café was your idea, as I recall. We talked about who would work there and about the potted plants. How was I to know there was a misunderstanding? Besides, when the railroad comes through, we'll have more than enough business for both stores."

"I did not say it would be in the Emporium —you tricked me. And why are you so certain the train will stop here?" she demanded. "No one else is so sure."

"It has to. Locomotives can go only so far

before they use up their water supply. They have to retank wherever water is available, and there's that big lake at the edge of town. Mellville is a natural stopover."

"The tracks aren't through here yet," Becca said stubbornly as she swung with more vigor. "How are we both going to survive until then? You'll take away my business."

"It all goes in the same bank account," he reminded.

"That has nothing to do with it. I don't want you in competition with me. And I will not open a café!"

Matt sighed and crossed his arms over his chest as he leaned back in the chair. For a while he regarded the darkening twilight. "We have to leave the competition at work, honey. I'm not trying to hurt your business. I really thought you had agreed to open a café."

"And I was under the impression you had."

"Doesn't it make more sense to you for the wife to go into the cooking business?"

"No! Not if she dislikes cooking as much as I do. Besides, you like to cook and you're better at it."

"You're being stubborn, Becca."

"Most likely. I've been accused of it before." For a few minutes, only the creaking of the swing broke the silence. "Did you tell Harvey Willis to stop painting the café sign?"

"He had already finished it. I had his men put it in the barn for now."

"In *my* barn?" She stopped swinging abruptly.

"In *our* barn," he amended. "He did a good job. Do you want to see it?"

"No." Again she put the swing in motion.

Matt glanced at her and said, "I've been thinking about how to arrange the counters in my store. Do you think women's notions, like hair ribbons and silk flowers, should go up front?"

"You're asking me?"

"We aren't enemies, Becca, and I value your opinion."

She observed him for the space of two swings. "Of course they should be displayed in the front. The bright colors draw people in. But if you leave the same ones there too long they'll fade."

He nodded as if he were memorizing her words. "And boots and shoes?"

"In the back. Men and women can share that department, so you don't need as much space as, say, for clothes, that have to be kept separate."

Matt got up and joined her in the swing. "I don't see why we can't work together on this. If we don't, in fact, Mellville will be gossiping about us from dawn to dusk."

"I know. They already are." She looked up at his shadowy features as distant thunder rumbled. "I never in my life said angry words in public, but I have twice since I met you. No one ever saw me fall in the creek before, either."

"You look lovely when you're wet," he grinned.

"That's neither here nor there. I've spent most of my life trying not to draw attention to myself. With my penchant for saying what's on my mind, it hasn't been easy. Now I find I not only shock people by voicing my thoughts, but I wade in creeks and argue in public."

"And have a hell of a lot more fun than you ever did before," he laughed. "Tell the truth now, Becca. When you were laying into me and my carpenters today, didn't you feel the thrill of battle? Didn't you feel alive, down to your toes?"

"I felt embarrassed to my very core, if that's what you mean."

"No, you didn't. Not at the time. I saw fire in your eyes and color in your cheeks. If you ask me, you were almost enjoying it."

Becca looked at him as if he had lost his senses. "I most certainly did not!"

"Well, you should have. You gave me as good as you got. I wasn't embarrassed in the least, and I don't think you should be, either."

As she digested this odd turn of perspective, she stared at him. Now that he mentioned it, the embarrassment she'd felt hadn't been noticeable until afterward. At any time during the argument she could have refused to answer back, or she could have insisted they discuss their differences at home. She smiled. "I don't think you're very good for me, Matt Prescott."

"On the contrary, Becca Prescott, I think we fit each other perfectly." He reached out and stroked her cheek as the first fat drops of rain spattered onto the lawn.

Becca wandered through the aisles of new merchandise. In general she approved of Matt's stock, but she had some reservations about his arrangement of it. The Emporium was laid out quite differently.

"What do you think?" Matt asked as he joined her. "Tomorrow is the big day."

"It all looks very inviting, but I'm curious as to why you put the vases and decorative bowls so near the front."

"You said the bright colors will draw customers."

"So would the silk flowers and scarves. I'd have put the giftware further back."

"Let's see how it does up front," Matt said with a smile. "I like your new dress, by the way."

"Thank you." It was one of a style she and Nell planned to offer in the handmade section. Small pleats of soft cotton enhanced the bodice, and the baby blue fabric was embellished with tiny wild flowers and berry vines in white embroidery. She was wearing it in the hope that other women would compliment her on it and she could inform them that it was one of the Emporium's newest additions.

Becca lifted a pair of boy's trousers and looked up at Matt. "These are going to be displayed here?"

"Of course. All the men's and boys' items are to the right. Women's and girls' to the left, just as I arranged it in Memphis."

"But these are for children. Their mothers won't want to invade the men's half of the store in order to buy for their sons. It's inconvenient. And look over there. Someone has put the yard goods on shelves instead of up-ending the bolts on a table." He had asked her advice on how to arrange things and had ignored everything she had suggested.

"I did that myself." Matt said in a testy voice. "It's neater that way."

"Maybe so, but it's less convenient. The shorter ladies won't be able to reach the top bolts."

He looked at the colorful rolls of cloth and frowned. That hadn't even occurred to him. "A salesclerk will be around to help."

"She'd better be tall. Besides, a woman likes to finger cloth before she buys. Your clerk will be lifting bolts all day just for inspections."

Matt didn't answer; his eyes were becoming veiled.

Becca strolled down the aisle toward ladies' gloves. "Really, Matt," she laughed as she lifted a pair of lace-trimmed bloomers. "This is rather risqué, isn't it? I mean, I can sell them, but everyone in town knows you're a man."

"I haven't tried to keep that fact a secret," he said.

"But what woman will buy bloomers from a man?" Another display caught her eye and she frankly stared. "Face paint! In Mell-ville?"

"Only face powder, and kohl for the eyelashes. All the city stores carry these items." His voice was growing curt.

"Mellville is no city. Both our preachers will be up in arms. They may be, anyway, over the bloomers! I do wish you had consulted me about these things."

"If they don't sell, I won't restock them, but I think most of the younger women will buy."

Becca frowned and looked at him from the corner of her eye. "Are you saying I'm outdated?"

"No, of course not. Only that there should be a choice."

Slowly Becca walked further back. "I wouldn't have put the rack of clothes so far into the store. Ladies like to see them easily and not have to search them out. And I've always kept the men's work clothes against the wall."

"Becca, I'm not trying to reproduce the Emporium. This is my store and I'm going to organize it my way."

"That's obvious. I was only offering suggestions," she pointed out huffily. "I know what Mellville wants."

"Thank you, but I don't need your help." In a softer tone, he said, "I'll meet you after work and we can walk home together. I don't have to stay late today."

"All right," she agreed reluctantly. "Do you want me to help you move the bolts of cloth to a table before I go?"

"Good-bye, Becca," he said as he firmly propelled her toward the door. "I'll see you after work."

Becca went back out into the sunshine and paused for a moment to study the historic Emporium, with its corniced and crenellated roof rising above the neighboring buildings. The clapboard front was painted a robin's-egg blue, the trim a pristine white. The store's name was boldly stated in a brilliant red-and-gold style reminiscent of circus wagons. Its two front windows were made up of many panes, several of which caught and reflected the sunlight. The Emporium had dignity. Stability and quality seemed to be typified by the shiny brass bell that tinkled whenever the door opened.

Satisfied with the comparison between the Emporium and Prescott's Dry Goods, Becca crossed the street. The day promised to be a hot one, and she could already feel the heat from the red bricks of the pavement through the soles of her shoes. She turned the brass knob and entered her domain as the bell announced her arrival.

"Is he ready to open tomorrow?" Nell asked as she looked up from the baby caps she was straightening.

"Yes, but he certainly has his merchandise arranged oddly. No one will be able to find anything."

"What a shame," Nell said. "I thought you said he was in the dry goods business before he moved here."

"He was. I guess things are done differently in Memphis. Well, perhaps he'll have some customers. You know how people are about anything new. Then, after his business plays out, we can sell his merchandise here and use the new building as a café."

"Mr. Prescott has agreed to this?" Nell asked with interest.

"I haven't mentioned it. But you and I both know Mellville can't support two dry goods stores."

"I just hope this gets worked out without hard feelings between you two," Nell observed dourly. "It's hard enough to have a good marriage without asking for trouble right off."

Becca glanced at Nell with amusement. Nell had married young, and the two of them had only been together a few months before he died after having been thrown by his horse. Nell had been so upset by the turn of events that she never remarried. Yet, Nell was a self-styled expert on marital affairs.

"Nevertheless, I do hope he has enough customers to keep up his spirits. People won't turn their backs on the Emporium, of course. I can afford to wait a few days to get them back." With a satisfied nod of her head, Becca went to the back to rearrange her new linen display.

Chapter Eight

BECCA CROSSED HER ARMS AND FROWNED AT the view from her store window. Everyone in town seemed to be flocking to Matt's grand opening. Her bell hadn't sounded even once. The first day, she had been happy for him. She hadn't minded the second day when the same thing happened. But this was the fifth day and she was getting miffed. Part of the reason for Prescott's popularity was a sign in Matt's window that proclaimed a week-long sale on his entire stock.

Resolutely she turned her back and began running a feather duster over the display of giftwares. "Nell, how is the dress coming along for Mrs. Whiteside?"

"It's almost finished," Nell called out from the millinery room. "She is to come in today for the last fitting."

"She should be here soon. I just saw her go into Matt's."

"I have an idea for a hat to go with this dress. I thought I would use those little silk rosebuds from the last shipment and a length of that midnight blue ribbon."

"That sounds adorable." Becca's eyes wandered again to Matt's door. His sale had even lured out old Mrs. Peabody, who was practically a recluse. Her aging daughter, the church organist, was with her. Becca's dusting toppled over a china shepherdess.

As she was righting it, Mrs. Whiteside came bustling through the door. She was a large woman in both height and breadth. Her gray hair was crimped into curls around her face and slicked back to a small bun squarely on the back of her head. Years of good food had plumped out the skin where wrinkles might have formed, and she powdered more heavily than good taste would warrant. Her ample figure was encased in slick black taffeta that rustled loudly as she walked—if Mrs. Whiteside's purposeful gait could be described as merely walking. In her gloved hand she carried a large round box.

"Good afternoon, Mrs. Whiteside," Becca said as she tried to avert her eyes from what could only be a hatbox. "Are you here for your fitting?"

"Yes, I am. My goodness, your husband certainly has a fine establishment. And he's so gallant! He could turn a woman's head in no time. Not, of course, that he *would,* dear. My, come to think of it, you two did have a rather hasty courtship, didn't you? Well, that's neither here nor there. Where's Nell?"

"In the back," Becca managed to say as the woman plotted her course to the fitting room. "Go right on in and I'll get your dress."

Becca hurried to the millinery room and took the dress from the clothing dummy. "Mrs. Whiteside is here."

"Could I have overlooked her?" Nell said with an uplifting of her lips that in a more frivolous woman would have been a smile. "Do you want me to fit her?"

"I'll do it." Becca glanced at the door to the fitting room. "She has a hatbox."

Nell looked up as she bit the thread she was sewing. "A hatbox? Are you certain?"

"Nothing else looks even remotely like a hatbox. She must have bought it from Matt."

"See if you can get a look at it. That milliner of his seems to be rather snippy for my taste. I'd like to know if she is any good."

Becca nodded and hurried across the store. Mrs. Whiteside hated to be kept waiting. "Here it is," she beamed. "I think it's Nell's best one yet." Good business made her refrain from pointing out it was also Nell's first.

Mrs. Whiteside stood in her petticoats, stays, and thick cotton chemise. Scarcely more skin showed now than had when she was fully dressed. She made an encouraging comment and let Becca help her into the new garment. The dress was the deepest of blues, with smocking across the bodice. The skirt was pulled toward the back and puffed out behind. It was a dress for compliments, not comfort.

"You look lovely," Becca said with poetic license. "Do you like it?"

"Don't you think it makes me look rather large?" The woman turned and preened in front of the full-length mirror.

"Dark colors are very slenderizing," Becca said hastily.

"Could Nell take it in a bit in the waist?"

Becca tried to find spare cloth at the waist, but the fabric was tighter than Mrs. Whiteside's own skin. "Perhaps she could. Would you like for her to design a hat for you to go with it?"

"No need for that." Mrs. Whiteside whipped open the box that sat in a chair and pulled out a hat. "I had the Prescott milliner run this up for me." She perched the unlikely concoction of papier-mâché fruit and ribbons on her head. "How lovely. That woman is a genius, and much faster than Nell. Now don't you tell her I said so. Neither one of them. Do you have any gloves in that I haven't seen?"

"No, not yet," Becca said, trying to keep up with the conversation.

"What a pity. I found some adorable ones at Prescott's. Navy blue with tiny jet beads on the back. Simply perfect with this dress. I don't suppose you would run across and get them for me?"

"No. I wouldn't." Becca looked at her in disbelief.

"No matter. I'll go myself. There might be some shoes I want as well. Do you recall that pin tray I bought last week for my niece? Well, I'm going to bring it back."

"You are? But whatever for? It's a lovely little tray."

"Prescott's has a nicer one, and for less money. We wives must watch our pennies, mustn't we? I'm sure you're the same way. By the way, how are you liking married life?"

"I like it quite well," Becca said stiffly. She had thought the pin tray was perfect for the Whiteside girl.

"The first part is always the easiest," Mrs. Whiteside said with brisk assurance. "The real test comes after the first few years. Of course, by then the babies are arriving and that gives a woman something to live for. I did dearly love my babies. Just precious, every one of them. I told Mabel Henshaw when you married that you would know about *that* soon enough." The woman gave a booming laugh. "Looks like we were wrong, though. You tell Nell I want to pick this dress up on Friday and to be sure and take it up in the waist. It positively hangs on me!"

"I'll tell her," Becca said frostily. So her

neighbors had thought her pregnant, had they? After all those years of such strict propriety. The very idea made her angry. She fastened the last button up the back of Mrs. Whiteside's black dress and stepped away. "I'll see you on Friday," she said in clipped tones.

"Friday. Yes. That's just what I said." Mrs. Whiteside plopped the beribboned hat back in the box and picked it up by its cotton string. "Do give my regards to your handsome husband and tell him how very much I appreciate all he is doing for Mellville, won't you? My goodness, he is certainly a benefit to this community."

"Yes, I'll tell him all right," Becca promised. "Good afternoon, Mrs. Whiteside."

"Good afternoon, Miss Simpson—I mean Mrs. Prescott. Heavens, I can't get your name straight, no matter what I do." With a flick of her ridiculously small hand, Mrs. Whiteside sailed away like a ship heading for the open sea.

"You bet I'll tell him," Becca muttered as she carried the dress back to Nell. Hadn't she just said she was going over to Matt's? It was hard to tell with Mrs. Whiteside.

"Did it fit?"

"It's a bit snug in the waist and needs to be shortened about an inch. She says it hangs on her and you're to take it up."

Nell shook her head. "I'll let it out a little. How did the hat look?"

"Like a bowl of fruit salad. Mrs. Whiteside has very little taste."

"I wasn't aware she had any at all," Nell observed dryly. "Was that the bell I just heard?"

"Couldn't be. Prescott's is still in business." Becca poked her head out and smiled. "Aunt Agatha! How good to see you. Did you just get into town?" Belatedly Becca realized she had forgotten to tell her aunt about her marriage.

Agatha Simpson was as tall as Mrs. Whiteside, but angular where the other woman was circular. Her long face was held at a regal tilt and her pale blue eyes hid no sense of humor. Steel gray hair was pulled back and braided in a knot on the nape of her neck. Her dress was unrelieved mourning of heaviest crepe despite the warm weather, and a small bonnet of the same color nested on her head. Even her gloves were black, unsoftened by any stitching, and her only adornment was a heavy black mourning broach. On the broach was a gold weeping willow and a funeral urn. Inside the broach was a lock of her dead brother's hair. Becca knew this because it was almost identical to the one she had discarded on meeting Matt.

"Rebecca, dear child! You're not wearing your mourning?" Agatha's contralto tones were shocked.

Becca self-consciously looked down at her daffodil yellow dress. "I've left off mourning,

Aunt Agatha. Father has been dead over a year now."

Agatha sniffed at the blunt word and said, "Your father has been *gone* scarcely thirteen months. As you can see, I'm still in strictest mourning. I expected you to show him the same respect. You might have gone to grays or even lavender by now, perhaps, but *yellow*?"

With a shake of her head, Becca went to her aunt and embraced her. "Dear Aunt Agatha, don't be upset with me. So much has happened, I hardly know where to start."

Agatha returned the hug and patted Becca's shoulder. "I had hoped you would come live in Jefferson with me. We are, after all, two women alone in the world. We could be such comfort to each other."

"I'm not quite as alone as you may think," Becca said with a nervous laugh. "However, this is not the time nor the place to go into that." She turned back to her assistant. "Nell, you remember my aunt?"

"Good afternoon, Miss Simpson," Nell said politely. "I had no idea you were coming for a visit."

"My niece appears to have forgotten it, too," Agatha said with faint amusement. "I wrote nearly two months ago and have not heard a word from her since."

Becca and Nell exchanged a look. "I think," said Becca, "I should take the afternoon off."

"That seems to be an excellent idea," Nell

quickly seconded. "I'm sure you have a great deal to talk about."

The walk home was filled with reminiscences about Agatha's dead brother, to whom she was now attributing the qualities of a saint, and gossip about Becca's various cousins, aunts, uncles.

Agatha's luggage was piled on the back doorstep just as the stage driver had left it. There seemed to be a great deal of it. Becca unlocked the door and lifted one end of a steamer trunk as her aunt picked up the other.

"We will have to make several trips," Agatha said as she shouldered past the screen door, "but I may need it all. Somehow I never learned how to pack. Probably never will."

Becca mumbled in reply, but saved most of her strength for the stairway.

"Should I take dear Ezra's room?"

The trunk slipped from Becca's fingers and thudded to the step. "No, Aunt Agatha, I don't think that's a good idea. You see . . ."

"You're right, of course. How foolish of me. No doubt you've preserved your dear father's room just as he left it."

"Not exactly. I . . ."

"No need to explain. I'll use the spare room as I always have. I will sleep better there anyway, since I'm accustomed to it."

Becca wondered how to break the news of her marriage to her aunt. To bluntly blurt it out seemed insensitive. Yet she had to tell her soon because it was almost time for Matt to come home.

At last all Agatha's belongings were stacked neatly in the spare bedroom and Becca was trying to catch her breath as she put fresh sheets on the bed. Agatha was busily hanging her clothes in the wardrobe and giving Becca detailed instructions for elderberry jelly. Becca decided to tell her news after Agatha had finished unpacking.

Matt came into the kitchen and looked around. "Becca?" he called out. When there was no answer, he went to the library and looked there. "Becca, are you here?"

A voice spoke words he didn't quite catch, but he smiled. She was upstairs in the guest room for some reason, probably spring-cleaning. Matt was in a particularly good mood and he wanted to share it with Becca. Prescott's had brought in more money in its first five days than he had expected in the first two weeks. He knew Becca would be glad to hear it.

He went upstairs and started to go into the guest room. She was in there, all right; he could hear her moving around. She seemed to be talking to herself, but he decided she must be singing. Becca had no talent for tunes.

His grin broadened. Quickly he pulled off his coat and loosened his tie. He seldom got a chance to surprise Becca and this was a golden opportunity. In no time at all, all his clothes lay in a heap in the hallway. Still grinning, he opened the door and strode in. "Hello, honey. I'm home."

Becca's mouth dropped open at the sight of all of him; an elderly woman shrieked and staggered backward, making gobbling noises. Matt stared at her, too startled to react. "Becca?" he began. "Who . . ."

At the sound of his voice, the older woman screamed again and fell sideways onto the bed. Becca grabbed up a blanket and threw it at him. Matt caught it deftly and hastily wrapped it around himself.

"Aunt Agatha," Becca said, "I'd like you to meet my husband, Matt Prescott."

"I don't think your aunt likes me," Matt whispered as they sat in the front parlor.

"How can you tell? She hasn't said three words to you."

"But it's been four hours since we were . . . introduced. She wouldn't let me wash the dishes after supper."

"I know. She isn't used to seeing a man do these things. You gave her quite a turn upstairs," Becca said with a suppressed grin. "When you insisted on cooking supper with us, she was nearly as shocked as at your . . . introduction. But not quite."

"Why didn't you tell me we had company?" Matt peered around the corner toward the kitchen where Agatha was finishing the dishes.

"I forgot she was coming. After that, I had no chance. Do you suppose she'll ever come back?"

"From the looks of her luggage I wonder if she'll ever go."

Becca jabbed him in the ribs and nodded toward the doorway. Matt stood as Agatha came, with great dignity, down the hall. As she passed him, she paused, sniffed the smelling salts in her handkerchief, and sat primly on the edge of one of the blue velvet chairs.

"Lovely weather," Matt ventured as he sat down beside Becca.

"It seems unseasonably warm to me, Matthew," Agatha stated.

"Matt," he corrected, "not Matthew."

Agatha looked through him to the English floral print framed above the sofa. "Supper was delicious, Rebecca."

"Thank you," Becca and Matt said together.

"Bad luck," Agatha prophesied. "You should knock on wood right away."

"I'm not superstitious, Aunt Agatha," Becca said, then realized she had probably offended her again. "I should have written you about Matt and myself. I was very remiss in not doing so, but everything happened so quickly . . ."

"How quickly?" Agatha asked in her precise voice.

"Well, he came to town on a Monday," Becca began, "and . . ."

"She means we have known each other

WILLOW WIND

quite a while," Matt amended hastily. "But we decided to marry at once rather than wait and . . ."

"We got married the following Wednesday . . ."

"After a long and proper courtship, of course," Matt added. He could see Aunt Agatha was in danger of icing over.

"Correct me if I'm wrong, but are you two discussing the same wedding? Your stories vary greatly."

Becca sighed and took Matt's hand. "He is trying to spare you. The truth is, I met Matt for the first time about two months ago. We fell in love at first sight and were married two days later. I know it was terribly sudden, but we don't regret it."

"After an entire two months?" Agatha said wryly. "I doubt you've had time to become accustomed to your new name yet. Marry in haste, repent in leisure, I always say."

Matt leaned forward, his eyes as unyielding as green flint. "You are my wife's aunt. You are a guest in our home. One more remark like that, and only one of those statements will be true."

Becca raised her fingers to her forehead and wondered if it would help matters if she fainted.

"Young man," Agatha said regally. "You are not my favorite person in this world, nor do I suspect you will ever be. However, Rebecca has seen fit to bring you into our family, so I

136

accept you. Welcome." The last word dripped frost.

"Thank you," he replied in kind.

"Coffee, anyone?" Becca said too brightly as she sprang up from the sofa. "I know I want some, and I need some help. Matt?"

"He helps you make coffee, too?" Agatha observed. "I thought it strange enough that he helped you cook supper. Do you assist him in chopping firewood?"

"We haven't needed any yet. Do you take cream and sugar?"

"Yes, thank you."

Becca walked hastily down the hall to the kitchen. She felt Agatha's eyes boring into her every step of the way. Once the door was closed behind them, Becca took the coffeepot from the cabinet and poured a generous amount of ground coffee beans into the metal cup. "You've got to stop picking fights with my aunt," she hissed.

"Me! She's the one that's doing it." He bent and prodded the dying fire to life in the stove.

As Becca pumped water into the pot, she glared at him. "That's just her way, Matt. She's my favorite aunt and I want you to be nice to her."

"She's your favorite?" he said incredulously. "The others must be dragons!"

Becca avoided his eyes as she clapped the lid on the pot and sat it on a burner. "They are. Couldn't you try a little harder? You managed to charm me fast enough."

"My charm only works on nubile young women like yourself."

"I said charm her, not seduce her." She took out a tray of lacquered wood, enriched with tole painting. Moving with natural grace, she added the rose china sugar bowl and creamer and tiptoed to reach three cups. The last one slipped from her fingers, but Matt caught it inches from the floor.

"Don't be so nervous," he said as he put the cup safely onto its saucer. "I would prefer for her to like me, but if she doesn't, it won't be a catastrophe. After all, she's only here for a visit. Right?"

"Of course." Becca recalled the mounds of luggage and wondered how long the visit would be. As she waited for the coffee to strengthen, she rearranged the dishes and silverware Agatha had misplaced. "You will try, won't you?"

Matt sighed. "I'll do it for you, but for no other reason."

"Thank you," she said with a smile that brought her dimple into play. "I love you."

"I love you, too. If your aunt hadn't been here, we would be upstairs in that feather bed."

"Later. The night isn't done yet." Becca used a cup towel as a potholder to remove the vessel from the heat. She put a metal spoon in the china coffeepot to absorb the heat and slowly poured in the black liquid. Then she removed the spoon and covered the coffee while she washed the metal pot.

Agatha had taken out her knitting, and the click of her needles sounded in the room as they returned. Matt put the tray on the table and Becca poured each of them a cup of coffee. Agatha gave Matt a severe look, but said in a conversational tone, "I suppose you have heard about Abe Rothschild being tried again."

"No, I haven't," Becca said, glad of any subject to break the silence.

"Who?" Matt asked.

Agatha glanced at him as if he were being deliberately dense. "Abe Rothschild. You've never heard of him? He and his pretty young bride came to Jefferson six years ago. In 1876 it was. A fine, handsome couple, we thought at the time. Rich, too. She was wearing diamonds all over her. Bracelets, earrings, necklace, rings. You name it. She wore them all the time and folks started calling her 'Diamond Bessie.'

"Then one morning in January they were seen walking out to the woods. Had them a picnic dinner. Later that day, Mr. Rothschild showed up, but not Bessie. He said she had gone to visit friends. We all thought that was odd, but it was just as odd to have gone on a picnic in January, and they had done that.

"The next day, Mr. Rothschild left town. Two weeks later, somebody came upon

Bessie's body in the woods at the edge of town. The poor thing was shot twice in the head and was as dead as a doornail. I had heard gossip that those two had lived in sin before they got married, but that's a terrible thing to have happen to a woman. Especially in a town as nice as Jefferson. Of course, neither of them was from there. They were from somewhere up north. She was a Moore by birth. They got married in Linden just a little while before coming to town. Honeymooners, they were, and to end up like that."

"I thought Mr. Rothschild had already been tried for her murder," Becca said.

"He was. They're going to try him again. Everybody knows he did it."

"There must be a doubt somewhere or he would already have hung," Matt put in.

"Not in my mind there isn't. I saw that young woman after they brought her body in and it was disgraceful. As dead as anybody you'll ever see, and her in her prime. All those diamonds were gone, too. I guess that's how Mr. Rothschild got off the first time, saying why would he give her diamonds and then shoot her to steal them back."

There seemed to be no reply to this, so the silence loomed into the room. Only the tick of Agatha's flying needles and the occasional click of a coffee cup broke the heavy stillness.

"I read in the newspaper the other day that Jay Gould is coming to Jefferson," Matt said at last. "Have you heard any news about the railroad?"

"Railroad!" Agatha spat out as if it were a curse. "There will be no railroad coming through Jefferson if we have any say in it. Dumping Yankees and foreigners on our doorsteps. Making a racket day and night. We don't need it. The Big Caddo River brings us all the trade we need. Jefferson is one of the most important ports in Texas! What do we want with a railroad, Matthew?"

Matt looked at her blankly for a moment. "Matt. It's progress, for one thing. The rails will bring in more trade. One train can carry more goods than a dozen riverboats."

"And be a hundred times noisier in the bargain. No, sir. You give me a riverboat any day over a train. Dirty, smelly old things! A riverboat has dignity, style, quality. It takes a banty rooster like Jay Gould to like a train."

"I've never ridden on one," Becca broke in. "Nell has, and she says they go ever so fast."

"They do, and it's unnatural. Tearing along that fast, a person could suffocate."

"Suffocate?" Matt asked cautiously.

"I said it clearly, did I not? Lungs weren't meant to draw in air whipping by at that speed."

"But in a storm the wind blows faster than—"

"More coffee?" Becca interrupted. "This is such a good batch of beans. Mr. Henshaw over at the general store ground them for me just this morning."

Agatha glared at Matt and ignored Becca. "If we have anything to do with it, no train will ever roar through Jefferson."

"I sincerely hope you have your way, Aunt Agatha," Matt said firmly, "because the only other choice is for a water stop in Mellville."

"'Aunt Agatha'!" the elderly lady exclaimed. "I never gave you leave—"

"Could I have your recipe for lemon pie?" Becca interposed frantically.

"Any aunt of Becca's is an aunt of mine," Matt affirmed with a maddening smile.

Becca leaned on the arm of the couch and shaded her eyes as she slowly shook her head.

"Headache, honey?" Matt asked solicitously.

"Sit up straight," Agatha commanded as if Becca were a child. "With posture like that, your spine will grow as crooked as ten miles of bad fence."

Becca automatically straightened.

"Her posture is just fine," Matt growled. "And her back is perfectly straight."

"A miracle, to be sure," Agatha countered.

"I'm going to bed now," Becca announced. "Excuse me, please, and I'll see you in the morning."

"What's this? You have separate rooms already?" Agatha demanded.

"She meant you," Matt snapped. "Not me."

"I should think separate rooms would be

rather convenient, myself," Agatha stated. "Rebecca's room is quite small."

"We share the large front room," Becca found herself explaining. Quickly she shut her mouth.

"Ezra's room?" Agatha gasped.

"Not that I've noticed," Matt replied.

Becca made a strangled noise and stood up to clear away the coffee.

"I think I'll retire, too," Agatha said. "I've had a rather trying day." She glared at Matt, who only smiled.

When she had washed the cups and joined Matt in their room, Becca leaned against the door and let out a pent-up breath. "That was your idea of trying?"

He had already removed his shirt and shoes and was about to take off his trousers. "I think I'm beginning to understand her," he informed Becca cheerfully. "She enjoys arguing."

"How do you know, Matt? You did nothing else."

"I can see now where you get your spunk. Aunt Agatha takes it a bit too far, but I can learn to overlook that."

"If you ask me, you two have more in common than she and I." Becca unbuttoned her dress and stepped out of it as Matt shucked off the rest of his clothes. She discarded her petticoat and sat at the mirror to brush her hair.

"Have I told you today how beautiful you

are? Particularly when you have no clothes on."

"Hush, Matt! What if Aunt Agatha hears you?"

"Do you suppose for a minute that she thinks we sleep fully clothed?" he teased. "I believe I'll ask her tomorrow."

"You'll do no such thing!" Becca gasped before she saw the laughter in his eyes.

"What'll you give me if I don't?"

She crossed the room and pretended to scowl down at him. "It's more a question of what I will give you if you *do!*"

His arm snaked out, and he tumbled her, laughing, onto the bed. Becca let out a startled shriek before she could stop herself. Instantly she clapped her hand over her mouth.

Matt nuzzled the ticklish part of her neck and ran his fingers over her ribs. Becca burst out laughing.

"Stop that!" she hissed. "Aunt Agatha will think you're beating me with all this racket going on."

"That's not what she'll think," he grinned down at her. "Besides, your old room separates our room from hers. Unless she has ears like a hawk, she can't hear us."

"Hawks don't have ears," Becca giggled.

"You know what I mean." His teasing gradually mellowed and a new light sparkled in his moss-green eyes. "I love you, my Becca."

"Now, Matt, I know that look. What if she *does* hear us? She will be scandalized."

"Let's see how quiet we can be. It'll be a challenge." His lips nibbled at her ear, and his breath made a tickling path along her temple. She sighed with pleasure. "Shhh," he whispered. "We haven't even started yet." He reached across her and turned down the lamp.

Chapter Nine

"It was pretty embarrassing when Aunt Agatha asked what you do for a living," Becca said as they walked to work.

"Oh? I thought the dry goods business is considered aboveboard. Even desirable," Matt replied as he tipped his hat to one of their neighbors.

"Not when it's in direct competition with the Emporium. I thought she was going to have a seizure."

"Not Aunt Agatha. She couldn't be felled with anything less than a cannonball. Don't let her bluff you."

All her life Becca had heard her father bow to the whim of his younger sister. He had frequently, and at great length, extolled her fragile femininity and helplessness. To hear Matt say exactly the opposite was almost blasphemous. "She is a Woman Alone in the World, Matt," Becca reminded him.

"And she probably prefers it that way. Everyone hops to do things for her and to see that her every suggestion becomes law. If she had a husband and a family to raise, things would have been put in perspective pretty fast."

"I don't think my parents would have cared for you at all."

"Probably not," he agreed with a grin. "Do you mind?"

"No, I don't in the least." She walked beside him along the shaded white fences draped with honeysuckle and wisteria. Summer had begun to settle in earnest and already the air was warm enough to bring dampness to her brow.

Her dress was aqua silk, as cool to the appearance as the deep porches of the same hue. The sleeves fit her arms snugly to the elbow, then billowed in pleated ruffles of creamy white organdy. At her throat a bow of the same fabric set off her slender neck and was met by more pleated ruffles to form a jabot. The silk dress was quite plain in the front, relieved by darker turquoise cording in curlicues and swirls. Another swath of creamy organdy circled low on her hips and made a cascade of pleated ruffles behind her in a look reminiscent of the bustle of the last decade. Her hat was small and sported an aqua silk bow that almost hid the white felt.

Becca felt very stylish beneath the shade of her red-and-white parasol, and she hoped her new chicness would bring her more trade.

Unfortunately for her business, Matt looked equally dashing in tan trousers, golden buff vest, and chocolate coat. Also, he was making a point of speaking to everyone and calling them by name. Becca frowned slightly. Her husband was becoming very popular, and when it came time to make purchases, people might take their trade to Prescott's. From Matt's point of view, this was good business, but Becca felt it was somehow underhanded. Perhaps, she thought, this would be a good time for a sale on summer dresses.

"I've hired a new employee," Matt mentioned as he tipped his hat to Mabel Henshaw.

"You have?" Becca said as she nodded her head in passing the woman. "I thought you had the counter help already. Who is it?"

"A man I knew back in Memphis. Percy Winthrop."

Becca suppressed a smile. "Is that his real name? It seems to me this Mr. Winthrop is coming a long way to work a cash register."

"Percy's not a cashier. He's a tailor."

"A what?" Becca's smile was fading. "Why do you need a tailor?"

"For the men, of course. I know nothing about sewing and I could hardly hire a woman to take a man's measurements."

"You intend to make men's clothing as well? In Mellville?"

148

"Why not?" Men like to dress as nicely as women do. My seamstress is turning out Sunday frocks and my milliner is making new bonnets to go with them. When the ladies are decked out in their finest, they will want their men to look equally well."

"None of the men in Mellville will have any use for a tailor. They are quite happy with rack suits."

"How do you know?" he countered. "What about the tall men who don't fit into an average pair of pants. What about Abner Brown, who's too tall *and* too broad to buy rack clothes?"

"Mrs. Brown makes all his suits and has for years. I know because I special-order fabric for her whenever she makes him a new outfit."

Matt gave her a superior smile. "Hasn't it occurred to you that she might not like to sew men's suits?"

"She told you that?"

"Yes, she did. That's what started me to thinking about Percy. He's a talented man. And, he owns his own machine."

Becca frowned. "You're overreaching again. If I were you, I'd listen to good advice. Don't hire a tailor."

"Is that my wife speaking or my business rival?"

"I've been in business in Mellville for years and I know what the people here want."

"Would you say it's sound business to take

professional advice from a rival? Besides, I've already written to him."

"Without consulting me?"

"Did you talk it over with me before you set Nell up as a seamstress?"

"Nell already worked in my store. You will soon have more employees than customers."

"It hasn't happened yet. I had a couple drive over yesterday from Ore City just to buy shoes for their children. They said they'd be back for clothes before school opens."

"*One* family," she snorted.

"They have nine children," he parried. "And they said they would tell their neighbors that it's worth the drive."

She walked beside him in silence for a while. Then she said, "This Percy Winthrop, is he a good tailor?"

"The best. He can sew a suit as fast as anyone I ever saw, and it fits every time."

"Somehow I can't imagine anyone I know going to a tailor named Percy. You'd better set aside money for his passage back to Memphis when it doesn't work out."

"We'll see." He tipped his hat to her as she left his side to cross the street to the Emporium.

"Percy!" she snorted. "His name alone will be a mark against him." With a swish of her skirts, she hurried across between two buggies. A tailor! She certainly hadn't expected that!

Becca unlocked the door and stepped into the shadowy store. This was one of the times of day that she liked best. The display of silk flowers and bonnets were shades of gray in the gloom, waiting for light to give them color. The aisles were corridors leading to cavern-like depths of the store, and the various wares were indeterminate shapes and bulges in the half-light. The racks of ready-made clothes stood like ranks of flat soldiers, the men to the right, the women to the left. There was an air of expectancy about the old store.

Becca raised the shades and let sunlight rush in to give life to the vibrant colors. As she did so, she reminded herself to change the window display. Across the street, Matt's lights were on and he was raising his own shades. One by one, Becca lit her gaslights and the remaining gloom disappeared for another day.

Nell called out a greeting as she let herself in through the back door. Her small house lay in that direction and she never bothered to come around to the front.

"Good morning, Nell," Becca answered.

Becca, who was already busy with her usual chores in preparation for the first customer of the day, stopped to study one of the clothes racks. "Let's mark down these summer dresses for a few days. They don't seem to be selling as fast as they might."

"It's the competition, if you don't mind my

saying so," Nell said as she removed her close-fitting navy hat. "Prescott's is bad for our business."

"It's only because the store is still a novelty. After the newness wears off, our business will pick back up. Let's put the bonnets on sale as well." Becca dusted the counter top next to the cash drawer. "You will never guess what Matt has done now. He has sent for a tailor."

"A tailor? In Mellville?"

"That's exactly what I said when he told me. Not only that, but his name is Percy Winthrop."

"Are you serious? His parents really named him that?"

Becca grinned and nodded. "Can't you just imagine what he must look like? Matt will have to label him so customers won't mistake him for the milliner."

Nell covered her mouth as she laughed and for the moment her mirth made her almost pretty.

"Rebecca, how you do go on!" She adjusted the dummy and slipped Mrs. Whiteside's dress over it. Taking up her cushion of pins, she started making alterations.

A rap at the door drew Becca's attention and she opened it to see a delivery man in the back alley.

"Delivery from Fairmont, Inc.," he said in a bored voice. "Sign here, please, ma'am."

She wrote her name on the line as the man

pulled three boxes from the back of his wagon. "Just stack them over there," she instructed.

With little regard for the contents, the man dropped the first box into the corner, then tossed the other two on top. He belatedly tipped his hat and left.

Becca pried up the end of one lid with a screwdriver. "It's the hat trimmings I ordered," she told Nell.

"Oh? I don't recall such a large order."

"Perhaps they're packed with extra paper." She rummaged through the box. "These are the papier-mâché cherries. The flowers must be in the other boxes."

"They came just in time. I used the last ones two days ago. Are the ribbons and laces there as well?" She turned the dress dummy and fluffed the ruffled bodice.

Becca put the opened box on the floor and went to work on the next one. "How strange," she said as she lifted a cluster of cherries from the crate. "These seem to be more of the same." She moved that box aside and tore into the third. "Nell, you aren't going to believe this."

"Not more cherries!"

"Three crates full."

Nell came over to look for herself. "Why did you order so many fruits?"

"Not fruits, only cherries. And I didn't order them." She looked more carefully at the order

153

form she had signed. "According to this, we have ten spools of velvet ribbon in assorted colors, fifteen bunches each of daisies, roses, and assorted leaves, twenty spools of lace, and ten bunches of fruit."

Nell poked in the nearest box. "I guess they made a mistake at the warehouse in Dallas."

Becca hurried out to the alley but the delivery man was gone. She came back inside and sighed. "He isn't here anymore. What on earth are we supposed to do with three crates of papier-mâché cherries?"

"Can't we return them?"

"Yes, but in the meantime, we have no other hat adornments and it will be at least two weeks before we can exchange these for our order."

Nell looked at the boxes as if she expected them to have some explanation to the problem. "Closer to a month, if you ask me."

Becca tapped the nearest crate with her toe. "I guess we might as well use as many as we need. Cherries are going to be in style in Mellville this summer. Perhaps we could put some on those sale dresses to perk them up a bit."

"Matt, where are the serving bowls?" Becca asked in exasperation. She had spent most of her day helping Agatha clean the attic and she was hot and tired.

"Look in the cabinet over the dry sink,"

154

Matt suggested. To escape Agatha he had spent the day mucking out the stables.

"They aren't there and the beans are about to scorch."

Matt took the pot from the stove and looked in the cabinet he had indicated. "What are jelly jars doing here?"

"Can I be of assistance?" Agatha's voice responded. "What are you looking for?"

"Serving bowls," Becca said with a minimum of civility.

"Above the stove to the right," Agatha answered.

Becca yanked open the cabinet and frowned. "What are they doing here?"

"I put them there yesterday."

"Why did you do that?" Because Becca so disliked cooking, she preferred to get in and out of the kitchen as quickly as possible. She hadn't rearranged her kitchen in years.

"They are much more convenient there by the stove. I have always kept my bowls in that vicinity."

"The silverware is gone!" Matt exclaimed.

"Don't be ridiculous," Agatha snapped. "I put it in the silver drawer of the buffet where it should have been all along."

Becca closed her mouth firmly, but her glance at Matt spoke eloquently. Finally she said, "I prefer my kitchen the way I had it, Aunt Agatha. In my opinion it was more convenient that way."

"Only because you were used to it. Believe me, this is a much more sensible arrangement. Besides, I plan to do most of the cooking while I'm here, so I ought to put things where I can find them."

"How long—" Matt began.

"You don't have to do that, Aunt Agatha," Becca interrupted hastily. "You are our guest."

"I don't want to burden you, and I insist. You'll find I also rearranged the cleaning supplies when I put them away. I'll do the housework, too, while you are at the Emporium." She cast a cool eye at Matt, then added, "And Prescott's."

"How long did you say you—" Matt tried again.

Once more Becca overran his words and threw him a warning look. "You will overtire yourself. Matt and I always cook supper after work. At least let us do that much."

"Rebecca Simpson, I never in my life ate food cooked by a man and I don't aim to start now."

"Her name is Prescott," Matt reminded with a scowl. "And I'm a damned fine cook!"

Agatha drew herself up and her expression became glacial. "*I* will tend to the kitchen. Starting now. Both of you clear out of here and give me room to work."

Matt made a growling sound low in his throat, but Becca caught his arm to lead him out onto the porch. When the door closed, she said, "Aunt Agatha has always loved to cook. She enjoys preparing supper especially. Let's stay out of her way."

"How long is she staying?" Robert asked bluntly.

"Probably not much longer," Becca soothed. "When my parents were alive, she never stayed more than three or four days at a time. You see, she and Mother rarely got along and . . ." Becca looked back at the door, then shook her head. "No, no, I'm sure she will be leaving soon."

"Good. I can't work as fast as she can dream up chores." He sat on the top step and pulled Becca down beside him.

The huge willow tree had leafed out, and its fernlike foliage of emerald stirred in the late afternoon breeze. A cardinal fluttered into the upper branches in search of a haven for the night.

"I think the cardinals have a nest up there," Becca said. "I've seen them up there a lot. Maybe we'll soon have a tree full of red birds."

"Maybe so." The air was cool after the heat of the day, and Matt began to relax.

The orchard trees were fat and bushy with their summer leaves. Hard knots of peaches, pears, and plums grew in their depths. Becca's vegetable garden was lush and promised a good harvest. Matt breathed in the sweet aroma of the four-o'clocks and smiled with contentment. This was the sort of life he had always wanted. He took Becca's hand and stroked her delicate fingers.

"A strange thing happened this week," he said idly. "Every woman who came in the store wanted a hat or dress with cherries on it. Mrs. Whiteside, who appears to be the trend-setter, is wearing cherries this season and everyone else is wanting them, too."

"Oh?" Becca asked innocently. "Why don't you sell them cherries?"

"I wish I could. I ordered three crates but all I got was a handful of ribbons, a few flowers, and some laces. I tried to catch the delivery man, but he was gone before I had noticed the error."

Becca looked at him. Suddenly she realized what had happened, and laughter welled up in her throat. "I have your order," she explained. "The man brought it to the Emporium by mistake. You have my hat trims."

He grinned. "I never thought of that. Do you want to trade?"

"Perhaps. But now that cherries are suddenly so fashionable, I don't want to give you all of them. How about a split—fifty-fifty?"

"But it's my order."

"It's in my shop."

"All right. Fifty-fifty." He pretended to bite her finger. "You drive a hard bargain."

"What were you going to do with all those cherries?" she asked curiously.

"The milliner needed some for hats."

"Three crates full?"

"The rest I was going to have made into Della Robbia wreaths along with some other artificial fruit." He kissed her palm.

"Wreaths? Christmas wreaths? It's still summertime, Matt."

"No point in waiting until the last minute. They take a while to assemble."

"You're already thinking about Christmas?" she asked incredulously. "Are you serious?"

"Of course. Aren't you?" He looked at her guilelessly.

"Well, certainly," Becca stammered. "My plans are well under way."

"What do you have in mind?"

"I'd rather not discuss that with the competition," she informed him primly. He was using the tip of his tongue to trace the lines of her palm, and she felt a tingle run through her. "Stop that," she said without pulling away. "What will Aunt Agatha think?"

"She will think she missed a great deal."

Becca pulled her hand back and smiled at him. "She would be absolutely right."

Matt stood and held out his hand to her. Together they strolled beneath the willow. Night was spreading across the sky, and the tree's feathery leaves were silhouetted against the purple and rose dome. The branches trailed to the ground, trapping twilight in their midst. All around the couple, the leaves swayed in a dance with the wind.

"I wish," Becca whispered up into the tree, "that Matt and I will always be as happy as we are today."

"I wish our guest would go home," he whispered in turn.

"Matt! That's not very hospitable."

"I wasn't trying for hospitality, Becca, only the privacy to chase you around the house."

She considered his idea for a moment and nodded. "That sounds good to me."

"I'm tired of having to whisper at night," he said as he put his arms around her and pulled her close. "She slows you down."

"She does no such thing. At least not much."

"Let's go on a picnic tomorrow, just the two of us. Somewhere far into the woods."

"We have jobs, remember?" Darkness hid her face but longing was in her voice.

"Nell can take care of the Emporium and Miss Fuller can handle Prescott's."

"What will Aunt Agatha say?"

"We won't tell her," he breathed into her ear. "By the way, I like your new hairstyle."

"I didn't think you'd noticed." Instead of her usual bun, she had swept her hair up into dark coils that cascaded down the back of her head. Shorter hair would have been easier to manage, but she knew Matt preferred it long, so she had compromised with the less severe style. The result was more youthful and was flattering to her heart-shaped face.

"I notice everything about you," he said as he nibbled at her ear.

She sighed and swayed closer to him.

"Here's our plan for tonight. After the dishes are put away, feign a headache. I'll look concerned and mildly surprised. You lay your hand on your brow, palm out, and say you feel faint. I'll look a bit more concerned. Then you say you want to retire early. I'll agree that you should. Then I'll lock Aunt Agatha in the broom closet and come upstairs and ravage your body."

"Except for the part about the broom closet, I think you've stumbled onto a good plan."

"Rebecca?" Agatha called stentoriously out the back door. "Come to supper. You, too, Matthew."

"How about if I lock her in the barn instead?" he growled.

"Now, Matt." Becca smiled. "You're the one with all the understanding, remember?"

"I still wonder when she plans to leave," he muttered as they walked back to the porch.

"This seems terribly illicit," Becca said as she climbed into the buggy beside Matt. "I've never left the Emporium to go on a picnic in the middle of the day."

"Nell can take care of everything."

"What about Aunt Agatha? She will be sure to wonder when we don't show up for supper."

"No she won't. She plans to have supper at Mrs. Whiteside's house."

Becca opened her parasol as protection against the bright sunshine. "It still seems odd for a married couple to slip off on a picnic."

"I didn't do much courting of you before our wedding, so I plan to do it now." He whistled to his horse and they drove away. "Do you regret that we married so quickly? Most women put a great deal of stock into being wooed and won."

"I have never regretted marrying you so quickly. At times I wish I could have paraded our courtship around—after all, as Town Spinster I could have been the talk of the county. But these are modern times and I can't see any use in the old courtship rules our parents had to follow: walking to church in a group, eventually a chaste kiss on the cheek, gifts no more personal than candy and flowers. That sounds like a waste of time to me."

"Yet that is exactly what most ladies would expect. I was quite prepared to go through all that for you."

"I never have fit into conventions." She contentedly watched the town recede and the countryside slowly unfold. Plumes of white clouds billowed above her and two scissortail doves looped and skipped in the warm air. A breeze brushed invisible fingers through the tall grasses of the meadow and gently shook the tops of the nearby trees. The hard-packed road meandered into the woods and cool shade enveloped the couple.

Soon they were driving beside the lazy creek that would eventually merge with the Little Cypress. Dragonflies darted and hung in the air and clouds of midge flies clustered over the banks. A half-submerged log provided a sun deck for several turtles, none of which paid any attention to the horse and buggy.

As they drove off the well-traveled road and onto a grassy, older path, the trees arched high above them. Small birds flitted from tree to tree, and below, tiny white and yellow butterflies fluttered like freed flowers in the grass. Ahead of them, a startled doe pricked her scooped ears and bounded into the dense foliage. On their left, the creek made one of its hairpin twists, nearly making an island of a finger of land.

"This looks like a good spot," Matt said as he pulled the horse to a stop.

"It's lovely." Without the sounds of the horse and buggy, Becca could hear the gurgle of a minute waterfall. The grass was strewn with pink and yellow flowers and a huge black walnut tree shaded the ground.

Matt spread a quilt beside the mossy tree roots as Becca took the picnic basket from the back of the buggy. They ate slowly, savoring the peaceful surroundings and the luxury of their aloneness.

When they were finished and the remains of the meal had been returned to the basket, Matt lay back and pulled Becca down beside him.

She rested her head in the hollow of his shoulder and gazed up at the sun-spangled leaves. A warm drowsiness overtook her and she hid a yawn behind her fingers. "I would live here if I were a bird," she murmured sleepily. "My nest would be in that fork right up there."

"Our nest," Matt amended. "Wherever you go, I go, too. Even if it means sprouting feathers and living in a tree."

"You must love me a great deal," she said, turning her head to look at him.

"I do. More, perhaps, than you even realize." He kissed her forehead and the pulse that beat at her temple.

With a happy sigh, Becca rolled over and kissed him. His lips were warm from the filtered sunlight and opened invitingly for her. Her tongue met his and she explored the softness inside his lips.

"Are you planning to have your way with me?" Matt asked with a smile.

"Just close your eyes and think of England, like Queen Victoria did," Becca suggested.

"Where did you hear that?" Matt laughed.

"Word gets around," she answered sagely.

"I feel sorry for the late Prince Albert." Matt pulled the pins from her hair and let it cascade over his fingers to form a dark veil around her face. "I would much rather have you think of me when we're making love."

"I always do. England never enters my

mind." Becca tickled his ear with the tip of her tongue. "I love you so much."

Slowly he unbuttoned her dress as his eyes gazed deeply into hers. At the same time, her fingers released the fastenings of his shirt. Bending over him, she ran her tongue over the smooth muscles of his chest. He groaned at the sensations that provoked in him, and pulled her dress aside to bury his face in the curve of her neck.

Becca sat up and removed her dress as he pillowed his head on his arm and watched. His eyes traveled over her, taking in the proud lift of her breasts under her nearly transparent chemise, and the slender circumference of her waist. Becca stood and pulled the ribbon that held up her petticoat. It floated to the ground to lie in a swirl at her feet.

"Now the chemise," Matt directed softly.

She released the pale blue ribbon and raised her arms to pull off the garment. Her breasts were full and rounded, her nipples rosily taut. Moving seductively, she took off her shoes and placed her foot on a burl of the tree. Sensuously she rolled her stockings down the shapely curve of her legs. With the grace of a Circe, she untied her bloomers and stepped out of them. She stood before him in all her glory, her long hair blowing ever so slightly across her breast.

"You're like a goddess, standing there," Matt said hoarsely. "You're beautiful."

"I never was until you came to town. Our love has made me beautiful, if I am."

He stood and ran his palms over the curve of her arms. "You were beautiful the first time I saw you. From that day on, you have been the center of my world. You are my reason for getting up in the morning and my reason for working all day. At night I fall asleep with a smile on my face, all because of you."

"My Matt," she said softly. "I love the way you show me your love, and the way you accept mine, with no conditions, no holding back."

Matt gathered her to him and she slipped her arms beneath his open shirt. "You feel so good," he spoke into her hair. "You smell good, too, like that rose-scented soap you use."

She placed a string of kisses beneath his jaw and tiptoed to nibble his earlobe. "Why are you still wearing so many clothes? You're overdressed for the occasion." As she spoke, she removed his coat and shirt and tossed them to lie beside her dress. Then she lay down and watched as he finished undressing. "You're beautiful, too," she said when he was finished.

Matt's muscles rippled as he lowered himself to the quilt and stretched out beside her. He hungrily claimed her lips until the passion of her kisses equaled his own. Slowly he moved his attentions down her throat and over the sweet curve of her breast. Becca entwined her fingers in his thick hair and led him to the place he sought.

His tongue sent shivers of fire through her as he flicked the tip of her breast before taking it into his mouth. Becca arched her back to give more of herself to him and moaned with pleasure. Matt's hand massaged her rib cage and waist, then glided over her slender hip to cup her firm buttocks.

Becca held him tightly and rolled over so that he lay beneath her. With her hands to either side of his head, her proud breasts teased him seductively. Matt took one in each hand and caressed them lovingly. Unable to wait, Becca slid lower until she engulfed him and they became one. For a moment she paused, becoming accustomed to him and to the new position she had discovered. Then she began a gentle rocking motion that made him moan with pleasure.

As she became more proficient at her movements, Matt's hands slid down to her hips and he aided her in her sensuous undulations. Slowly the fires built in her and she closed her eyes to savor the intense feelings. Unexpectedly, Matt lifted her forward and took her taut nipple into his eager mouth, sending her soaring to her completion. Wave after thundering wave roared through her, and at the same time, he held her closely in his own release.

Becca lay on his broad chest and felt the

hammering of their hearts. Her entire body seemed to float in a golden haze. "How could I ever have been afraid of this?" she murmured drowsily. "Is it this wonderful between all couples?"

"Only the ones in love," he answered as he stroked her silky hair.

Chapter Ten

NELL PINNED THE LACE INSERTS INTO THE train of the pink and gray striped taffeta on the judy. "There's a stranger in town," she reported. "He's staying over at Cooper's Boarding House."

"Oh?" Becca was lettering a sign for her window to announce a sale on galoshes and rainwear.

"He's rather nice looking," Nell continued. "His clothing was impeccable, if I do say so. Fit him to a tee. I wager a tailor had a hand in that design."

"I wonder what a stranger would be doing in Mellville." She looked up from her paint pot. "Do you suppose he could be from the railroad?"

"Perhaps. We weren't exactly introduced, so I couldn't say for sure."

"What do you mean by 'exactly'?" Becca printed a large *R* on the sign.

"Just as I was passing Cooper's I accidentally stepped out in front of a carriage. This nice young man grabbed my arm and pulled me to safety." Nell's cheeks blazed with color. "Well, not *too* young, actually."

Becca looked up again. "Good heavens, Nell. You weren't hurt, were you?"

"No, no, not at all. As I said, he pulled me back in time to prevent an injury."

"What is his name?"

"My goodness, we didn't strike up an acquaintance on the street! I would never be so bold. I imagine he is passing through on his way to Dallas and only stopped here for the night."

"You say he was handsome?" Becca asked with a smile and an appraising glance.

Again Nell flushed with color, and rosy cheeks lent youth and prettiness to her otherwise plain face. "I believe 'nice looking' was the term I used."

"Yes," Becca said with amusement, "I believe it was." In all the years she had known Nell, she had seldom heard the woman heap such praise upon a stranger. "Incidentally, you do remember you are having supper with us tonight?"

"Yes, I have it written on my calendar. Are you certain I shouldn't bring anything?"

"Nothing at all. Aunt Agatha has everything under control."

"How wonderful it must be to have her there to help you. She certainly is a jewel of a woman to give of herself so freely."

"Yes, isn't she." Becca wondered if this jewel had settled in the spare room forever. Agatha had been there over two weeks and still showed no sign of leaving. Becca felt disloyal, but she was tired of the constant war between Agatha and Matt.

The tinkle of the bell over the door announced a customer and Becca's thoughts were laid aside for the time.

"Percy Winthrop is in town," Matt announced as they walked home together. "He came in last night."

"Who?"

"My new tailor, remember?"

"Oh, yes. The tailor."

"You certainly don't sound very excited about it."

"Forgive me, Matt, but news like that isn't going to be the highlight of my day." The rainwear sale had been unsuccessful and Becca was in no mood to be gracious to the competition. Especially since Prescott's shoe sale had drawn all her customers. "You know, Matt, we really do need to discuss when we are going to have sales. We seem to be working against each other."

"Your business isn't going well?" Matt asked in genuine surprise.

"I wouldn't say that exactly," Becca said

hastily. "Only that we shouldn't undermine each other."

Matt frowned. "Why don't you put something on sale? That always draws customers for me."

"That's what I was just saying," she said testily. "And you needn't sound as if I'm going bankrupt."

"You are? I had no idea it was so bad. Becca, I really think you ought to give in and open a café. Think what a great place the Emporium would make. It has the perfect location. I'll even absorb your stock so you won't lose any more money."

"I'm not losing money! Quit twisting my words!" She quickened her pace in her anger.

"I'm doing no such thing. I'm only trying to help you out of a difficulty."

"I don't need your help," she snapped as he drew up beside her. She walked faster. "And I don't want to hear about your employees."

"What is that supposed to mean?" He was frowning as he overtook her.

"I'm referring to this Percy Winesap."

"Winthrop!"

"Whatever! Bringing a tailor in will only take away more of my business." She hadn't intended to say that and she clamped her mouth shut. By now she was all but trotting down the street.

"You're afraid of the competition," he accused. "Should I stock inferior goods and have no employees just so the Emporium can prosper?"

"Why not?" she said maddeningly. "I was here first!"

"Then you will have to brush up your own business tactics and keep up with me!" He stepped out in strides that threatened to leave her behind. "And you will have to hear about Percy because he is my friend as well as an employee and he happens to be eating supper with us tonight."

Becca stopped so quickly he was several feet away before he halted. "Tonight! Nell is eating with us tonight. Besides that, what will Aunt Agatha say?"

"I sent a note to her this afternoon. She expects him."

"Without even consulting me?"

"It's my house, too, Becca," he reminded her tersely. "If you would stop being so closed-minded, you might like Percy."

"Closed-minded! Me? You have no reason to insult me, Matt Prescott! And with a name like Percy Winthrop, how exciting can he be? He probably wears pink undergarments." She recalled she was on the street and blushed at her impropriety.

"I doubt it," Matt replied in frosty tones. "Why not wait until you meet him before you jump to any more conclusions."

Becca tilted her chin in the air and swept by him with an imperious toss of her head. "I always keep an open mind, Matt, but I can tell you now that I won't like him."

They stepped out briskly, neither wanting to be bested by the other, and they arrived breathlessly at the house. Agatha greeted them with her usual nod to Becca and a frown for Matt. The aroma of fried chicken permeated the house.

By eight o'clock Becca and Matt were seated uncomfortably in the formal parlor while Agatha reigned supreme in the kitchen. Neither was speaking to the other, and Becca had the uncomfortable sensation of not knowing what to do with her hands or where to rest her eyes. She wondered if Matt was looking at her, but she refused to glance over and see. If he was, he might think she was trying to patch up the quarrel, and if he wasn't, he might imagine she was staring at him. She settled for staring at a picture above the piano.

When the first knock sounded at the door, they stood up simultaneously. Abruptly, Becca sat back down just as Matt did, too. With a sigh, she glared at him and went to answer the door.

"Nell." She beamed at her guest as though she had not seen her in a very long time. "Won't you come in?"

Nell looked at her curiously, as she had been with Becca only a few hours before. She untied her small bonnet and gave it and her crocheted shawl to her hostess. She held a covered bowl in her capable hands. "I couldn't come to eat without bringing something. It's a blackberry cobbler."

"You shouldn't have, but I'm glad you did." Becca turned as her aunt came into the hall to greet the first guest. "Look, Aunt Agatha. Nell brought a cobbler."

"How nice," Agatha replied as she took the dish. "So thoughtful of you. Supper is ready if our other guest ever gets here." She cast a baleful eye toward the parlor before taking the cobbler back to the kitchen.

"Other guest?"

"Yes, it seems Matt has invited his tailor tonight as well." Lowering her voice, Becca said, "Don't expect too much. His name is Percy Winthrop, you remember."

"How sad," Nell said with a smile. "But what a perfect name for a tailor."

They were still laughing when they entered the parlor, but Becca felt her gaiety melt in Matt's presence. She returned to her former seat and Nell perched on the edge of the settee, her shoulders several correct inches from the tufted back. Silence grew uncomfortably tense in the room.

"I've always admired that watercolor of the Seine," Nell ventured.

"Thank you," Becca replied. "It's one of my mother's." Again there was silence.

"Made any hats lately?" Matt tried lamely when he could stand it no longer.

"Our hat business is doing fine," Becca answered for her. "Especially the ones with cherries."

Nell moved uncomfortably. The strain was relieved by a loud knock on the door. All three jumped.

"Excuse me, ladies," Matt said to Nell.

Soon the sound of male laughter came to them, and then Percy Winthrop entered the parlor. Becca stared. The man was tall and as dark as Matt was fair. A neatly trimmed moustache furred his lip, and his cheeks were clean-shaven. His face was somewhat too perfect to be called handsome, and his build was lean and well muscled. After a polite word to Becca, he turned with interest to Nell. "I believe we met earlier—almost."

Becca realized her mouth was open and closed it. "You're Percy Winthrop?" she asked.

"Yes, that's right. It's certainly easy to see why Matt decided to settle in Mellville. All the prettiest women are here." Again he smiled at Nell, who colored and lowered her eyes.

"And you're a tailor?" Becca queried.

"Didn't Matt tell you?" He grinned at his friend. "I know he used to keep me in the shadows before he married, but I expected more from him these days."

"Come now, Mr. Winthrop," Nell protested coquettishly. "Surely no one could keep you in the background."

Becca's stare swung to her shop assistant. After all the years she had known Nell, she would have sworn there wasn't a flirtatious bone in the woman's body. Yet here she was acting as coy as the belle of two counties.

Percy smiled and again his lips lifted in a lopsided fashion. "Please call me by my first name. It's Percy, short for Percival, I'm afraid."

"How lovely. Like the knight of King Arthur's Round Table," Nell observed.

"I believe supper is ready," Becca said. "I'll go help Aunt Agatha put it on the table."

To Matt's chagrin, Agatha, too, seemed to melt before Percy. At one point in the meal she actually made a sound that in a lesser mortal might be termed a titter. Matt stared at her, and Agatha's more accustomed expression surfaced.

Percy was an accomplished conversationalist, and by the chatter around the table it wasn't noticeable that Becca and Matt weren't speaking. Indeed, neither Nell nor Agatha had eyes for anything but the darkly handsome guest. He, in turn, bestowed smiles and compliments equally to all the ladies and jovial comments to his host.

Matt watched as Percy retrieved Becca's fallen napkin, and wondered if he had made a mistake in bringing him here. Percy had made a name for himself with all the ladies in Memphis and had secured the attention of more than one damsel that Matt had singled out for his own. Until this moment, however, Matt hadn't considered that Becca might find

Percy appealing. His eyes narrowed speculatively. Percy was engrossed by someone, and he knew it was neither Aunt Agatha nor himself. But years of observing Percy on the stalk of prey confirmed his suspicions. Becca's laughter rang out in clear tones as Matt cursed himself for a fool.

When Agatha served dessert—her own banana pudding and Nell's blackberry cobbler—Percy overflowed with compliments. Both cooks humbly refused to take any credit, but both were immeasurably pleased. After the meal, Agatha insisted on needing no help in "her" kitchen, so both couples retired to the parlor.

Becca returned to her chair as if it were a lodestone, and Matt did the same. Percy, however, sat on the piano stool and opened the keyboard. Expertly he ran a scale up the ivories.

"Lovely voice," he announced. "Such a tonal quality."

"Do you play, Percy?" Nell exclaimed.

"Only a little," he admitted with practiced reluctance.

"I can hardly believe that," Becca said to escape the former strained silence she dreaded would fall. "Please play us something."

"Only if you ladies will honor me with a song."

"I have no musical talents at all," Becca protested, "but Nell has a beautiful voice."

"How can you say that?" Nell laughed blushingly, but with little conviction.

"Come now," Matt said with forced gaiety. "I've heard you sing in church. Give it a try."

Nell allowed herself to be persuaded, and self-consciously she took her place by the piano. "Do you know 'Jeanie with the Light Brown Hair'?"

"Do I know it? It's one of my favorites." Percy rolled a scale down the keyboard and launched smoothly into the familiar melody. Nell began to sing, shyly at first, then more confidently as Percy harmonized his voice to hers.

Becca pasted a smile on her face and hoped the evening would end soon. The tension between Matt and herself was creating a dull throb in her temples. She only wanted to be left alone with him so they could resolve their differences in the cozy haven of their bedroom.

Percy started the strains of "Walking Nelly Home," and Nell blushed and lowered her eyes in a coy manner. By the time they had worked their way through "Drink to Me Only with Thine Eyes," Agatha came into the parlor. Surprisingly she joined her wavering voice to theirs and warbled her way through "Annie Laurie."

Percy insisted on seeing Nell home. By the time her guests left, Becca's headache had grown to awesome proportions, and her face ached from smiling and her back muscles felt rigid.

"Well," Agatha said with the smugness of a successful hostess, "it was a delightful evening. I approve of Mr. Winthrop. It wouldn't surprise me in the least to learn he can call kin to the Jefferson Winthrops. They are among the bedrock of our fair city." With a quick nod of her head, Agatha bade them good night and in a rustle of stiff taffeta retired to her room.

Suddenly finding herself alone with Matt, Becca felt uneasy. Abruptly, she went back to the parlor to put out the lights.

Matt watched her uncompromisingly straight back and he frowned. More than anything else he wanted to put things right between them, but Becca seemed determined to avoid him. He snuffed the candles in the dining room and waited at the foot of the stairs for Becca, who was locking the back door.

Only one candle remained burning in the entry, and when she emerged ghostily from the shadows of the kitchen, he looked long at her. Their eyes met and he saw the misery in her brown depths. With a sigh, he held out his arm to her. She came to him and silently gazed up at him.

"I like your friend," she said at last. "I was wrong to prejudge him."

A small muscle tightened in Matt's jaw. "He seemed rather taken with you, too." She looked so small and vulnerable as she stood there looking up at him. A wave of possessive protectiveness rushed over him. "Are you sleepy?"

"Not very, but I'm terribly tired. Let's go to bed."

He smiled and caressed her cheek. Miraculously her headache began to dissipate. Arm in arm they went upstairs, with the faint glow of the candle lighting one step at a time.

"Go start picking the cucumbers, Rebecca," Agatha said briskly. "We almost forgot to put up the pickles."

"Do we have to do it today?" Becca protested. "I'm still tired from all the jelly we canned yesterday." She thought of the precise rows of blackberry and strawberry jelly and wondered how she and Matt would ever eat all of it.

"Today is the day. The moon is on the wane and you know as well as I do that it takes two weeks to make pickles. If we don't get at it, we will be in a new moon and they will taste soft and slimy, no matter what we do to them."

Becca sighed and bowed to the inevitable. As she went outside, she saw Matt mowing the lawn. With a peck basket in hand, she went out to him, and when she caught his attention he called to his horse to stop and the mower whirled to a halt. "Good news, Matt," she said wryly. "In addition to four batches of jelly we will also have pickles all winter."

He wiped his sweaty brow on his sleeve and groaned. "Becca, you know I can't stand pickles."

"I can't help that. Aunt Agatha has already decided to pick the cucumbers. Will you get the crocks out of the storage shed for me? We will need all four."

"Four crocks of pickles?" he asked incredulously. "Four?"

"Two to soak the cucumbers and two to change the brine when we rinse them. It's all I have that's large enough to hold that many cucumbers."

"How many cucumbers would you say two crocks would hold, Becca?"

She thought of the heavily laden vines and the baskets on the back porch and said, "Quite a few, Matt. Quite a few."

"After she puts up the pickles do you think she will leave?"

"That's hard to say," Becca answered evasively.

"There is something you aren't telling me. What is it?" he demanded.

"It takes two weeks to make pickles."

He frowned down at her, then turned on his heel and stalked off toward the storage shed behind the barn. Becca shook her head as she went down to the garden. She, too, had had enough company. She brushed aside the hairy leaves and started pulling the cucumbers and laying them in the basket. The sun was warm on her back and she enjoyed the earthy smells of her garden, but she really wasn't in the mood to start making pickles today. Her fingers were still stained from the berry juice of the day before.

"Rebecca," Aunt Agatha called as she joined her. "You forgot your garden bonnet. Your hair will be the color of corn syrup if you let the sun get at it. Not to mention freckles."

With resignation Becca took her faded pink bonnet from her aunt and tied it under her chin. The heavily starched brim shaded her face, but also obscured her vision. The back of the hat covered her hair and a short ruffle shaded the back of her neck. Becca detested garden bonnets. Agatha was wearing a lavender striped one that looked incongruous with her usual mourning. Although the voluminous black cotton of a style more popular years ago must have been hot, Agatha moved briskly down the rows of cucumbers.

Becca soon filled her basket and emptied it into a bushel, then went back. When she started back down the row, she could see Matt washing the dusty crocks under the big yard pump. He still looked upset. Becca was beginning to wonder if Agatha had come to stay. Even though this was her favorite aunt, Becca sincerely hoped not. She wanted to be alone with her new husband.

Her muscles were tired from the berry picking, and by the time the vines were denuded of cucumbers, her back ached. She straightened gingerly and stretched to relieve her strained muscles. Agatha frowned disapprovingly at her and Becca promptly lowered her arms to a more decorous arrangement with her elbows lower than her shoulders. Agatha was waiting for her beside one of the large baskets, so Becca took the other side. Between them they carried the produce to the back porch.

By the time all the baskets were beside the screen door, Becca was more than ready to collapse into the wooden chair. She decided it was fortunate that peeling cucumbers was a job best done while sitting down. While Agatha put a huge kettle of water on to boil, Becca took her paring knife and a bowl from the kitchen and went back to the porch.

She mopped the dampness from her forehead as Robert came across the lawn with the tan crocks. Their eyes met and a silent message was passed. Becca was tired of housework and both were ready to be alone. He shoved two of the crocks toward her and upended the other two to drain on the weekly newspaper.

Methodically, Becca began peeling the cucumbers over the bowl and sliced them lengthwise into quarters. The peeled sections were dropped into the first crock, where they looked very small.

"You have a long way to go if you're going to fill both these crocks," Matt observed.

"There are plenty of knives in the kitchen if

you want to help." She began paring another sliver of dark green from the pale meat.

"I'll help later," Matt said hastily. "I need to grease that squeaky axle on the buggy."

"Uh-huh," Becca said in an unconvinced tone.

Heavy afternoon clouds were piling up behind the barn, their underbellies a sooty gray. "Looks like we're in for some rain," Agatha said conversationally as she rejoined Becca on the porch. "I noticed the earthworms making little hills in the garden. By suppertime we may be in for a storm."

Becca glanced up at the clouds. "At least we got the cucumbers in and Matt finished mowing the grass. Wet grass is almost impossible to cut."

"True, how true." Agatha's blue-veined hands expertly shaved the skin off a cucumber, quartered it, and tossed it into the crock before Becca could finish the one she held. "I tell you, girl, I've seen a world of improvement in my life. Mowing grass, white fences, neat towns. Texas sure has changed from my heyday."

"In what way?" Becca asked, as she knew she was supposed to do.

"When I first saw Texas we had just won our independence from Mexico. A sovereign state, it was, with our own flag and our own president. Glorious days, those were. Your father was as upset as I was over Texas joining the Union. We both wanted it to stay sovereign, but it seemed like everyone else wanted it to become a state. And they got their way." She shook her head and clucked disparagingly. "Now you see what a mess the War Between the States got us into."

"That was twenty years ago, Aunt Agatha. I can scarcely remember it."

"There's a pity," Agatha said, pointing her paring knife at Becca to punctuate her words. "That's something nobody ought to forget. We nearly lost your father in that free-for-all. You could have been a fatherless child and your poor mother a widow woman."

"But Father did come back . . ." Becca began.

"He never healed properly. That awful war put him in an early grave."

Ezra Simpson had died at seventy-two of a stroke, but Becca wisely held her tongue. When Aunt Agatha started in on the War Between the States, a prudent soul gave her no back talk.

Matt was lying on his back beneath the wagon, smearing green-gold grease onto the dry joint. He had bought the buggy new in Jefferson just before he came to Mellville and it shouldn't have needed repair so soon. Still, he decided, it had seen a lot of use. He crawled out from under the wagon and dusted himself. The wheels were looking worn, too, he noticed. It might be a good idea to have new rims put on at the wheelwright's. The blacksmith was next door and he could have the gray gelding reshod at the same time.

He picked up a rag and wiped the greasy mess off his hands. Working on the wagon was one job he didn't especially care for. When his hands were as clean as rubbing could make them, he went out to the big pump, whistling as he went. He pulled off his grimy work shirt and hung it on a nail in the wash shed. One of Becca's squares of lye soap lay waiting for use on the board and Matt took it with him.

By working the iron handle he produced a stream of cold water. Thrusting his head under it, he splashed water over his entire torso. Still whistling, he soaped the work grime from his hands, face, and arms. The soap made a yellowish lather that smelled faintly of pine tar. He scrubbed all the grease from his hands, then worked the pump handle again to rinse off the soap.

A portion of a broken mirror hung on the rough boards of the shed and gave him a wavery image as he combed his wet hair into place. Before suppertime he planned to take a proper bath, but at least he was presentable.

The sun was already drying the beaded water from his skin as he started for the house. He could see Becca and her aunt sitting on the porch and he frowned slightly. He had no clean shirt at the barn, and his work shirt was streaked with axle grease and dirt. Just seeing him in his shirt sleeves had once brought a disapproving grimace from Agatha.

A view of him half-naked would likely give her palpitations. He remembered their introduction and grinned in spite of himself. Still, there was no point in courting trouble.

Keeping the barn between himself and the women, he skirted the house. To go in the front door was out of the question since it was clearly visible from the street. The kitchen window, however, was invitingly open. Matt eased it open wider and swung his leg over the sill.

Just at that moment Agatha decided to check on the kettle of water. Her shriek at seeing a half-naked man climbing in the window could have been heard for blocks.

"Good afternoon, Aunt Agatha," Matt said with formal politeness. "Lovely weather for this time of year." He nodded to her as she fell back against the cabinet and fled to the porch. Matt continued across the kitchen in as unhurried a gait as if nothing untoward had happened.

"Did you call out?" Becca asked as Agatha plopped back down in her chair.

"No, I most certainly did not." Agatha's clipped tones revealed her agitation as much as the way she sliced at a cucumber. "That man has got to comport himself with more dignity!"

"Matt?" Becca asked. "What do you mean?"

"He's right in there in the kitchen and as naked as a savage. I caught him climbing in the window." Agatha hacked the cucumber into the crock and grabbed another.

"Climbing in the kitchen window? Matt?" She leaned forward to peer around the corner. "Aunt Agatha, I don't see anyone."

"Well, he's in there, as big as life. Stark, staring naked!"

Becca looked at her aunt, then back at the empty kitchen. The sun had been hot that day and Aunt Agatha had been bending over a great deal. Perhaps, Becca surmised, she was hallucinating. "I'll speak to him, Aunt Agatha. Why don't you go lie down and put some rose water on your brow. That always made Mother feel better."

"There is nothing ailing me. I'm not some hothouse flower to swoon over nothing. He was there, I tell you!"

"I believe you." Becca watched her aunt closely and hoped the spell would soon pass.

Agatha thinned her lips in an uncompromising line and glared at the barn. "Why Matthew can't be more like his friend, I don't know. You would never catch Mr. Winthrop naked in your kitchen, I wager."

"I agree. That is rather unlikely. Would you like a cool glass of tea?"

Agatha snorted and jumped as Matt, fully clothed, stepped out onto the porch. "Good afternoon, ladies. You seem to be making the most of the shade." He sat down by Becca and took a cucumber out of the basket. Using the peck as a receptacle, he pared away the thick green skin. "This is rather like whittling, isn't it?" he said amiably.

Becca looked at his damp hair and well-scrubbed face. "Yes, it is."

"And how would you know about whittling, miss?" Agatha demanded. "Your father would never have allowed his daughter to do that."

"Matt taught me," Becca informed her. "He also showed me how to fish." She glanced at Matt and they both grinned.

"It's unnatural for a lady to do either. Next you will want to ride astride."

Becca looked up thoughtfully and her paring knife slowed. That would be more comfortable than her sidesaddle, and probably safer once she learned how. She decided to ask Matt to teach her as soon as possible.

Matt recognized the expression on Becca's face and his grin broadened.

"I was just telling Rebecca about the War Between the States," Agatha said to make conversation. "I don't suppose you were in it, Matthew?"

"Matt. No, I was only a boy. My father fought, though, and took a bullet at Vicksburg. My two older brothers and my uncles were involved, too. My oldest brother lost his life." He shook his head and dropped the cucumber into Becca's crock. "That was a bitter time. As young as I was, I can recall the hard feelings."

"Oh? What hard feelings are you referring

to?" Agatha inquired in a tone that said she was not interested in the least.

"Between my brother that lived and my father. He and my uncles fought for the South, and it was years later before Papa would speak to them."

Agatha's knotty fingers slowed, then stopped altogether as the implication of Matt's words sank in. "You're the son of a Yankee!" she gasped.

"Aunt Agatha, it was twenty years ago!" Becca reminded her hastily. "All the rest of his family fought for the South."

"Except two cousins," Matt added helpfully, "and they were killed."

"Fetch my salts!" Agatha instructed Becca in a voice that sounded far too angry for her to be in danger of a fainting spell.

Becca threw Matt an accusing glance and ran for the smelling salts.

Matt regarded Agatha with wry amusement. "You and I both know you aren't given to swooning. Why do you pretend that you are?"

The shock of his words made Agatha's eyes fly open and she regarded him with hostility. "You are hardly an authority on my frailties."

"You are no more frail than I am." Matt grinned. "If you don't like what I have to say, why don't you stand up to me and say so, like Becca does. She's as feisty as the day is long and I like that in a woman."

"Feisty, indeed! She was brought up to be

191

genteel and not to raise her voice to any-one."

"I know, but I've almost got her past that."

Becca came out onto the porch in time to hear herself mentioned. "Are you talking about me?"

"I was just telling Aunt Agatha how much I like your spirit," Matt told her.

Agatha took the small cylinder, broke it open, and whiffed the contents. The faint odor of ammonia drifted in the air. Becca patted her aunt's shoulder and said, "Matt, were you in the kitchen a little while ago?"

"Naked," Agatha added in a pitifully weak voice.

"Only from the waist up," Matt amended. "Below that I was fully clothed."

Agatha fanned herself with the tail of her apron and glared at him. "Disgraceful!"

"Matt, how could you? You know how easily distressed Aunt Agatha is."

"I was trying to spare her distress, Becca. After I washed up from greasing that axle, I had nothing to change into. So I climbed in the kitchen window and was about to go upstairs. I had no idea she would catch me in the kitchen."

"I believe I will go lie down," Agatha said in a wavering voice.

"You could have put your shirt back on," Becca told him.

"It was greasy!"

"But to climb in the kitchen window!"

"Like a savage," Agatha prompted.

"Go lie down, Aunt Agatha," Becca snapped before she thought.

Agatha's head jerked up and her pale eyes became flinty. "Very well. If that's the way I'm to be treated, I will!"

"No, no, please don't be hurt," Becca pleaded. "I'm tired and I spoke to both of you more harshly than I should have."

With regal poise Agatha stood. "I, too, am tired, Rebecca. After all, I have been hard at work. And all, I might add, for you." With a twitch of her somber skirts, she sailed by Becca and into the house.

Thunder rumbled in the distance and emphasized the silence on the porch. Matt reached over and took Becca's hand. She frowned at him accusingly.

"She brought all that on herself, you know," he said gently.

"Aunt Agatha isn't as young as she once was. Don't blame her."

"None of us are getting any younger if it comes to that. It's no excuse for troublemaking."

Becca tried to pull her hand away, but he refused to release it. "Don't be angry with me. If I was out of line with her, I'll apologize."

"Matt, she is all the close family I have left," Becca tried to explain. "I rarely see my aunts on Mother's side of the family—they live in Austin and have never cared much for me. Aunt Agatha is all the tie I have left with my parents and my childhood." Her large, dark eyes filled with tears. "Please don't ask me to choose between you, Matt, because I will choose you and lose my roots."

"No, no, honey. I would never want you to do that." He scooted his chair closer so he could take her in his arms. "Aunt Agatha and I are about to reach an understanding," he explained as he cradled her head on his shoulder. "We may even get to like each other once she accepts who I am."

Becca looked up at him and he kissed her forehead. "Why didn't you ever tell me your father fought for the North?"

"I guess it just never came up. It didn't seem right to say 'Pass the potatoes, my father was a yankee.' Is it important to you?"

"No, but if I were you, I wouldn't spread the word around town. Memories are long around here and there isn't a family in town that the war didn't touch."

"It's that way all over, Becca," he said sadly. "War is a terrible thing. But this one is over and done and it need not come between us."

She sighed and watched the distant rain slant downward onto the fields beyond the barn. "You're right, Matt. We have enough to bother us between Aunt Agatha and the dry goods business without worrying about the War Between the States."

"You're right," he agreed as he hugged her. "Did I mention I plan to order a shipment of chinaware? I don't believe anyone in the entire county stocks dishes. The market is wide open." When she sat upright he reached for another cucumber. "Doesn't that rain smell good? Let's get some more of these peeled before the thunder drives us inside."

Chapter Eleven

MATT LOOKED UP FROM HIS LEDGER BOOK AND watched as Percy went out the door and into the sun-washed street that separated Prescott's from the Emporium. He paused and looked up and down the street, consulted his large watch, dropped it back in his vest pocket, and ambled across the street. Just as he had every day for a week. Matt replaced his pen in the ink pot and leaned back in his chair. As Matt thoughtfully stroked his chin, Percy disappeared through the Emporium's many-paned door.

At first Matt had been curious about Percy's dinnertime excursions. Now he was becoming suspicious. Only two people worked in the Emporium. Nell, with her plain face and angular figure, and Becca. Matt stood up and shut the ledger book.

"Miss Fuller?" he called to the milliner, "I'll be gone for dinner if anyone needs me."

She nodded around her mouthful of pins and continued fastening a swath of voile to a hat.

The heat of late summer hit Matt as soon as he left the shade of his store. The air shimmered in glassy mirages over the brick street, and even the large trees in the distant yards looked wilted and tired. Business was slow in the early afternoon, because people preferred to wait out the worst of the heat in their airy sitting rooms. He was almost alone on the street. Quickly he strode across to the Emporium. The high ceilings trapped the heat and left the lower levels relatively comfortable, though the store had no customers. Matt looked around for Percy as his eyes adjusted after the harsh sunlight. Voices led him toward the back room.

Becca looked out to see who had come in, and when she saw Matt, her smile broadened. "Come on back here," she called out in greeting. "Percy is telling us the most delightful tale."

With an effort, Matt arranged his lips into a smile and followed Becca into the office. Percy was leaning indolently against Nell's fabric-strewn worktable. As he talked, his handsome features were as animated as his hands. Matt crossed his arms on his chest and listened to the familiar anecdote. At the proper times he smiled, but he was paying no heed to Percy's words. Instead he was watching Becca and Nell and wondering why all women seemed to find Percy Winthrop so irresistible. Had he known Becca would fall into this classification, he might not have hired Percy as his tailor.

The story finished, Becca and Nell laughed delightedly. "I know," Becca said. "Why don't we all have dinner together? Aunt Agatha sent more than Matt and I can eat."

"We could put our food together and have a picnic of sorts," Nell agreed. "Won't you stay, Mr. Winthrop?"

Percy held up his hand to emphasize his words. "Only if you call me by my first name, Miss Nell."

Nell lowered her eyes and her lips tilted in a smile. "Very well, Percy."

Matt helped Becca clear a space on the table, but he found his appetite was flagging. When spoken to, he answered congenially enough, but he made no effort to further a conversation.

Becca looked at him closely. "Are you feeling well?" she asked with a little concern. "You seem so distant."

"I feel fine," he answered.

"Come now, Rebecca," Percy said smoothly. "Matt is merely being a stick-in-the-mud. You mustn't worry about him just because he isn't talking. Why, I remember one time when we were boys . . ."

Matt managed a smile as Percy launched into another tale. Becca looked at him with questioning eyes but soon turned her attention back to Percy. Matt ate a piece of cold ham and hoped it would get past the knot in his stomach.

Dinner seemed to last forever to Matt. By the time they ate the last boiled egg and drank all the sugared tea, he was painfully convinced that his darling Becca was all too friendly with his tailor. He interrupted Nell's laughter at Percy's latest joke to say, "Don't you have a fitting at one o'clock, Percy?"

Percy consulted his watch once again. "I have a few more minutes." He began helping Nell replace the remains of their meal into her dinner basket. "This has been truly delightful," he said, "as always."

Matt glared at him sharply. Had Percy been eating with Becca and Nell every day? Matt had been so busy with the store, he had seldom taken time to eat before supper, even though Becca always brought his portion of dinner to him in his cluttered office.

"Tomorrow I will bring a pecan pie," Nell suggested. "You do like pecan pie, don't you, Percy?"

"It's my favorite, Miss Nell."

"I thought your favorite was chocolate meringue," Matt said testily.

"Perhaps he has changed his mind," Becca suggested with a warning glance at her husband. "Nell's pecan pie is a masterpiece of cooking."

"I see." Matt looked from one to the other. "Let's go, Percy. We have just enough time to get back before the fitting."

"He's right," Percy said as he made a small bow to each lady. "Until tomorrow, *adieu*."

"I'll be here, too," Matt added quickly, and smiled as an afterthought. "I wouldn't miss one of your pies, Nell."

Becca watched the men leave and she frowned slightly. Matt had acted so strangely. Yet he hadn't appeared to be feverish. Still, his appetite was less than normal. "I think Matt is working too hard," she confided in her friend.

Nell sighed and her eyes were dreamy. "What a charming man, that Percy Winthrop." She looked as if merely saying his name was a pleasant experience.

Becca suppressed her smile. She had seen the same awed look on Percy's face as he had watched Nell unpack the dinner. When she went out into the shop, Becca heard Nell humming under her breath.

Matt sat on the back porch and creased his newspaper so the wind wouldn't ruffle through it. On the front page was an interview with Jay Gould, in which he stated that his railroad was approaching Shreveport and would soon be into Texas, but just where in

Texas it would go had not yet been decided. He boasted that his railroad didn't need to seek out established commerce, but rather created it from nothing. Wherever he deigned to lay his steel tracks, business would prosper. It was a high-handed attitude, but one that Matt knew was true. Trains could carry more goods and transport them faster than wagons or steamboats. Already towns were flourishing in Jay Gould's wake. And others were doomed to fade when he had capriciously skirted them. Within the next few months, it would be decided if the tracks would go through Jefferson or Mellville. And at the moment, Jefferson seemed to be the most likely target, according to the speculation of the reporter.

Matt laid down the paper and looked unseeingly at the tall willow. He had hoped to see the rails being laid further to the south, making Mellville a more likely target should the tracks move westward in a straight line. But with Gould's unpredictability, who could tell for sure?

Becca came out and sat beside him. Her face was flushed from the warmth of the kitchen but she smiled at him. "Aunt Agatha has gone walking with Mrs. Whiteside. We're alone."

He reached out and took her hand. "Let's walk out to the orchard. There seems to be a breeze out there."

Hand in hand, they crossed the lawn. The grass felt dry under her feet and she looked up at the coppery sky. Even though the sun was low over the trees, the blue had a harshness about it. "We've had a hard summer," she commented. "What little rain we've had has been baked out again the next day."

"Fall will come before long," Matt said. "It always does, just in the nick of time."

They walked to the low white fence and Becca cast an appraising eye at her fruit trees. With the promise of evening's coolness, they were looking less parched. "Something is bothering you," she said without looking at him. "What is it?"

"Nothing. Nothing at all."

She bent and picked a sprig of mint that grew by the fence and was threatening to spread into the yard. "Why won't you tell me? Every day at dinner you act as surly as a bear. Even Nell asked if you are angry with her."

Matt ran his hand over the fence as if he were checking to see if it needed painting. "I haven't been acting any way out of the ordinary," he replied evasively. "You can tell Nell I'm not upset with her."

"Are you upset with me?" Becca pursued.

"I don't have reason to be, do I?" He tried to smile, but his lips felt stiff.

"No, you have no reason at all. Yet I think you are."

Matt flicked a curl of cracked paint from the

fence. "I need to put another coat on this when the weather cools." He looked back at the stately house and let his eyes follow the roof line. "Seems as if Percy has been spending an unusual amount of time at the Emporium. Has he been getting in your way?"

Becca laughed and shook her head. "It seems as if he's there every time I look around. I've learned to walk around him." To her surprise, Matt looked disturbed by her words. "He isn't in my way or I would ask him to leave."

"I see. That shutter up there needs fixing. It's worked loose." They wandered back to the willow and he swept aside the branches so she could enter. "I would rather you didn't act quite so friendly to Percy. He may get the wrong idea. He is in the Emporium far too often."

"What?" she said incredulously. He looked serious, but she could hardly believe he had meant the words the way they had sounded. "You mean he is shirking his job? Well, as your competitor, I can scarcely regret that."

Matt abruptly pulled her around to face him. "You aren't flirting with him to get him away from his work, are you?"

Becca stared at him. "If I thought you meant that, I wouldn't speak to you for a week! How can you even joke about such a thing?"

"I'm not joking, Becca. I want you to discourage Percy from coming to the Emporium."

Her head tilted upward in the stubborn gesture he knew so well. "I will do no such thing. And I don't flirt with anyone."

"Don't you? I had told you that story about the spotted cow, and when Percy told it, you laughed as if you had never heard it before."

"He told it differently!"

"My version was the accurate one!"

"Who cares? His was . . ." She realized what she was about to say and closed her mouth. Percy was a born storyteller, but there was no point in rubbing it in.

"Better? Is that what you were about to say?"

"No, funnier!" There. She had let it slip out anyway. Anger flashed in her dark eyes.

Matt drew himself up and glared down at her. "What else would you suppose he excels in?"

For a moment she frowned up at him; then understanding dawned. "You're jealous!" she gasped. "You are jealous of Percy and me! Aren't you!" Amazement made her eyes round. Never in her wildest imaginings had she ever considered causing a rivalry between two men as handsome as Matt and Percy. She was too flattered to feel angry.

"All right, I'm jealous. Any man would be. Why are you smiling?"

"Because I love you so much." She tiptoed

and kissed him on the lips. "You're so dear to me, Matt." She decided to savor this new sensation and tell him later that Nell was the magnet that drew Percy away from his work at Prescott's.

Matt drew her to him and cradled her fiercely against his chest. Her hair smelled of sunlight and fresh air and he rubbed his cheek on the umber tresses. His jealousy ebbed as her arms tightened around him. Surely, he told himself, he was being ridiculous. Becca loved him and he trusted her. It was Percy he doubted. "Let's go upstairs," he suggested in a tone that was unmistakable.

"Now? It isn't even dark and Aunt Agatha may return at any moment."

"Let's hurry." He caught her hand and they ran toward the house.

Laughing and tripping over each other, they hurried through the kitchen and hallway and up the stairs. On the landing, Matt stopped her long enough for a kiss, and again they ran upstairs. Becca held her skirts up and showed far more leg than Aunt Agatha would have countenanced even in a child. Matt ran ahead of her and she grabbed his coattail to pull him back. They reached their bedroom door at the same time and she managed to squeeze by him to enter the room first.

Her cheeks were pink from running and her chocolate eyes sparkled with fun. Matt swept her up in his arms and kicked the door shut.

In a few strides he crossed the room and dropped her in the middle of the downy bed. The feather mattress billowed around her as he threw himself upon her.

Becca tried to stifle her laughter in his neck as he made growling sounds in her ear. Her hands were as busy removing his clothing as his were in stripping away her own.

"How strange it feels to be making love in the middle of the day," she said. "I feel positively wanton."

"Good. I approve of your decadence." He lowered his head and nuzzled her breast and nipped through the fabric at the erect bud in the center of the lush softness.

She smiled at him as the delicious sensation made a warm glow spread through her body. The sunlight streamed through the open windows and laid a patina of gold over his shoulders. Faint sounds from the street drifted up on a current of wind. She sighed happily.

Matt moved his attention to her other breast and she arched her back toward him. She pulled his arms from the sleeves of his shirt and ran her hands over his smooth skin. That wasn't enough, so she drew out his shirttail and tossed his shirt to the floor. Admiringly she ran her fingers over the swelling muscles of his back and felt the power of his shoulders.

He sat up and drew her to a position facing him. Slowly he pulled her dress down until she sat before him with only her thin chemise covering her full breasts. The fabric was almost transparent and did nothing to hide her pouting nipples. Taking his time, Matt lifted the garment over her head and tossed it over his shoulder. "You're so beautiful, he said gently. "At times you still surprise me in your perfection."

Becca stroked her fingertips across his broad chest and traced a vein that appeared in his biceps. "You're beautiful, too. You're golden, like a Greek god."

He leaned forward and kissed her, their bodies separated by a breath. Gradually she lay back and her arms encircled his neck. Matt lifted her and pushed away her remaining clothes and shoved them off the bed. Within moments, his had joined them and he lay naked against her body.

She ran her hand down his narrow waist and over the rounded muscles of his buttocks. "I love you," she sighed. "I want you."

Again his mouth claimed hers, and she seemed to float and swirl as his tongue traced fire in her inner lips. His breath was sweet against her cheek, and his arms held her as securely as bands of steel but far more gently. She rolled him on top of her and opened herself to him.

As they merged into one, she felt the now-familiar but ever-new fire begin in her veins. Molten lava seemed to replace her blood as Matt moved sensuously inside her. Slowly the fires built until her entire being seemed centered in their loving. Then he changed his rhythm slightly and together they soared in the golden sparks of love.

The world came back to them gradually. Becca heard a carriage pass her house, and in the distance a dog barked as children shouted. She nuzzled his cheek and he smiled without opening his eyes. From the house below came the distinct sound of a door opening and closing and then two women's voices. Becca's eyes flew open.

"Damn!" Matt muttered into the pillow. He rolled off her and sat on the edge of the bed to retrieve his pants as she grabbed at her petticoats and bloomers.

"Rebecca?" Agatha called from the bottom of the stairs. "Are you up there?"

She exchanged a helpless look with Matt, who grinned and shrugged. "Yes, Aunt Agatha."

"We have company," her aunt reported. "Come down."

"I'll be there in a minute." She tied the ribbons that held her bloomers, and tripped as she tried to pull up her petticoats. The door caught her, but the thud could be clearly heard below.

"What are you doing up there?" Agatha asked.

"I'm just moving my trunk," Becca lied.

"Should I come up and help you?" Agatha

offered. "Your trunk is much too heavy for you to move alone."

"I'm helping her," Matt sang out.

There was a heavy silence below and Becca rolled her eyes to the ceiling. Matt grinned at her as he fastened his pants. Becca put on her chemise and dress and reached around Matt's feet to retrieve her shoes. As she smoothed her hair and replaced the errant pins, she straightened the bedcovers.

"Do I look presentable?" she whispered to Matt.

"You look beautiful," he confirmed. As she went to the door he added, "And also well loved. Your cheeks are pink and your eyes are bright."

Becca smiled back at him as she stepped out of the room and closed the door behind her. She caught a glimpse of her reflection in a glassed watercolor on the landing and she finished straightening her hair. With her head held high, she sailed downstairs to help her aunt entertain their company.

Dusk was beginning to gather, and Agatha had already lit the lamps in the parlor and entryway. The low drone of conversation drifted into the hallway and Becca turned her feet in that direction. When she entered, the conversation stopped.

"Good evening, Mrs. Whiteside," Becca greeted her cheerfully. "Your new dress is very becoming."

"We came home and the house was dark. I was rather worried about you," Agatha said. "How long had you been upstairs rearranging furniture? Come to think of it, there was no light in the bedroom windows either."

"I was still using the remaining daylight," Becca said. "Coffee, Mrs. Whiteside?"

"Gracious, no. I really must be running," the stout woman said. "It will soon be dark and I don't want to be late getting home." She heaved herself off the creaking settee and stood up in a jerky motion that set ribbons jiggling on her hat.

"Is that a new bonnet?" Becca inquired as they walked to the door. "I don't recall seeing it before."

"Miss Fuller ran it up for me. It is adorable, isn't it? I thought it was simply perfect with this dress."

"But Nell made you a bonnet especially for that dress. Didn't you like it?"

"Somehow next to this one, it seems so plain. I will be in with it tomorrow for a refund. I know you won't mind since I've done so much business with you and your father over the years."

"But . . ."

"Rebecca won't mind at all," Agatha assured her friend. "We know how long you have been a mainstay of our family business."

"I will see you tomorrow afternoon," Mrs. Whiteside promised. "Good evening, Agatha. We must do this again soon."

"I will be looking forward to it, Edith." Agatha shut the door and turned to go upstairs.

"Why did you do that, Aunt Agatha? I have a policy against the return of specially ordered hats. So did Father."

"I also disagreed with him," Agatha said lightly. "So often a woman thinks she likes something in the store and changes her mind when she gets home."

"In this case, it was after she wore the hat to church. Really, Aunt Agatha, I have to ask that you not do that again."

Agatha drew herself up to an impressive height. "Mind your manners, miss. Edith Whiteside is my friend and one of your best customers. Ezra wouldn't have been so hard-nosed about exchanging an item."

"Yes, he would. Especially since the hat has been worn. Not only that, it is much nicer than that one."

"Is there some problem?" Matt asked as he came downstairs.

"You sold Mrs. Whiteside an atrocious bonnet and now she wants to return the one Nell made."

"That isn't my fault. You should have told her no."

"Nonsense," Agatha put in briskly. "It's not good business to upset a customer."

Matt looked from Becca's angry face to Agatha's. "I need to go move another trunk now." He turned and went back upstairs. "I could use some help, Becca."

Becca followed him, but inside she was boiling. This was only one example of the problems she was beginning to expect from competition with Prescott's.

Chapter Twelve

BECCA PUT A GRAPE LEAF IN THE JAR, THEN added the last of the new pickles. She took the flat glass lid from the pot of boiling water and eased it into place with her kitchen tongs. Then she screwed on the zinc cap. When the jar was wiped clean, she put it in the row of other jars, all of which had wedges of dark green pickles and a grape leaf to make them crisp. Her kitchen smelled of vinegar and spices, but at last the chore was done.

She looked out the window at her bare garden. The last of the produce was canned and dried and stored on deep shelves in her pantry. She was finished for another year. Becca dried her hands on her apron and started testing the tightness of the lids before carrying the jars to the pantry.

"I saw Edith Whiteside yesterday and she

said Cyrus Johnson is selling his surplus sweet potatoes. I thought we might buy a few bushels and dry them."

"What?" Becca eyed her aunt intently. "We have more food now than we need."

"You never know, Rebecca. Times are hard in the winter. If you don't need them, someone at the church might."

"Aunt Agatha, I know you mean well, but I don't want to put up any more food. I don't like to cook and I'm tired of being in the kitchen whenever I'm not at the Emporium."

"I've been meaning to speak to you about that. It doesn't seem right for a married woman to be traipsing off to work. When you were single and needing to support yourself, it was one thing, but now you have Matthew to do that." Agatha punctuated her words by scrubbing at the metal drainboard and sink. "You ought to be home raising a family."

"But I enjoy working in the Emporium, and I have no children yet."

Agatha nodded her head firmly. "You had better be glad of it, too. Edith told me it was all over town that you had a reason for getting married so fast, but I put an end to that rumor. Still, if you got in the family way too soon, talk might crop up again."

Becca stared at her. "Mrs. Whiteside had the nerve to say that about me? Why, that old windbag!"

"Mind your tongue, Rebecca. She is still your elder and my friend. Besides, I told her it wasn't true. By the way, why *did* you get married so fast?"

"We love each other."

"Marry in haste, repent in leisure. If you didn't want gossip to circulate you should have followed the rules. Had a proper courtship. An engagement. A family ceremony you could be proud of in years to come."

"I'm not ashamed of my wedding ceremony. It was exactly what Matt and I wanted."

Agatha snorted and used a cup towel to dry the counter top. "A man can't be consulted in these things. It's the woman who values tradition and a wedding dress."

Becca's eyes darkened and her chin lifted. Agatha's finding fault with her was one thing, but when she started in on Matt, that was more than Becca could take. She opened her mouth to say so but Matt's entrance interrupted her words.

"Becca, have you seen my work clothes? I need to nail down that loose tin on the barn roof and my clothes are missing."

"Aren't they in the wardrobe?"

"No, I looked there."

Agatha flicked the last drop of water from the drainboard and said, "I gave them to the rag man this morning."

"What did you say? The rag man?"

"They were too worn to be serviceable and the boots were not worth mending."

"My work boots as well?" Matt asked in a growl. "You gave away my work boots?"

Agatha faced him with regal dignity. "They were long overdue to the trash bin. The rag man had use for them."

"What do you propose that I wear to mend the barn roof? My best suit?"

Becca laid her hand on his arm. "Matt, could I talk to you alone?"

"Not yet! Aunt Agatha, I know you must have meant well, but don't ever give away any of my things again without consulting with me." Suspicion crept into his voice. "You didn't give anything else away, did you?"

"As a matter of fact, I did. I got rid of a faded blue shirt and a serge suit as well."

"My blue serge suit!"

"Aunt Agatha, you really shouldn't have done that!"

"The elbows and knees were becoming shiny. I may as well tell you I gave him your pink housedress, too. It had been mended in several places and I saw no reason to keep it."

"My pink one? With the lace at the collar?" Becca looked at her aunt, a shocked expression on her face. "That is my most comfortable housedress."

"And your least flattering," Agatha added.

Becca closed her mouth firmly. The words that threatened to spill out would cause more trouble than the dress was worth.

Matt caught Becca's eye and he jerked his head toward the back door. Wordlessly she followed him outside. As when she was a child, Becca retreated to the shade of the willow tree.

Matt shoved his hands into his pockets and looked up at the leaves that swayed in the wind. "I have a wish," he muttered. "Get Aunt Agatha out of my house and back to Jefferson!"

Becca leaned against the tree trunk and sighed. "I can't ask her to leave, Matt."

"I was talking to the tree."

"She may be irritating, but she is my aunt. And the clothes were indeed old and worn."

"That's not the point." He picked up a pebble and tossed it at the barn.

"I know. Surely she can't stay forever."

"It already feels as if it has been that long. Maybe I could just hint that it's time for her to leave."

"No, Matt. You will do no such thing!"

"Will you do it instead?"

Becca gave him an exasperated look. "Be patient a little while longer. For me?"

"My patience is used up, Becca." He saw her expression and sighed. "However, my silence isn't. I'll give her a few more days."

"Thank you," she said, slipping her hands around his waist. "Let's walk down the road. I can't go back inside yet. My pink dress, of all things!"

Arm in arm they walked away their frustration.

* * *

Matt had become accustomed to Percy's daily rendezvous at the Emporium, and managed to arrive there first. As usual, the customers were scarce at this time of day, when families needed more attention than did shopping lists. Relations between Percy and him had grown strained, and Matt acknowledged his friend's arrival with a bare nod.

As usual, Percy more than kept up his share of the conversation and Matt had to paste a smile on his face as Becca and Nell laughed at Percy's jokes and hung on his words. Occasionally Matt would try to bring the conversation around to a topic that paired Becca and himself, but such topics were hard to work into a general discussion and seemed to serve very little purpose. They always reminded Percy of yet another amusing anecdote.

Matt ate mechanically as a means of justifying his presence. But his eyes followed Becca jealously. Every peal of laughter made him crawl deeper into himself and become even less sociable. On occasion Becca would look searchingly at him, and when she did, he tried to smile back at her.

The jingling doorbell proclaimed the beginning of the afternoon's customers and Becca went out to tend to her business. Matt decided Percy would soon finish his last deviled egg, so he made his good-byes and went back to his store. As he left, he passed two more ladies coming into the Emporium. He tipped his hat to them and wondered what Becca had put on sale to draw such attention.

While he crossed the street, he wondered what, if anything, he should do about Percy's evident affection for Becca. He trusted his wife and he never really thought that she would stray to Percy, but he didn't like any man flirting with her. Especially one with a track record like Percy Winthrop's. They had been rivals far too often in the past for Matt to be sure that a wedding band would deter him.

As Matt approached the door to Prescott's, he frowned. Someone had placed the Closed sign in the window. Could he have forgotten to remove it this morning? No, he was certain that he had. He pushed at the door and bumped into its unyielding surface. His frown deepening, Matt rattled the doorknob, but it remained closed.

He fished the key from his coat pocket and unlocked the door, only to find a greater surprise on the inside. His two clerks were hauling armloads of linens and boxes of flatware from the front of the store to the back. Miss Fuller, the milliner, was carrying a stack of men's hats to the counter that had once held ascots and gloves. There was a petulant look on her face.

Because she was nearest, he addressed her. "What's going on here? Why are you rearranging my store?"

"We were told to do it!" she snapped. "By that woman!"

"Woman? What woman?"

"Miss Simpson. She came in here about an hour ago and started driving everybody crazy. Changing this, changing that. I'm telling you, Mr. Prescott, I didn't hire on as a stock boy. I'm a milliner and I don't appreciate . . ."

"Wait, wait. Miss Simpson? You can't mean Becca is doing this!"

She glared at him. "I said Miss Simpson, not Mrs. Prescott. Her aunt is the one I mean."

Matt looked about in amazement that rapidly turned to anger. "She did this!" Everyone in the store heard his roar, and activity ground to a halt. "What exactly did she say?"

Miss Fuller's pinched face looked uncertain at the storm she had unleashed. "She said the goods are arranged wrong. That we were to put everything in the same order as the Emporium. She told us where to put things and saw to it we were all working before she left."

"Do you normally take orders from just anyone off the street, Miss Fuller? Didn't that seem a trifle odd to you?"

"She said you authorized her to do this. We all believed her since she is Mrs. Prescott's aunt. I tried to tell her I don't do stocking but she wouldn't listen. I thought she was going to fire me."

"Nobody can fire you but me, Miss Fuller. Now put everything back the way we had it."

"Mr. Prescott, I must remind you of my position. I don't—"

"Get moving, Miss Fuller, and get the Open sign back in the window." He strode out of the store and down the street. Now and then he passed an acquaintance but he was too angry to speak. At the corner he turned left and headed down the street lined with two-story houses. The brisk walk was helping to clear his head, but he had no intention of turning back. He took the front steps two at a time and slammed the door behind him. "Aunt Agatha!" he bellowed.

Her head popped around the corner. "What ever are you doing home at this time of day? You should be in your store attending to business."

Matt drew a steadying breath. "Good news, Aunt Agatha. We are going to Jefferson, and since we won't be here for you to visit, we will escort you home."

"Home? To Jefferson?" She came into the entryway and stared at him. "I can't go off and leave you to manage all this alone." She gestured with her dust rag. "It's all I can do to keep it running smoothly."

"We can manage," he said through clenched teeth.

"Not very well, you can't. I went in that store of yours and couldn't believe my eyes. Ezra would never have put the bed linens up front like that! And whoever put the yard goods on a shelf instead of on a counter must be mad! I couldn't even reach some of them."

Matt came two steps closer. "We are leaving Saturday morning. Early. Be packed."

Agatha jerked up her head. "You make it sound as if you're forcing me to leave! Rebecca won't like the sound of this."

With all the restraint he could command, Matt said, "Becca and I appreciate your intentions, if not your actions. I know you meant well. But frankly, Aunt Agatha, you are driving me to distraction!" His eyes bored into her blue ones.

When he refused to lower his gaze, Agatha snapped, "Very well! If that's all the thanks a poor woman gets when she has broken her back trying to help others, then so be it! Here I am, alone in the world, but throw me out! I'll go back to my own house and leave you to manage for yourselves!" She flounced away but paused on the first step to glare back at him. "That nice Mr. Winthrop would have been far better suited to Rebecca, if you ask me. I only hope she doesn't spend all her days regretting a certain hasty action."

Matt smiled maddeningly. "We have certainly enjoyed your visit, Aunt Agatha. It's been an experience."

She tossed her head and stamped up the stairs. Matt was smiling as he left the house. That hadn't been too difficult. He hoped Becca would be as receptive of the change in plans as he was. The idea of a trip to Jefferson had been an inspiration. He had read in the newspaper that Jay Gould would be there the following week, and it would be a perfect opportunity to learn of his exact plans for the railroad, maybe even firsthand, and at last put an end to the speculation between Becca and himself.

As he walked down the street he whistled a tune, but worried that he might have been wrong about the display of yard goods. And if that were so, had his judgment about the railroad been wrong, too?

When he reached Prescott's he noticed the Open sign was back in the window where it should be. Inside he could see people moving about. Instead of going in, he crossed over to the Emporium. Becca looked up expectantly as he entered. "How would you like to go on a honeymoon?" he asked hopefully.

"A what? We've been married nearly three months," she laughed. "Would you push that bolt of gingham across the table?"

He shoved the cloth as she had asked. "It's never too late for a honeymoon, Becca. Ever since we got married I've regretted not taking you on one."

"We can't just drive away, Matt. There are the stores to run, and Aunt Agatha is still visiting."

"I've already worked that out. Percy can manage Prescott's, and Nell can take care of the Emporium. Since you've been giving her more responsibility, she's proven she does well. As for Aunt Agatha, I've talked to her and she has agreed to let us escort her as far as Jefferson."

Becca looked at him suspiciously. "When did you see her?"

"I went by the house after I left here. She and I understand each other. After we see her safely home, we will board a riverboat and float away into the sunset."

Becca laughed and deposited the bolt of cloth on end with the others. "You're a dyed-in-the-wool romanticist."

Matt wound a loose length of lace onto the cardboard spool and dropped it into its slot. "Do you want to go? Say yes." He leaned on the counter and pulled on the twine in the metal ball holder.

"Quit unraveling my string," she said, slapping at his wrist. "Yes, I would love to go. Are you certain Aunt Agatha doesn't mind?"

"She said she would go back to her own house and let us manage for ourselves," he replied. "Where did you order these pearl buttons?"

"They came from Shreveport. We are going on a riverboat? How exciting! Where will we go?"

"Down the Big Cypress, across Caddo Lake, and as far down the Red River as you want to go. Would you like to see Alexandria, Louisiana, or maybe even New Orleans?"

"I've heard so much about those places! Could we really?"

"I'll telegraph for our reservations this afternoon." The sound of the front door reminded him of business and he straightened from the counter. "We will leave early Saturday, if that's convenient with you. I have some short business to attend to in Jefferson, but we can board the boat early in the week."

"I can hardly wait. I'll talk to Nell as soon as I have a chance."

"Good." He leaned over the counter and kissed her smiling lips. "I'll see you in a few hours." He nodded to the customers, Mrs. Whiteside and Mrs. Henshaw, who were watching the public kiss, their eyes opened wide. "Good afternoon, ladies," he said as casually as if he hadn't been near Becca's lips. "You're both looking beautiful today in your new dresses." He winked at Becca because they both knew the dresses bore Prescott labels. Then he went to check on the progress at his store.

Chapter Thirteen

Agatha's house was exactly what Matt had expected. The walls were papered in somber grays and tans with overblown bouquets of maroon flowers. All the woodwork was oyster white, except for a black oval on each door, around the doorknob. Matt could remember seeing this style in his grandmother's house, but it had burned in the war and he hadn't seen anything like it since. The black circles kept fingerprints from showing, but they gave the doors the aspect of having eyes.

Among the furniture were several chairs, padded in navy horsehair and protected from the gentlemen's pomade hair dressing with yellowing doilies. However, the safeguard seemed superfluous as Aunt Agatha rarely had male visitors. The side tables hulked on bowed legs in the shadowy corners, and the wooden floors were covered by oval "tied" rugs. The hall tree that received Matt's hat was of dark mahogany and of a size to dwarf the entryway. It's foggy glass scarcely gave back Matt's image.

Agatha sighed with the joy of homecoming and looked around her with relish. "It's always so good to be back." These were the first words she had uttered all day except in reply to questions. "Matthew, carry your trunks upstairs. Rebecca will show you the way." She went across the parlor and fitted a metal key in the clock's face. Soon the sound of ticking filled the house. The clock's tinny voice followed Becca and Matt upstairs as Agatha set it to the correct time.

Becca led him to the small guest room she had used as a child. Here, too, the furniture was dark and oppressive, and the tan garlanded wallpaper was broken by a few black-and-white prints from England. The windows were hung with heavy gold drapes which Becca pulled aside to reveal lace panels. She opened the windows to air the musty smell from the room.

Matt lowered the trunk to the floor and took Becca in his arms. "Soon, my Becca, I'll have you all to myself."

She sighed and laid her head on his broad chest. "Monday morning we will be on board a riverboat. Just imagine! Have you ever ridden on one?"

"Yes, once when I was a boy, my uncle took

me on one down the Mississippi. That was just before the war and I was pretty young, but I remember it all. He said he knew the war was coming and that no matter who won, our lives would never be the same. In some ways he was right."

"Will I ever meet any of your family?"

"Some day we will go to Nashville and I'll introduce you to all my cousins. My parents have died. The family house is gone now, but my aunt rebuilt in its place. I grew up there in the new house."

"I have only the haziest of memories about the war, but I do remember the day it was over. Bells rang in both churches and we all gathered on the green in the middle of town. The mayor announced the end of the war and that we had lost, then we all went home. Mother held my hand very tightly and smelled of lavender, but that's all I remember."

"I'm glad. Sherman was right when he said, 'War is hell.' I was home the night the Yankees burned our house. It was only luck that saved us."

Becca held him tightly as if she could comfort the small boy he had been. Even after twenty years the war haunted all the people it had touched, and she wondered if the scars would ever disappear entirely.

Matt hugged her and smiled. "Now what is this long face? You are on a honeymoon, sweetheart, or soon will be. Don't look sad. I know, let's go down and rearrange Aunt Agatha's kitchen."

Becca laughed and tiptoed to kiss him. "You're incorrigible."

They found Agatha making a shopping list of food they would need. Matt took her trunk up to her room and then was given the task of opening the windows to let fresh air into the house.

"Now Rebecca and I are going to the general store and the market. You may amuse yourself however you please and supper will be on the table promptly at seven o'clock."

"I'll come with you."

"Indeed you will not. The delivery boy will carry our purchases, and besides, this is woman's work."

Becca's eyes met his and she shrugged. Matt enjoyed helping her choose fresh produce and he could ramble through a general store longer than she could, but this was Agatha's territory. Matt took his dismissal gracefully.

He wandered down Alley Street, past two-story houses that were similar to the one he and Becca owned in Mellville. At the corner of Alley and Delta, he looked with curiosity at the large house topped by a square cupola. He had heard Aunt Agatha mention this house because each of the cupola's four sides was paned with a different color glass. It was said that from the inside, the view of the surrounding town had the appearance of each of the seasons, depending on which color you looked through. People were beginning to call it the House of the Seasons.

Taking a zigzag path that led him to Austin Street, Matt wandered into the wrought-iron trimmed Excelsior House. If Jay Gould was in town, he would almost certainly be staying here. But even so, how could he get a chance to talk to him? He asked at the desk, but the clerk gave him no specific information. It seemed that Mr. Gould valued his privacy. At least, Matt surmised, that meant that Gould was indeed in town.

Matt went out back onto the brick walkway. Flowers grew in profusion and fat bumblebees hummed in the heat amid the cloying scents of geraniums and marigolds. If he knew what Gould looked like, he might be able to arrange an introduction, he thought, as he looked at the deserted patio. The vine-covered walls blocked all but the most persistent breezes from the enclosure, so Matt went back into the cooler lobby.

Matt chose to sit on one of a grouping of sofas in the foyer so that he could think. If he could only find Gould he might be able to convince him to put the rails south through Mellville. With its busy port, Jefferson didn't need the railroad for commerce, and Agatha had been adamant that the citizens of Jefferson didn't want it built there, anyway. Matt crossed his arms over his chest and sighed audibly.

The only other man in the lobby sat across from him, half hidden behind the latest edition of the *Jefferson Jimplecute*. At Matt's sigh, he laid the paper aside and regarded him speculatively. "Anything wrong?" he asked.

"No, no. I was just thinking. By the way, would you know whether Jay Gould is still in town? I need to talk to him and the desk clerk here is no help."

"Oh? Are you a railroad man?"

"Far from it. My name is Matt Prescott. I own Prescott's Dry Goods in Mellville. My wife and I are here to catch a riverboat." When the man offered no information, Matt added, "Would you know Gould if you saw him?"

"From Mellville, you say." The man seemed to be debating his response to Matt's question. "Yes, actually, I know him quite well." The man's lips turned up in a smile that was almost obscured by his bushy black beard. The smile never reached his eyes. He coughed behind his hand and said, "I'll be playing poker tonight in his room. I'm sure he wouldn't mind if you joined us, if you'd like."

Matt stared at him a moment before answering, "I couldn't presume to barge in like that."

"Nonsense, you'll be my guest."

"What about the stakes? I hear Gould plays a rich-man's game."

"Not tonight. This is just a friendly game. There will be more politics passed around than money."

Matt looked thoughtfully at the slender man. Whoever he was, he was offering to introduce him to Gould and that was what he had wanted. He hadn't planned on a poker game, though. "All right. I'll be there. What time?"

"Come at nine. Upstairs to room two-fifteen."

"I appreciate it." Matt stood and held out his hand to the man. After a second's pause, the latter shook hands briefly. Matt walked away before the stranger could change his mind about the generous impulse.

After supper, Agatha folded her napkin into her silver napkin ring and announced, "Mrs. Victoria Arbuckle is giving an edifying lecture tonight on the evils of hard liquor. She is a rousing speaker and I'm sure we will enjoy hearing her."

"I'm afraid I will have to decline," Matt said as he lay down his own napkin. "I already have plans for tonight." Becca looked at him expectantly, and he added, "I have managed an introduction to Jay Gould over at the Excelsior House."

"That uncouth little man?" Agatha responded. "He and his railroad are not welcome in Jefferson. You would be much better off hearing Mrs. Arbuckle."

"I don't doubt that for a minute," Matt replied, "but I am going to see Gould instead. I hope to find out for sure that the railroad is going through Mellville. But if he's still undecided, maybe I can help him make up his mind."

"I would love to go with you, Aunt Agatha," Becca said hurriedly. Matt and Agatha hadn't argued in almost two days, and Becca didn't want the visit to end on a sour note.

"Everyone could profit from hearing about Demon Rum," Agatha objected with a pointed look at Matt.

"Take notes for me, will you, Becca? We can go over them on the riverboat."

Agatha sniffed and Becca smiled. When Matt used that tone of voice there was no swaying him. "Will you be late?"

"No, I don't think so. From all I gathered the game will break up early."

"Game?" Agatha asked suspiciously.

"Pinochle," Matt responded creatively. "For matchsticks."

"Good-bye, Matt," Becca said pointedly. Agatha's views on card playing were nearly as stringent as her rules about hard liquor.

He leaned over the corner of the table and kissed her. "I'll be home early." He nodded to Agatha and went out into the night.

Soon he was in the Excelsior House and knocking on the door of room 215. The door was answered by a portly man in ginger-colored whiskers who looked at him quizzically. "I'm Matt Prescott, from Mellville. I'm expected." Looking past the man, he saw the stranger from the lobby. "He invited me," he added, nodding toward the man he had met earlier.

"Mr. Gould? Very well, come in. We were just about to start the game."

Matt looked back at the slender, dark man. So that was Gould! No wonder he felt so confident in asking him up to join the game. Matt hid his surprise and followed the other man into the room, as he wondered why Gould hadn't introduced himself in the lobby.

A round table had been set up and chairs placed around it. An unopened box of cards and a box of poker chips lay on the table. The other players were already seated.

"You were almost too late," Gould said. "Gentlemen, I'd like you to meet Mr. Matt Prescott, a businessman from Mellville."

Matt sat opposite Gould, still puzzling as to why he had been included, and was introduced to the others. On Matt's right was the president of a bank. To the left, the owner of a riverboat line. Gould was flanked by another banker and a lawyer whose name Matt recognized as belonging to an aspiring politician. Two city officials sat away from the table, engaged in conversation with one of the town's leading merchants. With the exception of Matt, this could have been a meeting to decide the fate of the Jefferson railway.

Feeling rather uneasy, Matt pulled money

from his pocket and gave it to the man with ginger whiskers in exchange for a stack of chips. When they had gone around the table, Matt observed that his was the smallest pile and wondered if he might have made a mistake getting involved in this "friendly" game with such high rollers. The dealer opened the card pack, and passed them around for examination, then gave them to the lawyer for shuffling. When they were cut and given back to the lawyer, Matt felt tension build in the room. He tossed a chip, along with the others, into the ante pile and leaned back nonchalantly as the five cards were dealt.

As a youth, Matt had learned many things of a redoubtable nature, and five-card stud had been one of them. After the first round of betting, he laid two cards down on the table in front of him and was dealt two more.

"Perhaps," Gould said casually as he accepted three cards, "you could tell me why I should consider Jefferson over Mellville for my route." He smiled blandly at the banker.

The man looked up uncomfortably and said, "I don't believe we ever actually said whether we did or did not want the railroad. It would mean a big growth for our town, but there is a lot of public feeling against it."

"What about Mellville?" Gould said almost absentmindedly. "Is Mellville afraid of progress, Mr. Prescott?"

"No, not in the least." Matt was beginning to see he was a pawn in the railroad magnate's strategy. "Mellville would welcome the railroad."

"Naturally, Mellville has no river port," the lawyer spoke up. "It would mean transporting goods further south. Could be more expensive."

"Land is cheaper in Mellville," Matt said offhandedly as he added a chip to the stack. "Right-of-way is less expensive."

Gould looked at him speculatively. Matt smiled.

The other banker shook his head. "I can't countenance the railroad coming through here myself. It will bring all sorts of riffraff and unsavory vagrants. The port trash is bad enough."

"Think of the income though," the lawyer put in. "It would make Jefferson an important city like New Orleans."

"Do you want your children growing up in a big city?" the banker demanded. "I'm against it."

Gould looked at the man as if he were recording his face for future reference. He tossed chips into the pile. "Raise."

The lawyer folded, and after a brief deliberation the banker did likewise. "I'll see your raise." Matt's chips joined Gould's.

"I'm concerned about the appearance of our town," the other banker said. "A railroad is dirty and loud. We would have coal dust and ashes all over everything and a racket day and night."

"The sound of commerce," Gould tempered. "Without it, Jefferson will become a ghost town."

The lawyer looked offended and both bankers pulled back from the table. "I believe Jefferson can survive quite well without the Texas and Pacific Railroad," one said. "We have so far. Jefferson is the largest inland port in the country."

Gould glanced around the table. Anger was building in his narrowed eyes. "Call."

Cards slapped faceup on the table. Matt smiled. "I believe I won this hand, gentlemen." He raked in his winnings and the next hand started.

The lawyer, who had been riding the fence in his views, swung toward his townsmen. "I can't see that we will profit all that much by a railroad. Clearly river traffic is here to stay, and the Big Cypress isn't going anywhere." He was rewarded for this wisdom by guffaws from the bankers.

"That's not the way we see it in Mellville," Matt said as he examined the faces of his new cards. "We would welcome the railroad with open arms."

The man with ginger whiskers looked as if he regretted having opened the door to Matt. "Now see here, this is just a card game. We aren't here to decide anything."

Matt widened his eyes in innocence. "Far be it from me to try and sway anyone over a card game." He added a sizable number of chips to the growing pile. The man looked at him suspiciously and folded. "Of course in Mellville, we would build the coal yards outside of town," Matt added.

"Coal yards?"

"The trains run on coal. Maybe if you're really fortunate, they will find coal in the area and mine it here."

"A coal mine! In Jefferson?" The banker looked indignant. "Never!"

"I would rather see the Big Cypress run dry than have a coal mine in Jefferson," the lawyer stated.

"So would I. If I had to vote tonight, I would be against the railroad."

Gould's dark eyes smoldered. "Gentlemen, take my word for it. If the rails bypass Jefferson, you will see the day when bats roost in your church belfries and grass grows in your streets. The age of the railroad is upon us!" The outburst brought a return of his persistent, wracking cough, and he pressed a handkerchief to his mouth.

Matt raised the bet and watched the other men. Unless they began to pay closer attention to their cards and cooled their anger, he would leave the table a richer man. And Gould would soon be angry enough to bypass Jefferson just to spite the town. Matt laid down his cards and claimed the pot.

Becca joined the clapping as the illustrious Mrs. Arbuckle stepped from the podium.

There were few dry eyes in the room. The mayor of Jefferson, who was campaigning for reelection, took over the stand.

"Ladies and gentlemen," he intoned in a melodious voice, "I'm sure you are all, as was I, touched and enlightened by Mrs. Arbuckle's insights into the evils of intemperance. I do not now, nor will I ever in the future, touch a drop of Demon Rum. My lovely wife there can testify to that." He gestured with his palm toward a beribboned lady who rapidly bobbed her head to show she could indeed swear to it.

"Also foremost in our minds," the mayor rolled out, "is the question of Jefferson's future as well. We shall not, nay, cannot sit idly by and watch progress slip away from us. I'm speaking, my friends, of the Texas and Pacific Railroad. A railroad that could make Jefferson even bigger and better. A railroad to provide transportation for edifying speakers, poets, heads of state who long to visit our fair city but cannot due to lengthy travel routes of stage or riverboat. Think, ladies and gentlemen, of the resources that will be at our beck and call! Early produce from the southern climes, beef from the Fort Worth stockyards, merchandise from the faraway factories." The mayor, in his wisdom, refrained from mentioning the northern location of these factories. He leaned forward as if to impart a great revelation. "We will be as rich in trade as the biblical seaports of old. Our children will benefit by the influx of luxuries as well as the additional literature and art." He finished with a dramatic wave of his arm and the ringing tones of a Roman orator. "If reelected, I will see to it that all these delights are yours. I will bring the Texas and Pacific Railroad through Jefferson!"

He stepped back to thunderous applause. Becca followed suit with clapping, but her heart was heavy. The mayor seemed to be extremely popular and he was basing his campaign on the railroad.

"What do you think, Mrs. Taylor?" Becca asked Aunt Agatha's friend. "Will the rails come through here, or Mellville?"

Mrs. Taylor looked with wide eyes at Becca. "Here, to be sure. It's all but a foregone conclusion. My husband is a surveyor and he says lines are already being sighted for the project. They plan to start chopping trees next month."

"So soon? But if it is already so certain, why is the mayor using it in his campaign?"

The woman smiled superciliously. "That, too, is a foregone conclusion. This will be his fifth term."

Agatha nodded. "I don't want the railroad in Jefferson, but I plan to vote for him. He is a decent, upright man, and I believe him when he says he is temperate." She punctuated her words with a brisk nod of her head.

Becca joined the others for lemonade and

tea cakes, but her mind was busy with other matters. Matt was wrong! After the mayor's speech, she was positive of it. She was prepared to vote for him herself, and she didn't even live here! Surely he would be reelected, and then the railroad would be a certainty—if it wasn't already. Mrs. Taylor's husband was in a position to know.

She thought of the two dry goods stores in Mellville and nearly groaned aloud. Her ledger sheet had shown much less profit than it ever had. True, the money from both Prescott's and the Emporium went into the same bank account, but there wasn't enough business to operate both stores. Once more she thought what a nice café Prescott's would make. Geraniums in the big windows and gingham curtains would make it a charming eating establishment. Since Percy was already fond of Nell, she could add him to her staff. Miss Fuller would have to go, but she didn't seem too fond of Mellville anyway.

Mrs. Arbuckle had joined them and Becca drew her attention back to the meeting. Agatha was saying, "When you read that poem about the mother and children turned out in the cold, I wanted to cry. Truly, I did."

"It's so accurate," Mrs. Arbuckle said mournfully. "No matter how steady and upstanding a man is, hard drink can bring him down to the gutter. It's an evil we all must guard against in our men."

"What about women?" Becca said before she thought. "Surely ladies are just as susceptible . . ."

"No *lady* would ever touch a drop!" Mrs. Arbuckle said with horror. "Not even on pain of death!"

"Lips that touch liquor will never touch mine," Mrs. Taylor intoned. "It's from the Bible."

Becca opened her mouth to question this rather remarkable statement, but a look from her aunt shut her lips.

"In my family, we never imbibe," Agatha said primly. "Men *nor* women."

Becca thought of her father's medicinal brandy, the wine she and Matt occasionally served with supper, and Agatha's cooking sherry. She decided silence was her best course and was heartily grateful that Matt wasn't there.

She saw the mayor and his florid wife approaching and excused herself. If anyone knew for sure about the railroad, it must be him. She intercepted them at the lemonade pitcher and accepted another glass of the tart liquid.

"I am very interested in what you had to say about the railroad," she said after she introduced herself. "Will it indeed come through Jefferson?"

"It could hardly miss us," he boomed jovially. "They are already mapping out its path.

Once I'm elected, I will see to it that construction is as speedy as possible."

His wife and her ribbons nodded eagerly that this was indisputably true.

"And the elections will be held when?"

"Two weeks, ma'am. Mother and I plan to remain on board at least one more term." He smiled fondly at his wife, who nodded agreeably once more.

"My best wishes to you both." Becca had little patience with a man who addressed his wife as if she were his mother. She decided she wouldn't vote for him even if she could. Especially if he planned to bring the railroad through. Matt would be so disappointed when he heard the news.

Chapter Fourteen

BECCA AND MATT WALKED UP THE GANGPLANK and onto the green deck of the *Della Lane*. While a man carried their trunk to their stateroom, Becca and Matt leaned on the polished oak rail and waved to Agatha. The elderly woman stood just off the dock and waved her lace handkerchief as industriously as if Becca and Matt were bound for a world cruise instead of just to Alexandria. Dark men clad in homespun hauled bales of burlap-bound cotton onto the boat and more lowered the bales down into a gaping hold.

The dock seethed with life. Horses stamped and neighed as dogs barked and chased along the wooden walkways. Several young boys ran by, making more noise than the animals. Crates of live chickens squawked and crowed according to their nature. Ladies in gay colors

flocked aboard, escorted by well-dressed gentlemen, all looking like flowers come to life. A
flamboyant man followed by a red-jacketed
servant strolled onto the ship and Becca realized she was seeing her first riverboat gam-
bler.

Trunks and wicker baskets seemed to be
stacked everywhere. Somehow, miraculously, the proper ones found their way on board
and the others were claimed by departing
passengers.

Becca heard a rumble and a jolt as the
engines started to life and the broad blades
began to push the boat through the water. She
waved at Agatha and poked Matt so that he
waved, too. They were moving out into the
middle now and gathering speed. Silvered
diamonds of water dripped from the huge
paddles and smoke curled from the twin
smokestacks. Agatha, like Jefferson, grew
smaller with distance and was lost from sight
as they passed the turning basin where another boat waited for right-of-way.

The gray-green water slid by and frothed at
the boat's passing. Enormous cypresses shaded the banks and made the water around their
knees an inky black. Moss hung like trapped
fog in their branches, and in some trees
seemed to choke the life from them. An alliga-
tor slid from the bank to the water and disappeared without a sound.

Becca looked around in awe. The river was
entirely different from anything she had ever

seen before. Emerald fungus slimed the back-washes and water lilies bloomed in crowded profusion. A cloud of cranes took flight at their approach and their flapping startled smaller birds until the woods seemed alive with their cries and rustlings.

"Is it all you hoped it would be?" Matt asked. He was watching her rather than the scenery.

"It's even more wonderful! I can't take it all in. Help me remember it, Matt, every inch. Then when we are old we can relive it."

"This won't be our last trip, honey. Only the first one. When the memories fade, we will take another. Maybe even one every year."

The *Della Lane*'s calliope voice warned her approach to a curve and was answered by another voice out of sight around the bend. Becca stopped one of the passing crewmen and asked, "Is there room to pass? I heard another boat approaching."

"Yes, ma'am. That would likely be the *Lady of the Mist*. She was due in this morning. The Big Cypress is a deep channel. Naught to fear. There's not been a bad accident around here since the *Mittie Stephens* blew up back in 'sixty-nine." He looked thoughtfully at the captain's deck. "Course now, the *Lizzie Rea* went down about seven years ago, but only one man died. I wouldn't worry none." He tugged at his cap and went on about his duties.

"Blew up?" Becca said with a doubtful expression. "Did he say a boat blew up?"

"That was a long time ago and they were carrying hay on the deck and kegs of powder in the hold. I read about it years ago. The hay caught on fire somehow. Our cargo is cotton."

"Cotton burns, Matt."

"Do you know how tight the cotton is packed in those bales? There's no air space. Don't worry about it."

"You never taught me to swim," she reminded him.

"If we sink, I'll teach you then," he promised. "Look at the size of that magnolia tree." He put his arm protectively around her.

The lush beauty drove away her trepidation and Becca was soon enjoying the scenery. The smell of ever-shady ground and forever-damp trees drifted from the riverbank. Sunlight broke through the feathery cypress leaves to spangle on the river.

"This was once called the Soda River," Matt told her. "It's the English version of an Indian name for it."

"Where did you hear that?"

"I came partway by river from Memphis. A boatman told me about it. He also told me the Indian name. It was *Tso'-to* or something like that. He was an old man and kept referring to Caddo as Ferry Lake." Matt laughed. "I thought I was on the wrong boat until I asked the captain."

"When will we be on the lake?"

"Not too long from now. Do you want to see our cabin?"

Becca followed him to the door he indicated in the middle of a long row of identical portals. Matt fit his key to the opening and she stepped inside. The room was tiny. A bed scarcely large enough for two people filled most of the space. Their two trunks took up the rest of the room. Unlit lamps hung from chain cradles, and a dim light came in from the minute window.

"We will be rather crowded," he confessed, "but we will be on deck most of the time." He shoved the trunks away from the door and made a little more space.

"I don't mind at all. It's rather like a playhouse. And we have never needed much room in bed."

"That's true," he said as he maneuvered the door shut and locked it. "Maybe we should try it out."

"I suppose we ought to," she said demurely.

In spite of the cramped quarters, they soon had their clothes off and the covers down. After her own linens, the boat's sheets felt coarse on her skin and the pillow wasn't as full as her own. Beneath her, the boat flowed through the dark waters, and even though there was no rocking motion, she was aware of a sense of movement.

Matt slipped into her embrace and they held each other closely, savoring the sensation of the other's bare body. Matt touched his forehead to hers and rubbed his nose against her own. Becca smiled and kissed him, gently at first, then with greater passion. Matt ran his hand over her ribs and cupped her breast. She sighed with pleasure and moved against him.

He chuckled softly. "I think steamboats appeal to you."

"They do. So do you." She smoothed her hand over his hips and caressed his firm buttocks. Rubbing him to her, she moved sensuously against him. "I've wanted you for hours," she whispered in his ear. Her tongue followed the curve where his blond hair waved.

He nudged against her and she drew her leg up to lie over his hip. Still on their sides, he entered her. Becca closed her eyes as he gave her pleasure. When he lowered his lips to her breast and tugged gently, a hotness spread through her. His tongue and lips, combined with the lithe movement of his hips, brought her to her peak. She buried her face in his shoulder to silence her cry as ecstasy that was almost painful tore through her in throbbing heartbeats.

When her breathing slowed, he began the rhythm once more. Becca ran the tip of her tongue over his chest and tasted the faint saltiness of his skin. She loved the sight and feel of his powerful muscles as he moved with her. As she pulled him deeper into her, she tightened her leg over his buttocks, controlling the rhythm, making their pace long and slow. Matt gazed into her eyes as pleasure built in them both. Becca felt her body begin the climb to her peak, but she continued in the same pattern. Suddenly Matt cried out and held her tight and his ecstasy triggered her own.

They half dozed, rousing to kiss or stroke each other, then drifting again into a light sleep.

Twilight had turned the Big Cypress to an avenue of darkness before Becca and Matt returned to the deck. The fringed leaves of the cypress trees made Spanish lace against the amethyst sky. Handfuls of lightning bugs glimmered and vanished in the thick woods. Only the steady chug of the engine and the splash of the paddles broke the primeval quietness.

Then unexpectedly, the river broadened and yawned out into a glassy lake. The revealed sunset was a silent explosion of vivid reds and golds shot through with brilliant pink clouds. Slowly the swollen globe of the sun settled into the distant trees and the colors deepened to purple, then black, and a dazzling array of stars arched over them.

Becca looked up with wonder at the Milky Way. The dusting of diamonds over the velvet sky could be seen in a band that seemed to encircle the earth.

"See that bright star over there near the horizon?" Matt asked as he put his arm around her waist. When she nodded, he said, "It's the brightest one I see, so I'm going to give it to you."

She smiled and leaned back against him. "Thank you, Matt," she said contentedly.

Becca awoke first and lay in Matt's sleeping embrace as she gazed up at the ceiling. She had never been on a real trip before and she was enjoying it immeasurably. So much so, she was reluctant to think about returning to the routine of the Emporium. She had discovered that she enjoyed traveling, and even the inconveniences of living out of a trunk, little space, and virtually no privacy didn't really bother her.

She turned her head to look at Matt. His breathing was quiet and deep and his dark gold eyelashes lay on his cheeks. His fair hair was rumpled and he looked younger in his sleep. As always, he slept without a stitch, and of late, so had she. Giving up her nightgown had seemed terribly daring to her at first, but now she wondered how she had ever slept in such confinement.

Experimentally, Becca raised her finger to Matt's lips and traced their curve. He turned his head and brushed at her with his hand. Her finger next explored his ear, tickling him until he rolled his head back again to escape her. Once more she touched his lips just enough to create a sensation.

Without opening his eyes, Matt grabbed her

hand and pretended to be about to eat her fingers. She laughed and he rolled to his back, pulling her on top of him. "Good morning," she said as she looked down into his dark green eyes.

"You don't believe in letting a man sleep late, do you?" he growled, but amusement gleamed in his eyes.

"You can sleep late at home. This is our honeymoon and I want you to enjoy every minute of it."

He raised his head to kiss her lips. "I am. Are you?"

"Yes. I don't ever want it to end. Let's stay on this boat forever."

"Forever would end pretty soon. It only goes back and forth between Jefferson and New Orleans."

"Then we could change boats and sail around the world," she smiled down at him.

"My wife, the gypsy," he teased. "What happens when our money runs out?"

"We'll have Nell and Percy send us some more." She rolled over and pillowed her head on his shoulder. "I'm so glad you arranged this trip. Up until now I hadn't realized how much I needed time away from the Emporium."

"We will take a lot of trips. Once the railroad comes through we can hire managers for the stores and go to New York or wherever to buy our stock. No more ordering from lists and hoping it looks good when it's delivered."

Becca's smile wavered. "What will happen if the rails go through Jefferson instead?"

"I know they won't."

"There is something I haven't told you because I didn't want to spoil our trip. The railroad *is* going through Jefferson. I found out at the temperance lecture."

"No, it isn't. You should have mentioned it earlier and I could have put your mind at ease."

"They are already laying out the survey lines. By now they are cutting the trees."

"Who is 'they'? I was playing cards with Jay Gould, remember? If someone is clearing timber for the rails, it's news to him."

"The mayor himself told me," Becca replied, "and he's basing his entire campaign on bringing the line through as quickly as possible."

"He's wrong."

"I also talked to Aunt Agatha's friend, Mrs. Taylor, whose husband is a surveyor. He's the one laying out the route."

"He's wrong, too."

"Everyone can't be wrong, Matt," Becca said as her temper rose. "Isn't it just barely possible that you are mistaken?"

"No, because I got it straight from Gould. Before I left the game he said Jefferson would be damned before they saw one inch of Texas and Pacific rails. He was pretty upset at the time." He tried to nibble at her ear, but she pulled away.

"The mayor wouldn't lie. Neither would Mr. Taylor."

"How do you know? The mayor is up for reelection, and Mr. Taylor may be a fool for all we know."

"I've met him and he isn't!"

"Then he's misinformed! Becca, Jay Gould is mad at Jefferson and he is withdrawing his plans to put the railroad there. It will go through Mellville!"

"And I say it won't!" She glared at him.

He moved his arm and let her head drop to the bed. "People say things that other people want to hear during election years. Gould owns the railroad and his say is final, no matter what the mayor may wish is true!"

"How can you say that! You weren't even there! Maybe Mr. Gould lied to you in order to get the land cheaper in Jefferson."

Matt frowned. "A millionaire doesn't quibble over the price of right-of-way."

"I'll bet he does. How else did he get to be a millionaire?" she demanded triumphantly.

"I get the feeling you don't want the railroad to come through Mellville. You're sounding as closed-minded as your Aunt Agatha!"

"Leave my aunt out of this! I do want the railroad and all the prosperity it will bring, but I think we should look at both sides until we know for certain."

"I am certain!"

"Did your friend Mr. Gould happen to confide in you when this will take place?"

"No, he didn't."

"I thought not."

"He may not know himself yet! First the land has to be surveyed and a strip bought to be cleared."

"They are surveying and clearing in Jefferson," she repeated.

"Blast Jefferson! Also the mayor and Mr. Taylor! I know what I'm talking about."

"Do you, Matt?" she asked coolly. "We'll see."

"In a matter of months I'll be saying 'I told you so.'"

"We'll see." She sat up and managed to look regal as she clutched the sheet to cover herself. "Are you ready to go to breakfast?"

"No, not until we make up."

"I have no intention of making up with you, because I know I'm right." Her chin lifted defiantly.

"Who cares?" he growled as he grabbed away the sheet. "I love you and I couldn't care less about that railroad at this moment." He caught her as she tried to jump out of bed and pinned her under him. "Say 'Matt, I love you.'"

"I will not."

"Say it or I'll tickle you."

"No!"

He lowered his head and rubbed his chin in the hollow of her neck where he knew she was especially ticklish. Becca squealed in spite of herself and tried to wriggle free. "Say you love me," Matt persisted.

"I love you, I love you!" she gasped.

"Now that wasn't so difficult, was it? I love you, too. Now say you aren't mad at me anymore."

Becca regarded him rebelliously, but when he nuzzled at her neck, she burst out, "I'm not mad. Leave me alone!"

He raised his head and looked down at her. "Do you really want me to?"

With an exasperated sigh, Becca answered, "No, I don't."

He kissed her gently, then with growing ardor. "Are you really hungry?"

"Not in the least." She slipped her arms around his neck and laced her fingers in his hair.

Chapter Fifteen

"IT'S GOOD TO BE HOME," BECCA ANNOUNCED as she removed her bonnet and looked around the house.

"I don't understand you," Matt said as he lowered their trunk to the floor. "First you never wanted to leave the riverboat, then you wanted to stay in Alexandria forever, then you loved the river again. Now you're glad to be home? I must say you're easy to please."

"Are you making fun of me?"

"No, honey. I wouldn't do that." He took her in his arms and sent his hat sailing to a hook on the hall tree. "We haven't been alone in weeks. Do you want to run naked through the house?"

She laughed and swatted at him. "First I want to get unpacked so I will know I'm really home. If you'll carry the trunk upstairs, I'll get started."

Matt sighed and lifted the trunk onto his back. "Don't get in front of me. This is heavy."

While he carried it upstairs, Becca went out back to the huge willow tree and put her hands lovingly on the rough bark. "I missed you," she whispered to her childhood confidant. "I saw amazing sights, but they weren't my home. I'm glad to be back. And alone with Matt." The tree shimmered in a breeze and its leaves made an answering sound.

Becca wandered back inside, pausing to notice the array of bright yellow cannas that bordered the back of the house. They had spread beyond their borders during the summer and she made a mental note to thin them that fall. After her short absence, all the plants seemed taller or more abundant than she had recalled. Tasks that had seemed mundane before had a freshness about them.

She roamed through the house before going upstairs. It needed an airing, but a few open windows would soon take care of that. Matt was already unpacking, and when she came in, he handed her a stack of petticoats and bloomers.

"Matt, have you considered how nice it would be to have a café in town? Tonight, for instance, we wouldn't have to cook after our trip. We could just go down and order whatever we pleased."

He glanced at her as he put away his extra cuff links and collar stays. "That would be nice. In fact, I'm glad you mentioned it."

"You are?" She removed the small hand-shaped clip that she used to hold her handkerchief at her belt.

"Even though the railroad is coming through here, it'll be several months. A café would be a good moneymaking business in the meantime. Then, after the trains are running, we could buy another building and move the café to it and keep Prescott's and the Emporium where they are now."

"Why, what a good idea! I never thought of that. Somehow I thought you meant the café would be permanent. Will you ask Mabel Henshaw if she will manage it, or shall I? It's bound to be a success if she agrees. Her cooking talents are well known."

"I think your cooking is some of the best I've ever tasted," he said loyally.

"Thank you, Matt, but I'll be far too busy to tend to the cooking business. You, on the other hand, can cook as well as I do, and you enjoy it more."

"Me? But I have Prescott's to run."

"At the moment, yes. But after we merge the two stores, both of us won't be needed. I've been thinking how nicely geraniums would do in those big windows. All that sunlight would make them bloom nearly year around. If you like, I'll start the curtains tomorrow night. Do you prefer gingham or starched white eyelet?"

"Wait a minute." He dropped his shirts back into the trunk and turned to look at her. "Those geraniums are going in your windows, not mine."

She frowned as she shook the travel wrinkles from her yellow dress and hung it in the wardrobe. "Why would I want flowers in the Emporium? What name do you think would be best?"

"Rebecca's Café. The sign has been in the barn for months."

"That's the one you had painted just after we married. It's not the right size for Prescott's."

"It's the perfect size for the Emporium."

She wheeled to face him. "That's out of the question."

"What are you talking about? It was your idea! Didn't you just walk in here and suggest we turn the Emporium into a café?"

"I most certainly did not! I was referring to Prescott's!" She met his glare staunchly and threw her lace collars onto the bed.

After a while he sighed and shrugged. "I guess I misunderstood. But I'm not going to turn my dry goods store into a café."

"Nor will I!" she snapped.

"Fine! But just in case, I'm still going to keep the sign."

They finished unpacking in silence.

Nell jabbed her needle into the hat and drew the thread through before she said, "Rebecca, there's something I need to tell you."

"Oh? What is it, Nell?" Becca asked absently as she dusted the packing from the new shipment of sachet jars.

"As you know, Percy has been showing me a great deal of attention of late and, well, last night he declared his intentions." She blushed a bright red and lowered her eyes demurely.

"Did he? How wonderful!" Becca came to Nell and drew her chair up beside her. "What was your answer?"

"Why, Rebecca, you shock me!" Nell declared. "I may be a widow, but I'm not the sort to say yes on his first proposal."

Becca thought of her own speedy courtship and had to hide her smile. "Will you say yes next time?"

Nell smiled and her plain features became almost pretty. "I expect so. There is, however, one small problem. I don't want to be in competition with my husband. Oh, I know it's all right for you and Matt, but it wouldn't sit well with me."

Becca thought for a minute and smiled. "Then Percy can come to work here."

"He could? You wouldn't mind?"

"Believe me, Nell, I'd love it." She glanced toward the windows, where Prescott's latest sale sign was obvious. "That might just solve everyone's problem."

Two days later, Nell again approached Becca. "I'm to be congratulated, Rebecca, or rather Percy is. I mean, I've agreed to become his wife."

"Nell! How wonderful!" Becca exclaimed as she hugged her friend. "I'm so happy for you both and I wish you all the best."

"Thank you. We haven't set a date yet, but I am leaning toward a late fall wedding."

"We will start collecting your trousseau at once. I heartily recommend a riverboat trip for a honeymoon."

"Slow down, Rebecca," Nell laughed. "It's not as if this is my first time down the aisle, you know. A trousseau and honeymoon seem so . . . odd in a second marriage. I'm not sure it's even done."

Becca thought of Nell's very short marriage and her long years of widowhood. "It's done," she said firmly, "in the best of circles. A marriage is a marriage and should be conducted however you want it to be."

"In that case, I'll suggest to Percy that we might take a cabin for a short trip."

"Did you speak with him about his working here instead of Prescott's?"

"Yes, but he seemed to think I should work for them, instead."

"Nell! You wouldn't! I have no one else to depend on!"

"That's exactly what I told Percy. I said it's out of the question."

"Thank heavens," Becca said with relief. "You nearly gave me heart failure."

"Percy still says he can't leave Prescott's. He has been friends with Matt too long. I tried to tell him how I feel, but he doesn't understand."

"Did you tell him about the raise?"

"Raise? What raise?"

"Surely I must have mentioned that. How forgetful of me. Tell him I will give him twenty percent more than he is making at Prescott's." Becca heard the bell announce an entrance and she looked out. "Percy just came in. This will be a perfect time to tell him. Remember, Nell, be firm!"

"I'll try," Nell whispered uncertainly.

"Wait here. I'll send him in." Becca went to meet Percy. "Congratulations," she said. "Nell just told me the good news. I can't begin to tell you how happy this makes me."

Percy smiled. "I'm the happiest of men, Miss Rebecca. Is Nell in the back? I'd like to ask her something if she isn't busy."

"Certainly. Go right on in. She's expecting you." She clasped his hand firmly before he turned away.

At the window, Mrs. Whiteside looked over at Mrs. Henshaw and they both raised their brows.

"Perhaps we should go in later," Mrs. Henshaw suggested in an offended tone. "It would be rather embarrassing to intrude now."

"I can scarcely believe my eyes," Mrs. Whiteside affirmed. "Rebecca Prescott has always seemed so . . . proper! And to think Mr. Winthrop is her own husband's employee!"

Mrs. Henshaw made a clucking noise. "I don't know about you, but I think that nice Mr. Prescott should be made aware of this. Holding hands like that in a public place! Anyone at all might have seen them!"

"She's fortunate it was only us. At least Agatha is spared this."

The two ladies crossed the street and entered Prescott's. Unlike the Emporium's air of homey calm, Prescott's was the epitome of style and the many employees gave a sense of business even during its slack time.

Mrs. Whiteside pretended to look at the new shipment of gloves, but her eyes were on Matt. "Look how trusting, Mabel. He doesn't have the slightest inkling."

"Evidently not. I knew when I was called on to witness their hasty marriage it would be a bad day's work, but I never dreamed Rebecca Simpson would turn out to be flighty."

"Who could have guessed it? Ezra and Belle would roll over in their graves if they knew."

Matt came over with a smile and greeted

his two best customers. "Good morning, ladies. Can I help you find something today?"

"No, no. We're just browsing," Mrs. Henshaw said with great innocence.

"Yes, browsing," Mrs. Whiteside echoed in a pitying voice.

Matt looked from one to the other searchingly. Something was wrong, but he had no idea what it could be. "All right. If I can help you, just let me know." He started to walk away.

"Oh, Mr. Prescott," Mrs. Whiteside called out. "Is Mr. Winthrop here?"

"Why, yes, I believe he is in the back. Do you want me to call him?"

"No, no, don't do that. Are you ready to go, Mabel?"

"Yes, Edith, I think we should. Good day, Mr. Prescott."

Matt watched them leave and shrugged. Whatever the mystery was, he had no intention of asking. Just as they reached the door, he saw Percy emerge from the Emporium and hurry across the street. The two ladies paused with their heads together, glanced back at him, then to Percy, and hurried away. Matt frowned. Percy was spending far too much time at the Emporium.

"He turned down a raise?" Becca said with surprise. "Are you certain he understood it was for twenty percent more than he makes at Prescott's?"

"Percy is a loyal man," Nell said with pride. "He said he couldn't possibly leave Matt."

"Did you tell him he will have his own fitting room?" She knew this was a bone of contention between Percy and the seamstress at Prescott's.

"What fitting room?"

"Did I forget to tell you about that? We don't need such a large storeroom. I can wall part off for his fitting room for gentlemen. It will be just across from your own ladies' fitting room. How absentminded I've become lately. Be sure you tell him about it as soon as possible."

"He would like that," Nell said doubtfully. "I've heard him say that he can't get along with Miss Fuller."

"There! You see? It's perfect. You two will be so happy here." As Nell returned to the dress she was altering, Becca's mind was busy in planning the new fitting room. She would be pressed for storage space, but it would be worth it to gain her own tailor.

While she arranged silk flowers in a tall vase in the notions department, she happened to see Matt striding toward her front door. His face wore a foreboding expression and she wondered idly if he would mind Percy's change of employment. Probably not, she decided. Whenever she objected to his luring away her customers, he was always quick to point out that the money all went to the same bank account.

"Hello, Matt," she greeted him. "You look

positively threatening. Has Jimmy Little been stealing you blind again?'' With the opening of Prescott's, the youthful thief had switched his allegiance.

''I have to talk to you, Becca. Right now.''

She looked up in surprise at his tone and thrust the lifelike tiger lily into the vase. ''Certainly, Matt. What is it.''

''Put those flowers down and look me in the eye!'' When she did, he said bluntly, ''What's going on between you and Percy!''

Becca stared at him and her mouth dropped open. ''Have you been out in the sun without a hat? Come in the back room and let me get you a glass of water.''

''Don't patronize me, Rebecca!''

''You've never called me that! Stop talking nonsense before Nell hears you.''

''If she doesn't know, then she is blind! Even Mrs. Whiteside and Mrs. Henshaw know something is going on between you two!''

''Those two busybodies? What did they say to you!''

''Nothing! It was how they didn't say it that mattered!''

''Are you aware how ridiculous that sounds?''

''All I know is that Percy is over here every time I look around.'' He caught her arm and pulled her to him. ''What's going on!''

She shrugged away his hand. ''Absolutely nothing that involves me! You are going to feel like a fool, Matt, but I think he should be the one to tell you."

Matt paled at her words. "Then there really is something going on? Somehow I didn't quite believe it!"

Grabbing up another tiger lily, Becca brandished it beneath his nose. "You're talking crazy, Matt Prescott. Do you know that? You come charging in here accusing me of goodness knows what, and when I deny it, you take that as a confession! Just what do you think is going on? Do you think I have an opium den operating in the storeroom? Maybe you've decided the Emporium is a front for pirates? We're a little far inland for that, Matt!"

"I thought you and Percy were falling in . . . that is, that he and you . . ."

Becca swatted the counter with the tiger lily. "You honestly think I would look at any other man when I love you? Do you?"

He took the bedraggled flower away from her and threw it away. "What else am I supposed to think, Becca!"

"You might assume he is taken with *Nell!* That happens to be the truth!"

Matt stared at her. "Nell?"

"Certainly! And you needn't look so surprised. You've been here watching them every day at dinner."

"Nell? And Percy? Not you?"

"Keep your voice down or she'll hear you! You might congratulate Percy. They're going to be married!"

"Percy? And Nell? I don't know what to say. I was so sure he was interested in you!"

"He is far too honorable to try to steal away his best friend's wife, even if he was tempted —which he most assuredly is not. It was your idea that we be friends, remember!"

Matt stared at his angry wife. "But Mrs. Whiteside and Mrs. Henshaw seemed to think something is going on over here!"

"There is, but it doesn't involve me."

"You're right. I do feel foolish. I don't know what to say, Becca."

"Just be glad you confronted me first and not Percy!"

"I doubt he would have gotten as angry as you did. I owe you an apology, honey. Are you still upset?"

"Only a little," she conceded. "In a way, I'm somewhat flattered. Percy is a handsome man."

"That's why I never thought of Nell being the object of his attentions."

"Matt Prescott! You're making me angry all over again! Nell has far more sterling qualities than most people I know."

"Calm down," he said, glancing toward the back room. "I didn't mean that derogatorily."

"How else could I take it? Nobody can take liberties with my friends—not even you!"

Matt grinned at her. "Do you champion me as wholeheartedly as you do Nell?"

"Given the occasion, I would. But it seems

everyone in the county loves the illustrious Matt Prescott!"

"Even you?" he asked.

"Especially me. But at times you could try the patience of a saint!"

"I love you, too, Becca. I'm glad you're not philandering with my friend." His eyes were amused now, and a grin lurked just behind his lips. "Percy's a big man. That's why I decided to confront you first."

"Matt! How can you say such absurd things?" But she smiled in spite of herself.

"I have to get back to work. Will you still be mad at me by tonight?"

"Probably not," she said with a sigh and a resigned shake of her head. "We'll see."

"Good. We can make up properly then." Matt kissed her on the forehead and left as quickly as he had entered.

As he crossed the street, he was whistling. So Percy was about to join the married ranks! It was about time. Now that he gave it some thought, Nell was perfect for him.

Matt sought Percy out in the fitting room and slapped him on the shoulder. "Congratulations! Becca just told me the good news!"

Percy grinned self-consciously. "I was going to tell you later. I don't quite believe it yet. Nell only said yes last night."

"I think that's about the best news I ever had. Have you set the date? No, I guess it's too soon yet. When you do, take time for a honeymoon. I can give you the name to contact if you want to go by boat."

"Sounds good to me. I'll ask Nell." Percy brushed at a chalk mark on the pair of trousers he held. "Something is bothering me, however. Nell has this quirk about us working in competing stores. She is very adamant about it." He made a new mark just inside the seam. "Rebecca suggested we solve it by my going to work at the Emporium."

"How's that again?" Matt's grin faded. "The Emporium?"

"I told her I wouldn't. She even offered me a raise."

"She did? Well, of course I was just coming to that. As a married man, you will need more money. I'll match whatever she offered."

"It was twenty percent more than I'm getting now."

Matt blinked and swallowed. He was already paying Percy a generous salary. "That's no problem." So Becca had no compunction in trying to take his tailor! "We could solve Nell's problem nicely by bringing her into Prescott's."

"I suggested that to her, but she is also Becca's friend and she said that wouldn't do."

"Offer her a raise. Twenty percent," Matt said blithely. "Talk it over with Nell and see what she says." He again clapped Percy on the back, and went back to work wondering just what Becca had been trying to pull.

Chapter Sixteen

"WHAT DO YOU MEAN BY TRYING TO STEAL Nell?" Becca demanded as she jammed her parasol into the wooden umbrella stand and her hat onto the hall tree.

"Well, you tried to get Percy." He put his hat on the hook beside hers. "I wondered why you were so quiet all the way home. What are we having for supper?"

"Of all the underhanded things I ever heard of, this takes the cake! You know Nell is my only employee!"

"Percy is my only tailor." He wandered nonchalantly toward the kitchen.

"What would you possibly do with two milliners?" she demanded.

"I'll trade you Miss Fuller for Nell. Even Steven."

"I don't want Miss Fuller!"

"All right. Have it your way. Did Nell accept my offer?"

"Certainly not! She would never leave me alone and go to work for Prescott's."

"No? Perhaps I should double my salary offer and give her a longer yearly vacation."

Becca glared at him and put herself between him and the kitchen. "Don't you dare do this to me, Matt!"

"This can really be solved quite simply," he said with irritating composure. "Move your business into Prescott's and open a café. Then when we open the Emporium back up, Nell and Percy can decide for themselves where they want to work."

"That's absolutely appalling! I should have known that was at the bottom of this!"

"Actually, I only just thought of it. Excuse me." He lifted her out of the doorway and deposited her in the hall. "How about some of that pot roast from last night?"

"How can you be hungry in the middle of an argument?"

"Because I'm not having one, you are. Iced tea?"

"You could at least have the decency to get angry with me."

"Say that again?" He went to the icebox and got out the meat. After peering in the top of the box, he said, "I hope the ice delivery is tomorrow. This block is about gone."

"Then shut the door so the cold air won't escape," she suggested bitingly. "It's melting while you look at it."

"I hope cooler weather comes soon. This summer has been a scorcher."

"Don't you make small talk with me, Matt Prescott! I want you to promise not to take Nell away."

"You just assured me that was impossible. And what was this about a fitting room for Percy? Really, Becca, that's a bit much." He sliced the meat and put a wedge on each of their plates. "Let's eat under the willow tree where it's cooler."

"I have a proposition for you," she said haughtily.

"Oh? Can it wait until after supper?" He grinned at her.

"I can see that you will never give in and merge Prescott's with the Emporium. Am I right?"

"You are." He leaned against the counter and regarded her with interest.

"I propose a contest. A match between the two of us to see who has the best store. The loser at the end of a month will move his stock to the store of the winner."

"That's a ridiculous idea. Prescott's already has the best business."

"Then you're afraid to chance it?"

"Of course I'm not afraid. I just don't want to embarrass you."

"I wouldn't worry about that, Matt. Say that

you agree that the loser merges with the winner."

"I'd be a fool not to take that bet, but will you be mad if I win?"

"Have you ever known me to be less than reasonable? I will merge with Prescott's *if* I lose."

"But will you still be speaking to me?"

"We'll have to wait and see, Matt. You might prefer that I not be." She added a wedge of cornbread to their plates and got the ice pick to chop ice for their tea.

It was cool under the willow tree, and, preparing to eat, Becca balanced her plate on the lawn chair's wooden arm. Now that she saw victory looming, Becca was prepared to be more civil. "I went by the post office this afternoon," she ventured. "There was a letter from Aunt Agatha. She's well and sends her regards and is enjoying the jars of pickles you insisted she take home with her."

"I'm glad to hear it. She didn't mention anything about another visit, did she?"

"No, she says she has become much too involved in civic affairs to leave town. She read an article by Mrs. Annie Wittenmyer and is now trying to organize a branch of the Woman's Christian Temperance Union."

Matt regarded her with amusement. "It's a good thing we went to Jefferson when we did. Jay Gould might not have been as talkative over lemonade."

"She enclosed a pamphlet on the virtues of

temperance. It's addressed to you." Becca sipped her tea.

"Wonderful. That's just what I wanted to read." He let his eyes roam over the orchard where the first leaves were beginning to gild themselves for fall. "We really don't have to have this contest, honey. Now that you've cooled down, why don't we call it off?"

"Afraid I'll win?"

"Stop saying that, and no, I'm not."

"I have no intention of calling it off. In fact, I plan to have Harvey Willis paint a sign tomorrow, just so we are prepared. I think Matt's Café would be nice. Matt's Eatery sounds a bit cute."

"If I were you, I'd wait a while before I had a sign painted."

"Oh, but you didn't, remember? It's in the barn. I see it every time I go out to gather eggs."

"You can't win, Becca."

"Don't be too sure," she answered with a smile.

A cricket chirped in the tree and was answered by another in the thick grass. The whirring call of a locust added to the melody of dusk.

"Let's go for a walk," Matt said tactfully to change the subject.

Becca rose and held out her hand for his plate, but he took her plate from her instead. "These can wait until we get back."

Instead of going toward the street, he took her hand and led her down the side road that led eventually to the dairy farm. There was no traffic on the road and the powdery red dust lay undisturbed. Ruts from wagon wheels made two hard-packed surfaces just the right distance apart for Becca and Matt to walk side by side. Between them was a furrow of dust like that at the side of the road, where hardy nut grass grew in clumps.

"Are you ever sorry for all that's happened?" Matt asked after they had walked a few yards. "Your life was neatly ordered before I showed up."

"It was a wasteland. I have never regretted marrying you. What about yourself? From Percy's stories—as edited as I can tell they are—you led a far more exciting life in Memphis than you have in Mellville. Do you ever regret having given up all those wild oats you were sowing?"

"Not for a minute. Also I have to confess that Percy sometimes lies. My life wasn't all that exciting."

"Good," she smiled.

The song of the locusts followed them and the air became rosy with the colors of sunset. The scent of late honeysuckle drifted to them and lightning bugs began to appear along the side of the road.

"I do wish, however, that you had mentioned your occupation," Becca admitted.

"Would it have mattered?"

"No, but I could have counseled you not to buy the old feed store if I had known you had Prescott's in mind."

"Then we would have had the problem of two bosses in the Emporium," he reminded her.

"We will anyway," she answered demurely. "I think you should have an office beside Percy's fitting room."

"Don't start building it yet," he warned her. "I'm not sure if I should make room for your desk in my office or if I should convert my storeroom for you. Do you have a preference?"

"That's a decision I'll never have to make," she answered confidently. "Would you rather have tan wallpaper or blue?"

He glanced at her. "Yellow wallpaper or pink? You have your choice."

At the crossroads they turned and walked back the way they had come. Dusk was gathering into dark and there were occasional rustlings in the underbrush. An armadillo waddled out into the road and froze at the sound of their footsteps. As they approached, he scurried across the road and into the bushes.

"Let's plant a persimmon tree," Matt suggested.

"I don't like persimmons."

"Neither do I, but the leaves are pretty in the fall. Besides," he grinned, "I never heard

278

of anyone canning a persimmon, and the challenge will drive Aunt Agatha to distraction."

"I wish you would try to get along with her. She means well."

"I don't dislike her as much as you think. I rather enjoyed our . . . discussions."

"Battles, you mean."

"If I was fifty years older, I might have given her a run for her money."

"See? There you go again." But she smiled.

They crossed the back of the orchard and came up by the hen yard behind the barn. Already the chickens had flapped to the low limbs of a chinaberry tree and were settled down for the night. They had their heads tucked under their wings and looked like feathery muffs arranged along all the branches.

"Chickens have an easy life," Matt commented. "Nothing to do all day but cluck and lay eggs."

"And the rooster doesn't even do that much," she teased.

"He does his part."

They walked up the gentle slope of the lawn. The billowing willow tree waved its tendrils in the night breeze. Beneath its dome, darkness already ruled. Matt took Becca in his arms and held her close. "Don't ever stop loving me," he murmured into her hair.

"I never will. How can you even suggest that I might?"

"Call off this contest."

"Not now, Matt. I haven't won yet."

He sighed and held her a few more minutes before they went inside for the night.

Becca had learned a great deal by watching the signs in Prescott's windows. Sales were the bait to lure customers. The parched days of late summer had not yet given way to the torrential rains of fall, and it was the perfect time to mark down all her summer stock.

She went to the store early and made a sign to put in the Emporium's window. By the time the doors opened for business, several women were already waiting on the sidewalk. Becca welcomed them in and she and Nell started selling the goods.

All day there was a steady stream of customers. The dimity dresses went first, followed by the seersucker ones. Lacy gloves that had sat on the shelf all summer were selling so quickly that Becca wondered why she hadn't done this sooner. True, her margin of profit was low, but she was getting rid of stock that might be out of style by the following summer.

She and Nell spent a good deal of time dashing from the cash register to the office for charge account customers. By the end of the day, Becca was exhausted.

"We certainly did well today," Nell said as she locked the store door. "Do you suppose we had the dresses priced too low?"

"I think we did well because Prescott's has

taught people to buy at sales. Matt did us a good turn." She followed Nell to the office and opened the ledger. "He has also taught them to open charge accounts, unfortunately."

"I nearly ran my legs off," Nell agreed. "We need to revise our system of bookkeeping."

"We can't leave the ledger books unattended at the cash register. Jake Henshaw has a new gadget at the general store that we may need. It's a metal cage that travels on a pulley. You put money or receipts in it, pull the cord, and it goes zipping back to the office. Wally Henshaw could probably install one tomorrow."

"I never heard of such a thing," Nell said with amazement. "Do you suppose it works?"

"The ones in Prescott's do. I can get Miss Peabody to help us out in the office so we can both be on the floor at once. What do you think?"

"Well, she helps us out at Christmas time, so she knows how. But you know how flustered she gets."

"She can close the door and be quite alone in there. Only the metal boxes will go in and out. I think she can manage it. Besides, her mother is doing better these days and she isn't needed at home that much." Becca put on her bonnet and said, "If I hurry I can get to the general store before it closes. I'll also stop by the Peabodys' on the way home. See you tomorrow."

Becca hurried down the back alley and onto

the cross street that led to the Henshaws' store. By cutting across a vacant lot, she reached the door before Jake Henshaw locked it.

"Good evening, Mr. Henshaw. Do you still have any message carriers like the ones you sold my husband?"

Jake peered at her through his half-moon spectacles and looked blankly at his cluttered store. "Message carriers?"

"Those little boxes on a pulley. Like you sold to Prescott's."

"Oh, you mean a message carrier," he said with sudden insight. "Sure, those are over here. I've only got one left."

"One is all I need."

"How's that?" He stopped and turned toward her. "You don't need but one?"

"Yes, that's right." Even a short conversation with Jake was enough to tire Becca.

He shuffled behind the counter and caught the ladder to pull it along the metal track to the correct shelf. When he reached his destination, he paused and looked up before starting to climb the ladder. As always, Becca held her breath in fear for his safety. He fumbled with one hand through several boxes, retracted a long cylindrical one, peered at it myopically, and said, "You're in luck. There's one left." He put it under his arm and began the perilous climb down.

When his feet were firmly on the floor, he looked at the box, examined each end, and handed it to Becca. "Anything else? We've got eggs on for half price."

"No, thank you. Could Wally come to the Emporium tomorrow and install this?"

"Install it?" Jake lifted his head so he could sight down his nose to Becca. "The Emporium, you say? Wally?"

"Yes."

"Sure he could. He ain't got nothing else to do. I'll send him over first thing tomorrow."

Becca looked at the price on the box and took the money from her reticule.

Jake looked at the money, then held out his hand to take it. "You don't want that on your account?"

"I don't have an account here, Mr. Henshaw."

"That's right." He began his shuffle to the cash register. "You want to open one?"

"No, I prefer to pay cash."

"Just like your papa. I don't think Ezra ever charged anything in his life. A good man. I don't hold with charging myself. If you don't have the money, do without, is my motto." He punched a key and the drawer of the cash register flew open with a loud ping. "You going to put that up yourself, are you?" He nodded at the box. "It's a job, now. Be sure and get the screws good and tight."

"Could I leave a note for Wally?" she said in resignation.

"Wally? Sure."

Becca tore off a piece of white wrapping

paper and wrote a message to Wally. Then she folded it, wrote his name on the outside, and gave it to his father. She watched Jake stuff it into his shirt pocket; then she smiled. "Good evening, Mr. Henshaw."

"Good evening. Come back soon."

Becca walked past the boarding house and up a short street with small houses. At the third one, she went up the walk and knocked on the door. Almost at once it was opened by a thin woman who looked much older than her actual years.

"Good evening, Miss Peabody."

"Why, Rebecca Prescott. How good to see you. Come in off the porch." Like her body, the woman's voice was wispy and flat. Her black dress hung on her as if she had recently lost a great deal of weight, which she hadn't, and she had a habit of squinting as if she were nearsighted, which she wasn't.

"How is your mother?"

"Quite brisk lately, thank you. She's into her second childhood, if you know what I mean." Miss Peabody smiled her puckery little smile.

"I'm so glad to hear it."

"How are things going at the Emporium?"

"We were quite busy today. In fact, that's why I'm here. Could you possibly come to work for me for about a month?"

"Why, yes, I suppose I could. Things are slow at the church now with all the June weddings past. I won't be needed to play the organ except for Sundays. Unless, of course" —her voice dropped dolorously—"there is a death in our congregation."

"Hopefully there won't be. You'll work in the office as usual, and I'm installing a mechanical message carrier to make your work easier."

"Mercy, I don't know anything about machinery."

"All you have to do is read the messages as they come down the wire and record the amount in the ledger book. Then you close the metal basket, pull the cord, and send it back. It's very simple."

"What wire? What basket?"

"I'll show you when you come in. Could you start tomorrow?"

"Yes, I'll get someone to stay with Mama and I'll be in as early as possible."

"Wonderful. I'll see you tomorrow."

As Becca walked home she contemplated her plans for the Emporium. She had an ample stock to put on sale and she was confident that the month's profit would make her the winner.

Matt was sitting on the porch when she came home. "Hello," she called out. "Did you have a good day?"

"Fair," he said noncommittally. "And you?"

"I'm worn out. The Emporium was like a beehive all day." She came onto the porch and sat beside him on the swing. "Work, work, work, all day. My shirttail didn't hit my back, I was working so hard."

Matt regarded her with narrowed eyes. "This is only the first day. Don't overreach."

"Not me. I know exactly what I'm doing. I even hired a new clerk for the duration. Miss Peabody starts tomorrow."

"The organist?"

"Yes. She usually helps me at Christmas and is quite competent." Becca removed her hat and examined the spray of rosebuds. "Nell did very good work on this bonnet, didn't she?"

"I suppose," Matt said without looking at it. "Will your dress sale continue tomorrow?"

"Why, yes, it will," she said, as if surprised he would even question it. "Well, I guess I'll go start supper. Are you coming in?"

"I'll be in later," he answered. He was trying to decide what would get his customers back.

The next three days saw a flurry of activity in the Emporium that it hadn't known since the last Christmas shopping. Miss Peabody had been taught to unscrew the metal cage, record the amount in the ledger, and to send the cage back for the next message. She never quite adjusted to the whine and clatter as the boxes arrived and departed, but she was bearing up staunchly. As a sign of the Emporium's new popularity, light-fingered Jimmy Little returned to haunt the candy counter.

On the fourth day, however, the crowds diminished and Becca looked across the street to see Prescott's sign announcing a storewide sale. She countered by marking down school clothes and regained the lead.

The next day Matt got in a shipment of fall clothes, which he promptly put on the sale rack. All of Mellville seemed eager to brave the heat in order to stock up for the winter.

Becca and Nell baked all weekend, put the results in decorative tins, and called it a "home" sale. By the second day, all the cookies and fruitcakes were gone.

Matt refused to bake, nor could he bribe any of his employees to do it, so he had a "traveling" sale and marked down the walking shoes, sun bonnets, and steamer trunks.

"Don't you think you are going too far?" Becca demanded as she watched him laboriously lettering a sign announcing his entire stock would be priced at a third less.

"You started it," he said grimly. "My storeroom is larger than yours. Do you want to quit?"

"Never!"

"Becca, this isn't good business for you and me to be competitors. Why don't we call a halt to it before it goes any further."

"And keep both stores open?"

"No."

"You will move to the Emporium?"

"No."

"When you finish with the paint, I need it."
If Matt insisted on being so stubborn, she
could certainly be firm herself.

She took the rug she was making to the
front porch and sat in one of the wicker
chairs. As she unraveled the two long strings
of sheeting, she wondered why he was so
determined to have his own way. Since she
had always seen herself as the very soul of
docility, she found him incomprehensible.
She looped the completed end of the string
around the porch rail and took a four-inch
strip of wool jersey from the box of rug material. Holding the sheeting as if it were two reins,
she laid the wool on top and pulled the ends
under and up to form a cow hitch knot, which
she pushed down snug against the string of
others. When she finished tying the box of
wool strips, she would coil and sew the string
to make a shaggy rug.

Matt soon joined her and sat on the swing.
"I'm finished with the paint."

"I'll make my sign later."

He pushed the swing with his foot, then
looked over at her. "What are you putting on
sale?"

"I won't tell you." Actually she hadn't decided yet, but she saw no reason to admit this.

They sat in strained silence. Couples
strolled down the street, the men all dapper in

well-cut coats, the ladies resplendent in new frocks and parasols.

"We seem to be making Mellville a genuine fashion center," Becca commented wryly. "Everyone in town has new clothes."

Matt grinned with relief at her overture at conversation. "Look at Mrs. Whiteside over there. Where do you suppose she got that polka-dot dress?"

Becca looked and her smile dimmed considerably. "Aisle three. On sale last Tuesday."

"Oh. I thought she made it herself. Somehow the collar . . ."

"Don't try to talk your way out of it," Becca counseled. "You're only making it worse." She pulled the wool strip tightly into place and passed the length of rug over the porch rail to give herself room to add more strips.

She worked until it was too dark to see the colors in the wool. The silence on the porch was uncomfortable, but neither knew how to resolve the tension. The street had emptied of people, and as the lights came on in the house across the way, the windows looked like squares of butter.

"I guess it's bedtime," Matt ventured.

"I suppose so." Becca unwound the strip from the railing and coiled it into the box.

Together they went into the house. Matt lit a lamp to show them the stairs and they climbed upward in the circle of light. Still neither spoke. Becca pulled the pins from her heavy hair and let it sweep over her back like a veil. Matt longed to touch it, but she crossed the bedroom and kept her back to him as she undressed. Not to be outdone, he did the same.

Becca could hear the familiar sounds of his clothes being removed—the metallic click of his cuff links as they touched the shelf, the thud of his shoes on the floor. For the first time in weeks she took a nightgown from her shelf and slipped it over her head. Still without turning, she poured water in the wash basin and dipped a cloth in to wash her face. Next she brushed her hair and let it stream over her shoulders like a shimmering dark river. Behind her, she heard the creak of the bed as Matt lay down.

She forced her movements to be slow and unhurried as if this were a routine night. When all the tangles were out of her hair and it gleamed, she crossed the room to the bed. Without so much as a glance at Matt, she blew out the lamp and climbed into bed.

After a few minutes Matt rolled to his side and kissed her lightly. Becca managed to remain aloof. His hand eased over her stomach to cup her breast and she shifted slightly so that her arm pushed him unobtrusively away. He nuzzled behind her ear and again captured her breast.

"Please don't," she said coolly.

He lay back with a loud sigh and looked up at the ceiling. "You don't want to make up?"

"Yes, I do, but I don't want to be pawed over beforehand."

"I wasn't pawing over you. I was making love with you."

"If you want to end our argument, let's talk about it and find some way we can both reach an agreement."

"There is no way we can do that. We've tried."

"If you won't put out that much effort, then don't touch me." She lay stiffly in the dark and hoped he would understand what she was trying to say. After what seemed to be an eternity, he turned away from her and lay facing the far wall. Becca felt hot tears sting her eyes and her chin quivered in the dark. But she was far too proud to let him know, so she turned her back to his. A desert seemed to separate the two sides of the bed. Becca bit her lower lip to stop it from trembling and wished she knew how to explain to him that she only wanted to be cuddled and held close.

Matt lay awake and wondered what he had done that was so terrible that she would shun his love.

Chapter Seventeen

THE FICKLE SHOPPERS, SEEING PRESCOTT'S merchandise was a third off, turned away from the Emporium. Becca waited until noon, then announced her own goods were a half off. The customers returned. Along with the citizens of Mellville were new faces, for news had spread of the price war, and bargain hunters were flocking to town from as far away as Marshall and Longview.

Becca and Nell had their hands full as the customers grabbed items away from each other and shouldered their way to the register. Becca yanked the cord time after time to send the metal cage whizzing to the office, and no sooner did it return than Nell was waiting to use it herself.

The Emporium's merchandise was thinning and Nell had brought most of the stock out from the storeroom. Before she could even display it on the counters, the items were snatched up and taken away.

Suddenly the crowd began to disperse. Becca was ringing up the sale of some baby blankets when the customer shoved the purchase back at her and left the store.

Becca looked at Nell and they hurried to the front window. Matt had turned his sign over, and on the back it read, "Wholesale prices on all merchandise."

"He can't do that!" Becca gasped. "He won't make any profit at all!" She ran out of the door and across the crowded street. Buggies and horses were tied to anything that wouldn't move. People were jostling each other to get in the doors where Matt was welcoming them with a victorious grin.

Becca tiptoed to see over the crowd and spotted her husband. "Matt! You can't undercut me like this!" A few people turned to look at her.

"Yes, I can. You forced me to do it."

"This is ridiculous! Neither of us will make a profit!" A handful of people cheered.

"Call it off, Becca. Just say the word!"

Her mouth tightened angrily. "A pair of shoes *free* for every dress sold!" she called out. The crowd turned as one toward the Emporium.

"Free bed linens with each blanket purchase!" Matt countered loudly. The crowd surged back.

"A dozen men's handkerchiefs to the first two dozen customers!" Becca stood her ground, her hands on her hips as the frantic buyers again changed direction.

"Hold it! Hold it! What's going on here!" a man's voice demanded brusquely. A tall man, who wore a silver badge and bore a remarkable resemblance to Jimmy Little, elbowed his way through the crowd.

"We are having a sale at the Emporium, Sheriff Little," Becca explained, her cheeks flushed with anger.

"So is Prescott's!" Matt snapped.

The sheriff looked from one to the other. "What time do you folks close, anyway? It's after five."

Becca consulted the watch she wore at her broach pin and exclaimed, "It's nearly six o'clock!"

"All right, folks, the sales are over. Everybody go on home now," the sheriff bellowed. "Move on, move on." To Becca and Matt he gave a threatening glance that needed no interpretation.

Becca lifted her chin and glared at Matt. Once more he had succeeded in humiliating her! Full of righteous fury, she went back to the Emporium.

Nell had straightened much of the jumbled merchandise, and a very nervous Miss Peabody was craning her neck around the office door. Becca surveyed the appearance of her store and gave a despondent sigh. "The only saving grace is that Prescott's must also look this bad," she finally said.

"There sure isn't much left," Nell admitted. "Even those lavender brush sets went, and I never thought they would sell at all."

A lone glove dangled from the stem of a broken silk rose. Becca removed it and tossed it onto the counter. "Go on home. I'll come in tomorrow and straighten up."

"Tomorrow is Sunday," Nell reminded her.

"I know, but I can't leave it like this until Monday."

She let her two helpers out the back door and Miss Peabody scurried for home. Nell remained to walk down the alley with Becca. "This sure seems to be a strange way to fight competition," Nell said tactfully. "We didn't make much money when you figure it all out."

"Probably not. Well, people will have something to talk about for a while anyway. Next Monday we'll get back to normal."

"Good. I can't stand much more of this enterprise."

They separated at the crossroad and Becca slowly walked home. She imagined gossips at every window and thought what they must be saying about the eccentric Prescott couple. Perhaps Matt was oblivious to public opinion, but she was all too aware that she was not.

She went to the kitchen and poured herself a glass of buttermilk and crumbled some cornbread into it. The idea of cooking anything was repugnant to her. As she ate the concoction with a spoon, Matt arrived.

For a long time they stared across the room at each other. Finally he said, "What in the world is that you're eating?"

"Buttermilk and cornbread. There's more if you want it."

"Lord, no!"

She turned her back and looked out the window as she ate and hoped the food would find its way past the lump in her throat.

Matt sighed and ran his hand through his hair. "Look, this has gotten way out of control. We can't go on like this."

Instead of answering, Becca rinsed her glass and sat it loudly on the drainboard. With her chin in the air, she swept haughtily past Matt.

She went to their room and got a nightgown, a change of clothes for the next day, and a book she had been intending to read. Then she crossed the landing to her old room. Matt was coming up as she reached the door, and she glared at him frostily before closing it firmly behind her.

Quickly she undressed and put on her gown. Her throat was tight and her tongue felt heavy as she struggled to keep from crying. She would show him, she told herself. He would see she wasn't a woman to be ridiculed!

She threw back her covers and plopped down on her bed. The sheets felt cool and crisp and virginal. She propped her book on her knees and looked around. Somehow this room seemed smaller than she remembered it and the furniture was full of dents and scratches from her childhood.

Through the wall she could hear Matt moving around in the larger bedroom. This wasn't difficult, for the wall was thin and he was slamming the doors of the wardrobe and various drawers. Becca frowned and turned her eyes toward her book. Although she had read *Pride and Prejudice* before, Jane Austen had always been able to capture her attention. Until now. She reread the first page three times and glared at the wall. Matt was making an uncommon amount of noise. He sounded as mad as she was.

Becca fluffed her pillow and tried again to become immersed in the romance of Elizabeth and Mr. Darcy. Matt slammed another drawer and she jumped. Resolutely she read the page again.

It seemed strange, being in her childhood bed, in the room that had witnessed so many of her youthful dreams and defeats. She felt like a butterfly trying to crawl back into its cocoon. She sat up and put her legs over the edge of the bed. To let business come between Matt and herself was absurd! The thing for her to do was to apologize. She could start by saying she shouldn't have challenged him to a contest. He could reply that he shouldn't have cut prices so sharply. In return she could say she forgave him for trying to steal Nell and for being so pigheaded about the whole affair. Most likely he would then point out she had started it and the battle would rage again.

Becca lay back down and glared at the ceiling. She wasn't really angry any longer, but she couldn't see how to make up with him. From the sounds beyond the wall, Matt was quite angry and solitude might be the best thing for him. Once more she put her book in front of her face and struggled to make sense of the words.

Suddenly her bedroom door banged open and Matt strode in. He grabbed her book and tossed it onto her bedside table. In one easy motion, Matt picked her up and carried her out of the room. Becca shrieked with surprise and struggled, but he held her firmly. He strode into their bedroom and dropped her on the bed.

"Stay there!" he commanded when she tried to escape.

One look in his flinty green eyes, and she complied. She sat up and drew her knees against her chest and stared at her normally gentle husband.

"Listen to me and remember it well! In this house there will be no separate bedrooms. Do you understand me?"

She nodded, her dark eyes large in her pale face.

"This problem has gone on long enough! We are letting two stores rip us apart, and after today we have both suffered financially. Not to mention what the gossips must be saying about us."

Becca looked at him in surprise. "I thought you didn't care what people say about you."

"I lied. Mostly I care because I know it bothers you. Now, about our stores . . ."

"I won't agree to give in to you!"

"No one asked you to 'give in'! Listen to what I'm saying. This whole contest was wrong and I must have been out of my mind to agree to it in the first place."

"No, you just thought you'd win," she snapped. "You were wrong."

He drew a steadying breath. "We were both wrong."

"Not me!"

"Both! Or we are going to argue all night!"

"Both," she conceded reluctantly.

"We are going to settle this the only way I know how. By a coin toss." He dug in his pocket and extracted a silver dollar. "Look at it."

"I've seen dollars before."

"I know you have, but I don't want you claiming later that the coin has two heads."

She glared at him and took the coin. On one side she saw the familiar laurel-wreathed liberty profile, on the other an eagle with wings unfurled. "It looks like any other silver dollar," she confirmed.

Matt yanked back the rumpled covers and exposed a smooth surface of white sheet. "Do you swear to me that you will abide by this toss?" he demanded as he sat on the other end of the bed. "Yes or no."

"I will. Now you say you will, too."

He glared at her. "Of course I will. It was my idea!"

"I only wanted to be sure. Toss the coin," she said as she shoved it toward him.

"No, you do it." He slapped it down in her palm.

Becca looked from the dollar to Matt, then back again. "Heads," she said firmly. She balanced the coin on her thumb and forefinger and thumped it as hard as she could. It soared upward, spinning around, then landed on the sheet.

The silver eagle gleamed up at them.

For a while they neither moved nor spoke. Finally Becca said, "You won. I'll move my stock into Prescott's tomorrow." In spite of her effort, her voice quivered.

"Let's try for two out of three," Matt suggested with a scowl.

"No, we agreed to settle it on this one toss. I lost and that's all there is to it." Now that it was over she felt a curious relief. "I'll start packing things up after church and I'll have most of it in by Tuesday. There isn't much left to move after today."

Matt frowned down at the coin, then shoved it into his pocket. Having won, the victory seemed hollow. Especially since Becca was being such a good sport about losing. "There's no need to rush into this. We can pack it up next week."

"Why wait? I would rather get it over with." Now that the decision was made, she was determined to be magnanimous. "Will you talk to Wally Henshaw about building the tables, or shall I?"

"I'll do it," he growled.

"Good." She lay down and pulled up the sheet. "Pleasant dreams."

Matt frowned at her. Even having lost, she was able to take the upper hand. He wondered how she was able to do that. He blew out the lamp and undressed in the dark. The bed creaked as he lay down beside her and he was careful not to touch her still form. She shared his bed, but he felt as much alone as when she had been in her old room.

The bed quivered as she rolled over and her slender arm encircled his waist. Her breath was warm on his cheek as she nuzzled him with her nose. Matt lay still, not daring to hope that the estrangement was really over. Softly her lips found his and he returned her kiss cautiously, then with an almost desperate ardor.

"Matt, Matt," she murmured as he clasped her close. "What did we almost do? I would burn both buildings to the ground rather than hurt you. Forgive me. Please forgive me?"

"I do, my Becca. Will you forgive me? I let my pride get between us, but it will never happen again. I've learned something from

301

all this. You and I have to promise each other something. If we see something like this happening, we have to stop and make the other one listen long enough to avert it."

"That may not be easy," she whispered tremulously.

"I know you're a stubborn woman, but I can do it."

"Me! I meant you!"

"Hush." He gathered her back into his arms. "It's just barely possible that we are both stubborn."

"Perhaps." She held him tightly in the darkness and loved the way their bodies fit together so perfectly. He felt warm and secure beside her and she realized she no longer had to stand alone. All her training had taught her that she must be the bulwark of the family, the mainstay that kept it running smoothly. To discover this was no longer the case made her gasp.

"What is it? Did I hug you too tightly?"

"I just realized that I don't have to be the strong one," she exclaimed.

"I never said you should be."

"Somehow I never realized that! I don't have to prove anything to you!"

"Of course not."

"Don't you see, Matt? All this came about because I was trying to take the lead. I don't have to!"

"Hold on a minute. I don't want to be the supreme ruler either."

"You don't?"

"Becca, have you ever watched two mules pulling a wagon? If one pulls harder than the other, the wagon just goes in a circle. The same thing would happen if one of the mules stopped pulling as hard. You and I are more like those two mules than anyone I ever met. We've had a runaway wagon because each of us was trying to go faster than the other and finally the wagon—Prescott's and the Emporium—was going too fast and nearly ran over us."

"Did you just call me a mule?" Becca asked sweetly.

"Don't pretend you don't understand me. Isn't what I just said true?"

"I suppose so."

"You're going to be a mule to the very end, aren't you. As I see it, the only way you and I are going to be happy is if we match our strides. No one in the lead and no one subservient. Do you agree?"

She nodded. "You're a wise man, Matt. How do you propose that we do that?"

"I don't know. We'll have to work it out as we go along."

Chapter Eighteen

Becca had measured the windows of the
Emporium and used the bare counters to cut
the red-and-white curtain material. It wasn't
her first choice for café windows, but after the
huge sale, it was the only bolt left that was
suitable. Nell had offered to help, but she
turned down her offer. Seeing the Emporium
stripped of all its merchandise had bothered
Becca more than she cared to admit and she
needed something to keep her busy.

Wally Henshaw and half a dozen other carpenters had already arrived and were moving
the back counters out of their way. Their
voices and footsteps echoed hollowly in the
high-ceilinged room. Now and then someone
pulled a nail from a board and the loud
squeak was more abrasive than Becca could
bear.

As soon as she could, she folded the cloth and took it home to sew. Across the street, she knew Matt would be unpacking boxes of goods that she, or even her father, had ordered. Becca averted her eyes and hurried homeward.

In the last few days the heat had broken and silver clouds mounded above the small town. The still air was heavy with the scent of rain, but as yet the storm was pending. Leaves of the maples and sweet gums turned their lighter undersides upward and seemed to be waiting impatiently. Their leaves rustled as if a breeze were trapped within, but it never reached the street. A red dust covered the grass and bushes and begrimed the bottom of her skirt and her shoes. Far away she heard the low threat of thunder and her head started to ache dully.

Becca climbed her front porch and stamped the dust from her shoes. Again the clouds growled. When the storm arrived, it would be a fierce one.

She went inside and hung her hat by its scarf on the hall tree. Methodically she went through the house seeing that the windows were down before it rained. It seemed strange to be alone in the house during working hours. Soon she would start spending her days at Prescott's, but she wasn't ready for that yet.

Her sewing machine had been returned to the guest room. Slowly she climbed the dark stairway and went in. The cloudy skies made the room gloomy even with the curtains open, so Becca lit a reading lamp.

The sewing machine was a marvel of design, with a shiny black wasplike body and gold and red scrolls and curlicues. The needle moved whenever she pumped the wrought-iron foot treadle and she could sew as fast or as slow as she wanted. It was a recent purchase and a prized possession. Today, however, she took no delight in its use.

She recalled the empty Emporium and felt a twinge not unlike homesickness. A part of her life was being changed, and consequently destroyed, to birth a café. And she didn't even like to cook. At least she had insisted the sign be changed to read, "Mellville's Dining Hall." She preferred that to "Rebecca's."

As she threaded the various eyelets and levers, she gave herself over to self-pity. A pattering of rain against the window seemed to tell her that nature was in agreement with her. A pinkish flash of lightning told her the worst of the storm would miss the house, but a sheet of water was already falling from the ominous clouds. She turned the lamp brighter and eased the checkered cloth under the foot feed.

The storm buffeted the roof and made the willow droop in bedraggled folds of leaves. The wind increased and rattled the windows. Already the streets were sloughs of red mud and by dark would be impassable to heavy-laden wagons. Becca derived some comfort from not having to walk home in the rain from the Emporium.

Suddenly the front door banged open and she heard Matt bellow for her. She jumped and narrowly missed putting the needle through her finger. "Up here!" she called out as she rushed to the door. "What's wrong? Is it a tornado?"

Matt took the stairs two at a time, waving a sodden newspaper.

"Look at this, Becca! Just look what it says here!" He reached the landing and thrust the paper at her.

"Good heavens, Matt! You're dripping wet!"

A puddle was forming about his feet and his hair was plastered to his head as evidence he had run outside without his hat. "Don't worry about that. Read what it says here in the paper!" He shook the page at her.

Becca gingerly took the wet paper and squinted to make out the words. Between the darkness of the hall and the rain-soaked newsprint, she shook her head. "I can't make it out. The print is showing through from the other side. What does it say?"

"It says the railroad is coming! The tracks skirt Jefferson and are heading straight for us! Gould is still trying to negotiate a spur and a roundhouse at the wharf in Jefferson, but we will be the water stop! There's no need to close the Emporium!" He grabbed her to him and whirled her around until the front of her dress was as wet as his own clothes.

"You're sure?" she gasped as his words sank in. "There's no mistake?"

"None at all! That's why the surveyor in Jefferson was out sighting a line and clearing trees. The tracks go just outside of town. When the mayor said he would bring it through, he meant a spur, not the main line!"

"We were both right?" she managed to exclaim as he hugged her again.

"Jay Gould will probably be in town within the week to buy up right-of-way. I figure it will be just north of town toward the lake. Now if you recall, there is an old building there?"

"Yes, the old schoolhouse," she said in confusion. "But I don't see . . ."

"I went by and looked at it not too long ago and it's soundly built. Now I figure it would be perfect for a café. It's near the tracks and will be handy for travelers. What do you think?"

"What about the Emporium? I'm sewing the curtains and Wally's tearing out the counters and . . ."

"Damn! Is he there already? I'll have to go by there first."

"First?"

"I have to find out who owns that building and buy it before anyone else figures out where the tracks will lie."

"Slow down. You aren't going anywhere in this storm. Look at you! You're soaked." She pulled his coat from him and held it at arm's length. "Go get on some dry clothes before you catch your death of cold!"

"Becca, Becca, do you know what this means?" he said, ignoring her. "We're going to make a lot of money! You can have anything you want. I'll give you the world."

"All I want is your love," she answered with a smile. "Having so nearly lost it, I know its value all the more."

"No, honey," he said softly. "You never came anywhere near losing it. Even the two of us together aren't that muleheaded." He gathered her into his arms and she held him tight.

"I would, however, like one thing," she murmured in his ear.

"Just name it."

"The Emporium. I want to pass it on to our children someday."

"It's already yours. Don't forget we can hand down Prescott's, too."

"The Emporium will go to our daughters," she said teasingly. "I'm founding a family tradition."

He drew back and grinned down at her. "Don't you think you should found a family first?"

She smiled coyly and cocked her head to one side. "Do you know anything better to do on a rainy afternoon?"

Tapestry

HISTORICAL ROMANCES

Breathtaking New Tales

of love and adventure set against
history's most exciting time and
places. Featuring two novels by the
finest authors in the field of romantic fiction—every <u>month</u>.

Next Month From
Tapestry Romances

ARDENT VOWS
by Helen Tucker
DESIRE AND DESTINY
by Linda Lael Miller

POCKET BOOKS

____DEFIANT LOVE
Maura Seger
45963/$2.50

____MARIELLE
Ena Halliday
45962/$2.50

____FLAMES OF PASSION
Sheryl Flournoy
46195/$2.50

____THE BLACK EARL
Sharon Stephens
46194/$2.50

____HIGH
COUNTRY PRIDE
Lynn Erickson
46137/$2.50

____LIBERTINE LADY
Janet Joyce
46292/$2.50

____REBELLIOUS LOVE
Maura Seger
46379/$2.50

____LYSETTE
Ena Halliday
46165/$2.50

____EMBRACE THE STORM
Lynda Trent
46957/$2.50

____SWEETBRIAR
Jude Deveraux
45035/$2.50

____EMERALD
AND SAPPHIRE
Laura Parker
46415/$2.50

____EMBRACE THE WIND
Lynda Trent
49305/$2.50

Tapestry

____DELPHINE
Ena Halliday
46166/$2.75

____FORBIDDEN LOVE
Maura Seger
46970/$2.75

____SNOW PRINCESS
Victoria Foote
49333/$2.75

____FLETCHER'S WOMAN
Linda Lael Miller
47936/$2.75

____GENTLE FURY
Monica Barrie
49426/$2.95

____FLAME ON THE SUN
Maura Seger
49395/$2.95

____TAME THE WILD
HEART
Serita Stevens
49398/$2.95

____ENGLISH ROSE
Jacqueline Marten
49655/$2.95

____SNOW FLOWER
Cynthia Sinclair
49513/$2.95

____WILLOW WIND
Lynda Trent
47574/$2.95

Pocket Books, Department TAP
1230 Avenue of the Americas, New York, New York 10020

Please send me the books I have checked above. I am enclosing
$_____ (please add 75¢ to cover postage and handling. NYS and NYC
residents please add appropriate sales tax. Send check or money order—no
cash, stamps, or CODs please. Allow six weeks for delivery). For purchases over
$10.00, you may use VISA: card number, expiration date and customer signature
must be included.

Name _____

Address _____

City _____ State/Zip _____

749

☐ Check here to receive your free
Pocket Books order form

If you've enjoyed the love, passion and adventure of this Tapestry™ historical romance...be sure to enjoy them all, FREE for 15 days with convenient home delivery!

Now that you've read a Tapestry™ historical romance, we're sure you'll want to enjoy more of them. Because in each book you'll find love, intrigue and historical touches that really make the stories come alive!

You'll meet brave Guyon d'Arcy, a Norman knight ... handsome Comte Andre de Crillon, a Huguenot royalist ... rugged Branch Taggart, a feuding American rancher ... and more. And on each journey back in time, you'll experience tender romance and searing passion... and learn about the way people lived and loved in earlier times.

Now that you're acquainted with Tapestry romances, you won't want to miss a single one! We'd like to send you 2 books each month, as soon as they are published, through our Tapestry Home Subscription Service.℠ Look them over for 15 days, free. If not delighted, simply return them and owe nothing. But if you enjoy them as much as we think you will, pay the invoice enclosed.

There's never any additional charge for this convenient service — we pay all postage and handling costs.

To begin your subscription to Tapestry historical romances, fill out the coupon below and mail it to us today. You're on your way to all the love, passion and adventure of times gone by! Tapestry™ is a trademark of Simon & Schuster.

HISTORICAL *Tapestry* ROMANCES

Tapestry Home Subscription Service, Dept. TPTP 11
120 Brighton Road, Box 5020, Clifton, NJ 07012

Yes, I'd like to receive 2 exciting Tapestry historical romances each month as soon as they are published. The books are mine to examine for 15 days, free. If not delighted, I can return them and owe nothing. There is never a charge for this convenient home delivery—no postage, handling, or any other hidden charges. If I decide to keep the books, I will pay the invoice enclosed.

I understand there is no minimum number of books I must buy, and that I can cancel this arrangement at any time.

Name

Address

City   State   Zip

Signature   (If under 18, parent or guardian must sign.)

This offer expires July 31, 1984.

TPTP11

☐ Check here to receive your free Pocket Books order form.